PRAISE FOR LIBBY CUDMORE

"Negative Girl *by Libby Cudmore is a sharp subversive exploration of the PI novel that elevates the genre while never sacrificing the thrills. A fantastic book !"*

S.A. Cosby, bestselling author of *All the Sinners Bleed* and *Razorblade Tears*

"Libby Cudmore's Negative Girl *is a simmering neo-noir that crackles with verve and voice. Few novels can feel modern and timeless at once, but Cudmore pulls it off with confidence and a private eye duo that is up there with Lehane's Pat and Angie. I loved this book."*

Alex Segura, bestselling author of *Secret Identity* and *Alter Ego*

"Beautifully rendered with a cast of bruised, bittersweet characters, Libby Cudmore's latest absolutely crackles with life, charm, and above all, that secret, particular music of the human heart. Negative Girl *is the real deal."*

Matthew Lyons, author of *A Mask of Flies*

"Negative Girl *is a masterfully written PI novel and a love letter to Gen X music all rolled into a hardboiled treat. After you're done frantically flipping pages, build a playlist."*

Kimberly G. Giarratano, author of the *Billie Levine* series

Libby Cudmore

NEGATIVE GIRL

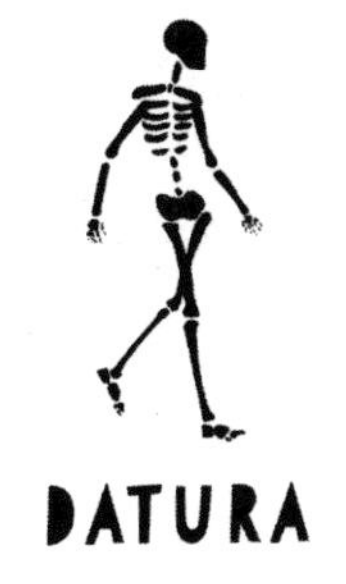

DATURA

DATURA BOOKS
An imprint of Watkins Media Ltd

Unit 11, Shepperton House
89 Shepperton Road
London N1 3DF
UK

daturabooks.com
twitter.com/daturabooks
L'alphabet en français

A Datura Books paperback original, 2024

Cover by Francesca Corsini
Edited by Daniel Culver
Set in Meridien

ISBN 978 1 91552 331 0
Ebook ISBN 978 1 91552 334 1

Printed and bound in the United Kingdom by CPI Group (UK) Ltd, Croydon CR0 4YY.

9 8 7 6 5 4 3 2 1

To everyone at the Barrelhouse Writer's Camp, past, present and future.

You left your cigarettes,
your faint regrets
Our lives out in the snow
It's hard to ever get warm again
When inside it's fifty below
The French Letters, "Fifty Below"

1

VALERIE

Martin had a migraine. I was fighting sleep at my desk with my third cup of coffee and games on my phone. We'd been out until 3am last night on the Russell case, making quiet conversation over the late-night jazz station while we took bets on who was using the family lake house without permission. I had guessed partying teens, or a family of clever raccoons, but it turns out it was Mr Russell and one of his students using the place for a little after-hours tutoring. After a year with the Wade Agency, Perrine's only licensed private detective agency, I should have guessed as much. Martin would meet with Dr Russell later in the week and go over the photos with her. I think it was a combination of muggy September weather and lack of sleep and a little bit of dread that left him useless, locked in his office with the lights off and a cold rag over his eyes. The day after a stakeout was always brutal.

I'd come back to Perrine two years ago under what my brother Deacon called "mysterious circumstances," arrived in Upstate New York after a three-day bus ride, wearing my pajamas and jacket and Doc Martens, without even a phone charger. I'd moved back in with my Aunt Gina, slept in Deacon's old bedroom, tended bar and wrote articles for the online music magazine *High Wire*. I met Martin on one such assignment; turns out the PI in the dusty little office above the vape shop on Becker Street used to be known as Basil Wise, infamous frontman of the French Letters, a brief flash of a band that was once destined to take their place in the post-punk court of jesters alongside The Smiths, The Replacements, U2 and R.E.M. I interviewed him and he brought me along on a couple of little cases, but in the end, I decided not to send in the article, let him keep his cover and instead joined the Wade Agency as his assistant. It was just part-time work at first, filing and taking appointments and going to the bank and post office, but in the last few months, he'd started letting me in on some of the secrets of the business, asking me to help with a tail or swap out a few hours of a motel surveillance mission so he could stretch his legs and get a bite to eat. He'd even let me take on a case when he had the flu.

And for the first time in my life, I actually liked my job. I made enough money to move out of Gina's, I bought a little beater of a car so I didn't have to take the bus, and I liked Martin. He was witty and dry, he played piano or put on records in the waning afternoon hours, he made good coffee and paid for lunch a few times a week. I'd hated leaving my alt-weekly back in Memphis, but at least I'd found a safe place to land.

I must have fallen asleep for just a moment, because when the buzzer rang, I nearly jumped out of my skin. A groan came out of Martin's office. I answered the intercom before it could ring again. "The Wade Agency, how may I help you?"

"Janice Archwood for Mr Wade, please."

Martin didn't have any appointments scheduled for the afternoon, but walk-ins weren't uncommon, especially in the divorce trade. "Please hold."

I knocked gently on Martin's door and slipped inside. He was stretched out on the couch, tie and watch in the desk's "Out" basket, jacket thrown over the arm of the blue chair, cuffs loose. "There's a Janice Archwood at the front door," I said. "Should I buzz her in?"

He sat up slowly. "Appointment?" he asked.

"Walk-in."

"How long was I out?"

"About an hour."

He let out a slow breath. "I think the worst of it has passed," he said. "Send her in."

2

MARTIN

I couldn't shake the feeling that I knew Ms Archwood from somewhere. There were plenty of gaps in my memory; nineteen years of sobriety couldn't restore what was lost in half a decade of addiction. She was slim and pretty and young, maybe mid-twenties, with hair the color of midcentury furniture piled high on her head. Hardly my usual clientele – shifty-eyed soccer moms, anxious husbands and stiff-armed corporate types angered about scaffold laws and workers' comp claims. But she had that nervous look I knew too well, her eyes flitting from the piano to me, the record cabinet to Valerie, then back to the piano. If I wasn't positive the slightest sound would detonate the dynamite kegs inside my skull, I might have directed Valerie to put on some music, just to fill the silence.

"How do you take your coffee, Ms Archwood?" Valerie offered.

"Black, please."

I motioned to Valerie to make it two. Normally I took mine with cream and sugar, but I'd learned that a client opens up a little easier if you give them something to subconsciously bond over. A shared drink order was a quick way to establish this, and I needed the caffeine – unsweetened, undiluted.

I gestured my client into the office and she sat in the blue chair. "This consultation is free," I began, easing behind my desk. "It doesn't obligate me to take your case and I don't take cases where drugs or violence are involved." That usually weeded out about a quarter of the clients, anxious parents who wanted us to search a teenage bedroom. Then there was the occasional tough guy who spoke in *wink-wink* terms about "taking care" of a neighbor or his ex-wife or a boss who fired him. I made sure to pass those kinds of clients along to an associate of mine, Captain Liam Hollander, Perrine PD.

Valerie brought in the coffee on a wooden tray. She brought two bottles of water too, and a small origami cup, made of notebook paper, with an Excedrin hidden inside. I set them aside. She gave me a look that said *take the pills*. Maybe later.

"It's nothing like that," said Ms Archwood. "My father was a drug addict who abandoned me and my mom. In the last few years, we've reconnected, but lately, he's been pressuring me to move back home. I'm studying violin at Raines, and I've only got another semester left. Does that make me an awful daughter if I just want him to… to back off a little bit?"

"Do you think he's dangerous?"

She shook her head. "No, just… overbearing. Like he's trying to make up for lost time. But my foster mother, she says she thinks he's trying to ask for money. I guess I just… don't know what to do. I'm not entirely sure he's still sober. He says he is, but…"

"But you've heard that before." So had I. Said it more than once myself, until I did the work to make sure I made it the truth. But it took the people I hurt time to believe that too. "So, what is it you want me to do?"

"I guess I'm not really sure," she said. "Maybe follow him for a bit, see if he's drinking or using?"

"I'm not a babysitter."

"Of course." She sighed. "If I gave you his number, would you call him and tell him to back off a little bit?"

So it was a White Knight gig. Easy enough. I got them every so often, skittish people who just needed an authoritative voice to speak up for them from the netherworld between a cop and lawyer, when lines were crossed but laws weren't.

"Leave his name and number with my assistant," I said. "I'll call him and ask him to wait out your answer. Hopefully, he's a good enough dad to give you some space."

I tried to give her a reassuring smile that felt instead like a knife splitting my mouth. "In the meantime, I'll call on him in the next twenty-four hours. Valerie will handle the deposit and set you up for a follow-up appointment later in the week."

I stood. She stood. She looked more familiar than ever. I scanned her like a TSA agent, searching for wires, searching for the faintest hint of who she might be. But if I was someone she knew, she didn't let on. "Thank you, Mr Wade," she said.

"Happy to help," I said. I held the door for her, directed her to Valerie, and closed the office door behind her. I sank back down on the couch, fighting dizziness. I cracked open the bottle of water. I swallowed both pills in one gulp.

Valerie knocked again. I let her come in. She handed me the memo. "Lem Chesterfield," she said. "He's staying at the Vanguard Hotel. She left his cell phone number, too."

My head throbbed. It wasn't from the migraine. Even that name had a ring of familiarity to it, lost and hollow. A half-forgotten movie, perhaps, or a name in a high school yearbook. A drug dealer, a session player or a roadie, a record executive's signature along the dotted line. Could be anybody. Could be nobody at all.

"C'mon," I said, pushing myself to standing. "Let's get lunch. I've reached the starving portion of this damn headache."

"Flower House?" she offered. "I bet Malee has something on the menu that could set your head right."

She was probably right, but I was craving grease and salt like it might absorb my physical misery. "Next time," I said. "Let's go to the Red Top."

3

VALERIE

We sometimes joked that the Red Top Diner was our other office. We were there frequently enough, and sometimes I even let Martin pretend like he discovered the place. When I first started working for him, he frequented Danny's, a greasy spoon where the cockroaches were such a common sight that they might as well have been busboys. I brought him to the Red Top and changed his mind. Well, maybe not so much me as Joan, the owner. I suspected he had a thing for her and I wouldn't blame him. Joan was the kind of woman a pulp writer might have described as a broad, a big redhead with a wide mouth and a hearty laugh and a heart to match all of it. There wasn't a man who came into the Red Top who wasn't in love with Joan.

She came by our table with the coffee pot and didn't even ask if we wanted coffee before she filled our cups. She knew the answer was yes, it was always yes when it came to coffee at the Red Top Diner. Though a whole series of high-end coffee shops had sprung up by Raines College, there wasn't a barista in Perrine who could make a cup as good as the one you got for $1.25 – with unlimited warm-ups, of course – at the Red Top.

"Haven't seen you in a few days," she said. "Was starting to think you'd gone back to your old ways at Danny's."

He laughed a little. "Valerie would never let that happen."

She reached over one manicured hand and smoothed a mess of stray silver hair off his forehead. "Big case?"

I could hear his heart pounding over Christopher Cross warbling "Arthur's Theme" on the radio behind the counter. "As big as cases get around here," he stammered.

"Then I guess I'd better get you guys fed," she said, pulling out her notepad. "What'll it be?"

Martin ordered breakfast. I ordered lunch. I watched her walk away, wondering if that wiggle was how she had always walked or if that was just for him. "When are you going to ask her out?" I asked in a low voice when I was sure she was out of earshot.

"She's not saying anything to me that I'm sure she doesn't say to all her other regulars," he said, pretending to be very interested in the yellow legal tablet in front of him. "Besides, it's generally not my policy to date married women."

"Her husband left her two months ago," I said. "Affair with one of his flight attendants. Surprised she didn't put you on the case. Could have racked up those frequent flyer miles."

Martin looked surprised at this revelation. His eyes darted towards the clock, then to the specials on the board, then to her left hand to see that, sure enough, she wasn't wearing her wedding ring. "Sorry to hear that," he said. "I'd hate to think of anyone hurting her."

That made two of us. Joan was always protective of the kids of Perrine, especially the ones like me and Deacon when we were growing up, kids who had seen some shit. I took a sip of my coffee. "How's your head?" I asked.

"Coffee helped," he said. "Meds are starting to kick in too."

"So talk to me about the case."

"It's not quite a stalking case," he explained. "Non-custodial parent, trying to make up for lost time. She might be having second thoughts, wants to make sure he's not just trying to get money out of her."

"Seems a little low-stakes for hiring a private eye."

Our plates came momentarily between us, set down by a waitress with a face too old for the rest of her body. I wondered if she was another of Perrine's seemingly endless supply of junkies; cash tips were a good way to fix up, and there wasn't a kitchen in Perrine that didn't have at least one dealer supplementing his income with the hard stuff. But more than a theory, it was the way Martin avoided looking at her that told me my hunch was right. He had just passed nineteen years of sobriety and it didn't take a PI license for him to spot a fellow zombie. "You think Joan knows?" he asked.

"Doubt it," I said. "She wouldn't keep her around if she did."

He looked back at Joan one more time and gave her a sweet, sad little smile. "C'mon, Martin," I chided. "Just ask her out. You don't have to marry her. Just take her to dinner. She clearly adores you."

"We'll see," he said in a tone that told me the conversation was, for the time being, over.

With nothing left in that line of inquiry, I hit him with the big question. "It sounds like it's just a telephone call," I ventured. "Why are you so anxious about it?"

He stopped like I'd thrown a bear trap on his plate. "Because I can't shake the feeling that I've seen her before," he admitted. He loosened his tie like he was trying to cheat the hangman, rolled his skinny shoulders slightly forward, mopped up egg yolks with a piece of toast and ate a little before he answered. "But I don't know where, and it's chewing me up inside."

I ran through scenarios in my head: a con artist; a wronged party from an old case now seeking revenge; an illegitimate daughter, conceived on a bender or a backstage fling, waiting to reveal her identity until she was sure he was her Real Dad before she put the squeeze on him. For all of what Martin refused to talk about, I wondered how much of it he even remembered. Heroin had got him fast and held him hard, haunting him even now. The track marks were long since gone, but there were scars on his soul that time would never heal.

"I could look into it," I said. "Make the call, keep you out of it, just in case." I couldn't help but be protective of him. Somebody had to be, and he'd bounced me out of trouble plenty enough. I owed him one. Hell, I owed him a couple if we were really keeping score.

He waved me off. "Thanks for the offer," he said. "But it's my name on the door. I'll make the call."

He didn't sound happy about it.

He paid the check, we said goodbye to Joan, and he drove us back to the office. He dialed the hotel number Ms Archwood had given me, putting the call on speaker. "Vanguard Hotel, how may I direct your call?"

"I'm looking to speak with a Lem Chesterfield," he said.

The desk manager didn't answer right away. "I'm sorry, sir, there's no one here by the name," he finally said.

An alias, perhaps? And why? I'd learned early on that the client could be just as shifty as whoever they wanted investigated, as if they were testing to see if we'd really put it all together. We always did. No sense trying to trick the brilliant mind of Martin Wade, Private Investigator.

"Did he check out recently?"

"No one has registered under that name," he repeated. "Is there anything else I can assist you with?"

I knew that look. Something had just clicked inside Martin's head. He ran the tip of his tongue across his upper lip and cleared his throat softly. "Maybe he's registered under a different name," he said. "Try Ron Carlock."

"One moment, please."

The phone began to ring. A man picked up. "Ron Carlock speaking."

Martin went as white as a wedding dress. "Ron," he said slowly. "It's Martin."

4

MARTIN

There are names you hope you never hear again. Voices you want to leave in the past. Nineteen years ago, another lifetime, one sometimes I imagined I dreamed. But unlike dreams, life has consequences. A dream can be forgotten. A life cannot be outrun.

The line got so quiet that I thought maybe Ron had hung up. I was hoping he would. He was the last person on this goddamn planet I wanted to hear from, now or ever. But after a moment, he spoke. "Martin," he said softly. "It's good to hear from you."

The pieces were all coming together, almost too quickly for me to catch hold of. I should have known it was Ron the second I heard that name, the same name he used to check into hotels under. And that meant Janice Archwood was really Janie Carlock, Ron's daughter. I could have kicked myself for not recognizing her. Now all grown up, she looked just like I remembered her mother, Sharon, used to look. But where did Archwood come from? Even that had the faintest taste of familiarity. "What are you doing in Perrine?" I asked.

"I came in to see some friends," Ron said. "I didn't know you lived here."

"Those friends include Janie?" I said.

Ron didn't respond right away. Valerie looked like she

wanted to shrink out of the room. I wished I hadn't put the call on speaker. I wished I'd never taken the case. She gestured to a legal tablet just past my left hip. I shook my head. No need to take notes. No need to have any record that any of this ever took place. "I just wanted to see my daughter," he finally said. "Is that so wrong?"

"It is if she told you she needs a little space to think."

"How are you involved in this?" Ron asked. "Why now, after all these years, do you even give a shit?"

"Because she hired me," I replied. "She asked me to mediate, to tell you she needs a little time to respond to your offer."

I was shaking, but I wasn't sure if it was from surprise or rage or fear. Why had she lied to me? Did she even know who I was? I was always Basil to her, the middle name I used on stage, the name I left behind.

The life I left behind.

Ron let out a sound that was more a bark than a laugh. "Sure," he croaked. "Sure, Martin, whatever you say."

He hung up. I set my phone down as gently as a baby in a crib. "Care to fill me in on what *that* was about?" Valerie asked.

"Not especially," I said, sinking into my chair. The room was spinning. Sweat was beading up all over my body like condensation on a cold beer. I had to hold it together long enough to get her out of the room so I could collapse into my own thoughts like a dying star. "Do me a favor and set up an appointment with Ms Archwood for tomorrow. I'm going to close out this case. We'll give back her deposit and destroy all the records."

The worst part wasn't the lie. Lies were the core piece of my business – hell, I'd told enough of them in my life to not take them personally. The worst part was how good it was to hear my partner's voice, as though the last nineteen years had been dust, easily blown away by a whistle. *No,* I told myself. *You put each other through hell. Do not go down that road again.*

Valerie read me well enough not to argue with me. She left the room and through the half-opened door I could hear her on the phone with Janie. I opened up my laptop. Janie had mentioned last seeing Ron at her mother's funeral. I did a quick search and sure enough, Sharon Lovette had died two years ago at her home in Santa Monica. Ovarian cancer, just shy of her fifty-first birthday. I wish I had known. I wish I had sent flowers. I wish I'd said a real goodbye nineteen years ago instead of just packing my piano into a U-Haul and disappearing to Minneapolis with a new phone number and no forwarding address. Like a fugitive. Like a coward.

Valerie knocked and let herself back in. "Ms Archwood will be in tomorrow at 11am," she said, arranging herself in the blue chair, one foot slung over the arm. "Are you going to be OK?"

I wanted to tell her. She knew little fragments of my past – that I was in recovery, that I had been a musician – but I was always hesitant to let out too much of myself. Just like I made her cover her tattoos so she wouldn't be recognizable in the field, I kept my own identifiers hidden. Anything that could hurt me. Anything that could be used against me somewhere down the line. "I'll be fine," I said, and changed the subject. "Plans for the evening?"

"Tacos at Topsy's," she said. "It's been a while since I've been over there. Besides, I'm too tired to cook. You want to come with me? We can drink Dr Pepper and fill up the jukebox. I got a hook-up."

I liked Topsy's – Valerie's aunt Gina booked good bands and we swapped stories from our previous lives as touring musicians, but tonight was the last night I wanted to spend toe-to-toe with temptation. "Think I'll go to a meeting and call it an early night," I said.

She did a quick tap-dance on her phone before I could even reach for mine. "There's a 6pm at the First Presbyterian Church," she said. "You could still make it. Or there's a 6:30 tomorrow morning."

I glanced at my watch. Time enough so that I could run home and get changed beforehand. Better than cutting my morning coffee short, and having to wait out a long evening. I lifted myself to standing once I was sure the shaking had settled. "You'll close up?"

"Of course," she replied with a decaffeinated smile. "Call me," she added. "If you need anything."

5

VALERIE

The best part about my day was always getting undressed at the end of it. I used to love showing off my tattoos, the full sleeves and ink on my thighs, but ever since Memphis I'd kept them all covered. I didn't want to be remembered, didn't want anyone to get the false impression that they knew me by the ink on my skin or the words I wrote. All of my work for *High Wire* had been published under "Staff Report" or, when absolutely necessary, the vague "VR Jacks." Working for a PI was the perfect cover, a career where no one was supposed to see you or recollect your face when they did. There are some things you just have to disappear from. But that moment when I could close my door and admire my brother's art always felt like the end of a long Halloween party, taking off a costume to reveal my true self once again.

Deacon had taken up tattooing right out of high school, apprenticing with a couple of award-winning parlors in Albany and Ithaca before coming back to Perrine to open up Arc Tattoo. He'd always been the more artistic of the two of us, illuminating his notebooks like historic manuscripts; test tubes and fire for chemistry, dancing bubble numbers in math, portraits of Shakespeare and Poe for English. And I was his willing canvas, traveling with him to expos and shows to stand at his booth in shorts and a tank top, skin bare and beautiful. *You're a nerd who never goes outside,* he told me. *Your pasty-white skin is perfect.*

Luckily, the scars of Memphis had missed the date on my wrist, 7/13/94, the matching ink Deacon and I had, the day our parents died. But going twenty-four hours without proper medical treatment had left a puckered white line nearly six inches long, from just below my left elbow to nearly my wrist, carving up the elaborate, watercolor-style scene of the front window of our old house on my forearm, with two little bluebirds sitting on the windowsill. My mom loved bluebirds and used to watch them from the feeder in front of that very window, and on the day we buried them, we saw two sitting side-by-side on a branch in the cemetery. Aunt Gina told us Mom had sent them to watch over us, and I still believed that. She and Dad must have been watching over me that night in Memphis, giving me enough strength to fight my way free, keeping me safe as I rode home through the night. Deacon was going to tattoo vines on it and fix what he could. We just hadn't gotten around to it yet.

I told myself I would never come back to Perrine, but what choice did I have? I couldn't go anyplace else while I was bleeding the way I was, wearing only pajamas and Dr Martens, without even a phone charger in my bag. Once I arrived, my city pulled me back in, like quicksand, like an addiction. Perrine was one of Upstate New York's many post-industrial towns in purgatory, always halfway between annihilation and redemption. Raines College kept some money here; the professors bought all the gorgeous old brick houses on the city's north side, high enough above the river so they never had to worry about a flood with their view. The students kept the skeeviest bar owners and the sketchiest landlords fed, but the rest of us had to fend for ourselves.

Luckily, there was music. That made things a lot easier. In the high times, Perrine had been known for making the radios that went in every drive-in in America, among other products, and with the conservatory at the college, it got a reputation as a music city that outlasted all the factories. Jazz in wine bars, metal clubs with concrete floors, nightly stages for dad-blues and classic rock, band concerts in the park on warm summer nights. Music was the only thing that could make this shithole worth living in. Knowing at the end of the day you could get a drink and hear a band – even if it was just a quartet of people struggling just like you – was the only reason most of us got out bed. Hell, even a jukebox could make the difference between a bad day and one that was all right in the end. And that wasn't even counting the college which had its own cloister of dance and opera and symphony performances. But there was always a quiet understanding that those offerings were not to be enjoyed by the likes of *us*.

There wasn't much to my apartment, a studio with a foldout couch I rarely unfolded, a kitchenette and a small bathroom, just enough space for a girl and her laptop. I'd never owned my own furniture and the handful of things I did possess had been left behind in Memphis. Probably in a pawn shop by now, sold for drugs under the pleas of *I need gas, I need to pay the babysitter, my kid needs his prescription*. I'd heard all of them even before I started working for Martin. I'd had enough of junkies for a lifetime.

I opened up my laptop and hit shuffle. Aunt Gina used to make us mix CDs like little love notes; music to play when we studied or cleaned our rooms or couldn't sleep. She had given up her own music career as the drummer in the Riot-Grrl band Icebox to raise us, but those mix CD melodies would always bind us as family. She introduced me to all her favorite artists: the B-52s and Garbage and Siouxsie and the Banshees, the Slits and Patti Smith and Dusty Springfield. I gathered all of them into my own collection until I had a patchwork assortment of bands I could love as my own.

Deacon used to joke that I was a music empath – that I absorbed everyone else's tastes – and it was true, to a certain extent. Even the cheesiest song can take on a critical meaning when you hear it at just the right moment: a kiss on the dance floor, on the radio while the windows are rolled down, a chord that slinks under your skin and wraps around your heart like a satin scarf.

Today felt like a Steely Dan day. I put on "Rikki Don't Lose That Number." My mom used to joke that this song was about her, that the original name was "Vickie," but that Donald Fagen had to change it so that my dad would never find out about their secret love affair. My mom loved Steely Dan to an almost absurd level; my brother was named after "Deacon Blues." But because she got to pick his name, my dad got to pick mine, and he chose to name me after a Steve Winwood song. I listened to both songs often, the last connection to the people who had been gone for nearly three decades.

The playlist was on shuffle. I let "Windmills of Your Mind" play while I changed into leggings and a tank top and a leopard-print cardigan. All of my clothes had been left behind in Memphis, but the upside was that I finally got to go through Gina's old boxes, pull out jackets and band shirts and babydoll dresses, leopard and plaid, all the Nineties thrift goodies that had been too big for a tit-less sixth grader in the age of flares and ringer tees. I was glad they were still boxed up in the garage, now that I was old enough to fit into them. I only had one fashion rule these days and that was that my arms had to be covered at all times. Not just at work, when a tail might remember the girl with the rabbit tattoo on her right shoulder. But more than that, I didn't want every drunk asshole asking me about my scar, as though their beer-soaked tenderness might get me to go to bed with them. I hadn't even shown my tattoos to Martin. We both had our secrets.

My phone buzzed. I hoped, for the briefest flit of a second, that it was Martin. I was worried about him. He didn't go to meetings often anymore, but he had something on his mind. Times like this reminded me that I knew very little about who he was before he arrived in Perrine – and worse, how easy it might be to send him back there.

But it was just Deacon on our family text chain: *Had a customer arrive late; put me back about half an hour,* he wrote.

NP, Gina replied. *Plenty of tacos. See you soon.*

So I had an unexpected windfall of time before dinner. The French Letters' "Shadowboxer" came on, appropriately. Even if I didn't know Martin, I would have loved his old band. To the uninitiated listener, The French Letters might have sounded like another Gin Blossoms clone, a slice of radio-friendly jangle-pop with a slightly sour edge. But this was 1986, the candy-drenched pop that dominated every party girl's concept of, like, the Eighties, was still in full swing. This would have been a welcome breath of fresh air, real and sweet, not quite as retro as garage rock or the heavily costumed air of rockabilly revival or as aggressive as the punk on stage at CBGBs just a few years prior. Martin – or rather, his alter-ego Basil Wise – had Morrissey's dramatic cadence and Paul Westerberg's gutter-blues sneer, but with none of the cruelness inherent in both of their voices. Instead, there was something oddly lilting, warm, even, with the glittery effervescence of New Wave, but grounded by Victor Van Owen's drums and Ron Carlock's guitar work.

Ron Carlock. He and Martin hadn't spoken in the decades following the band's dramatic burnout, on the courthouse steps where Martin had told the waiting paparazzi that the band was finished. The way he recounted it, it was news to all of them, especially their manager, but with terrible reviews of their fourth album, *Bullets for Breakfast,* and he and Ron waking up in the drunk tank after a weekend-long bender that culminated in a fistfight outside the Century Lounge, I don't think anyone was surprised that they self-combusted. Things only got worse when his fiancée Cecelia went missing. And she remained missing even now.

Hole's "Awful" came on shuffle. I hit skip. I wasn't in the mood for Courtney Love; I needed something soothing, something that would sink into the background as I worked. I settled on the Pet Shop Boys, "Opportunities." Moody and perfect.

Martin had taught me how to request arrest records and search court documents, and Ron's name quickly revealed a handful of drug arrests, a couple of domestic calls, a restraining order filed by a Sharon Lovette in 2009. One of the DUIs was from five years ago. Unlike Martin, it seemed, Ron hadn't fully reformed.

I tried Janice Carlock. Nothing. I tried Janie Archwood. Less than nothing. I tried Janie Lovette and finally found a few links. She was studying violin as a graduate student at Raines College, first chair of the Raines Orchestra and of the chamber ensemble; her recitals had garnered rave reviews, and the Raines College YouTube channel had a dozen clips showcasing her performances. For someone who went to the lengths of paying a man to protect her, she certainly didn't cover up her digital tracks very well. Most of us don't.

But I was still missing a whole section of the puzzle. I couldn't figure out why no one was being up front; the fake names, the garrote-tight silences. If it was all here to find, why lie about it? I could go over to Raines and ask her myself. I could call the hotel back and confront Ron. But for all the petty crimes, the adulteries and the fraud and the lifted jewelry, Martin still remained the one mystery I wanted to solve more than anything.

Topsy's was one of Perrine's best-kept secrets, an old speakeasy buried under what was now a sports bar where it wasn't uncommon to see a goth girl in full Victorian regalia or a genderqueer backup dancer in latex and platforms sharing smokes with hockey bros in Rangers jerseys. Gina kept the events as fluid as the bottles stocked behind the bar; one night it might be a screaming metal show, the next, a vintage PSA viewing party, the next, a Jimmy Buffet cover band, complete with beach balls and plastic parrot drinks.

Aunt Gina had picked up bartending shifts from the original

owners, Hank and Lena, when she first adopted us and, in turn, they adopted her. They'd invite us all over for Thanksgiving and to celebrate Hanukkah with them, made sure we had school clothes and bikes, became our doting aunt and uncle when our own aunt had to become our parents. And when they decided to retire, they sold the building and the business to Gina. Hank still tended bar occasionally, and Lena, a former Glamorous Lady of Wrestling, would offer to bounce when there was a band she liked on stage.

Taco Thursday was one of Gina's best additions to Topsy's. She didn't have a commercial kitchen, so she made a deal with a little Mexican place that opened last summer, just down the street from Arc Tattoo, to provide pans of ready-to-assemble ingredients. With two free tacos for the price of a drink, Topsy's quickly got the reputation for having the best damn tacos in town, but Gina wasn't one to hog all the glory, and routinely sent people to Garcia's Rose for the real deal. Last year, Garcia's Rose was awarded a *Perrine Courier*'s Best of the Best star in the Mexican Food category, an award that had, for a time, alternated between Moe's and Taco Bell. Some nights she would book bands, musica nortena and Latin pop bands, and once a punk band that covered Morrissey songs in Spanish. Tonight it was just the old Pizza Hut jukebox, loaded with all her mix CDs. Line Design's "Intensions" was playing, and the regulars were chowing down: a sweet young couple on a cheap date, a group of cheerful college boys with regatta-thick arms and nearly identical Raines University T-shirts, an older man with a hardcover book. Taco Thursday brought all types to Topsy's.

Deacon and Gina were seated at the bar with tin plates in front of them. "Better grab some now," Gina joked. "Your brother is going to clean me out."

"Today was insane," he said between bites. "I had back-to-back clients. No time for a lunch break. I'm *starving*."

She swatted him playfully. "Eat up," she said. To me, she added, "How many you want?"

I held up two fingers. I was still a little full from lunch, but I couldn't turn down free tacos. She had just handed me a plate when she waved to someone beyond me. Deacon and I both turned and saw a girl with hot pink sew-in braids and a floral-print bodysuit and cut-off jean shorts coming towards us. She looked like a dream, like a music video, like a catalogue model for a store with a velvet rope that might turn away anyone who wasn't as beautiful as she was.

Deacon got off his stool and hugged her. "Dott!" he exclaimed. "Are you playing tonight?"

"We are," she said. "But I'm here early. Didn't want to miss the tacos."

I forgot I was standing there until Gina said my name. "This is my niece, Valerie," she said. "Dott plays drums in Machine Gun Snatch, as well as The Chirmps. Machine Gun Snatch is playing as part of our punk showcase later tonight."

I'm sure I said something benign and idiotic, like *cool* or *yeah, I'll stick around,* words tumbling out of my mouth like stale Skittles down the metal sleeve of an old gumball machine.

"C'mon, sit, join us," Deacon offered, patting the seat next to him, the one my ass had occupied just a moment before. She could have it. She could have whatever she wanted.

She took my seat and I sat next to her as Gina got her some tacos. "I was just admiring your ink," she said to me. "Is it all Deacon's work?"

Before I could say anything, he jumped in. "Of course," he boasted. "Who else?"

But she didn't look at him. She put down her taco and pushed back her right sleeve to reveal a hand of tarot cards, surrounded by stars. I wanted to reach out and touch her perfect tight skin. "Got this one in Montreal," she said. "But Deacon did this one for me a few months back." She pushed back her hair to reveal a series of thorny vines that ran down her neck.

"So proud of that one." He beamed.

"They're beautiful," I said.

"So are yours," she said. "The ones I can see, anyways."

It had been a long time since I'd done anything that resembled flirting. My best friend Katy and I used to go out to clubs in Memphis and dance with pretty hipster boys who smelled like cigarettes and sandalwood, exchange a goodnight kiss and a promise to call that never materialized on either end. Katy always carried small blank cards and a pen, collected his phone number and wrote down a description on the back before storing them in a long wooden box. *Alex, hair like shark fins, gin and tonic, terrible dancer. Townes, faded ink, shy, Diet Coke with lime, just in town for the night.* Back then, Katy was pretty and quirky enough to get away with it, and I quickly fell into the mode of shy best friend. I liked boys, but I was always more natural with girls. Tonight, however, was testing that theory. And I wasn't going to let another thought of Katy – even one of the few happy memories left – make it any more awkward than it already was.

"You should stay for the show," Deacon said.

It took me a second to realize he was talking to me. "Yes, you should!" Dott clasped my hands. My whole body went electric. "Please say you'll stay. We're up third, but there are some great bands before us."

There was a yes on the tip of my tongue. But there was a no like a stone in my throat, someplace more pressing that I needed to be. "Next time," I promised.

She looked disappointed. "I'm holding you to that," she said, giving me a squeeze. She let go and eased off her barstool. "I've got to go help load up the van. I'll be back in about an hour."

"I'll save everyone some food," said Gina.

She thanked Gina for the tacos and then turned to me. "It was rad meeting you," she said. "See you at another show."

I watched her leave like she was disappearing into the fog. Deacon elbowed me in the ribs the second she was out the door. "She's cute," he teased.

"Shut up," I replied, stuffing the last of my taco in my mouth. I was a complete and total dumbass. With my social circle as small as it was – just Martin, Deacon and Aunt Gina – I had forgotten how to talk to anyone who wasn't a client or a criminal. I really needed to get some friends my own age.

But I wasn't going to do that tonight, not now that Dott had walked out of the room. I glanced at my phone: 7:49pm. I thought about calling Martin, telling him I wanted to come by, but he'd likely tell me no, that was unnecessary, that he'd see me in the morning. But I was worried about him, and with what I knew now – about Ron, about Janie – I had more reason to be concerned.

I said goodnight to my brother and aunt. I left the bar and turned the corner towards my car. I heard a woman and a man arguing in the alley, bodies half-blocked by the dumpster, faces shadowed by the lamplight. "How fucking dare you," she was saying. "I told you to leave me the fuck alone." The tall spikes of her mohawk created curious shadows on the brick wall behind her.

"I'm allowed to be here," he sneered back.

There was something familiar about her voice, but I couldn't place it. I guess she could have been anybody telling some guy to get out of her space. "Fuck off before I call the bouncer and the cops."

"I'm here to take promo photos of *your* band. Why are you being such a bitch?"

I was about to step in when I heard the door slam, followed by footsteps coming my way. I wasn't fast enough. "You got something you want to add?" he said.

Under the streetlights he was even less intimidating than his voice made him seem. He listed ever so slightly to one side, weighed down by the pin-and-patch-covered bag graffitied with the words BOMB SQUAD hanging over his right shoulder. His black canvas trench coat was two sizes too big, and he had quarter-sized gauges in his ears.

I wanted to laugh at him. Instead, I put my hand inside my purse and wrapped it around a roll of nickels I kept, just in case. I probably could have knocked this guy out if I breathed hard on him. "Go home to your Xbox," I said. "This is a fight you can't button-mash your way out of."

He wisely crossed the street.

6

MARTIN

I bought the house on Lido Avenue the day after my realtor showed it to me. I had all but given up on finding a place and had resigned myself to apartment living when he called and said the buyers had backed out and the owner was looking for a quick sale. It was a cozy little bungalow on a quiet cul-de-sac, built in the 1920s, with tucked-in front porch and a small backyard and four bedrooms, enough for an office and a guest room for when my sister Sandy brought my niece Gretchen out to visit, even a studio if I ever got around to writing music again. I kept telling myself I'd get a little trio together, play some jazz standards at weddings and hotel lounges for a little cash to keep me afloat in the lean months. The house reminded me, in a happy way, of the house Cecelia and I lived in back in LA. She would love it here. Or maybe she would hate it. Too quiet. Unless she decided that now was the time to reveal where she'd been hiding all these years, I'd never know.

I felt like Perrine needed me. The cops had their hands full of punks and drunks and dealers and the petty thieves. But sometimes you just wanted your jewelry back or your miserable husband caught with his girlfriend so you could finally get that divorce, and the Wade Agency had a package for all price points. Everything was negotiable; I could be a white knight or a peeping Tom. Life and lust and greed could be bought and sold cheap.

It was easy to get bitter about Perrine – Valerie frequently described her hometown as *so shitty* – but for the most part, I was comfortable here. The ex-punk in me enjoyed the gritty corners; the rest of me liked that my street was quiet and my mortgage was modest. I could never afford to live like this in LA. I knew my neighbors and the grocery clerks, and none of them wanted anything from me except maybe the total of my purchase or to pick up their mail while they were on vacation. It was the first place since Duluth where I felt like I could relax at the end of the day. Like I was finally home.

I was working my way through an ambling rendition of Dave Brubeck's "Strange Meadowlark" on the baby grand in the studio when I heard a knock on the door. I wasn't expecting anyone; it was after seven, but I got up and answered it to find Valerie standing on my porch with a grocery bag in her hand. "Everything all right?" I asked.

"Yeah," she said. She reached into the bag and pulled out a four-pack of ginger beer. "Just thought you could use some company."

It was easy to forget how well she could read me, that I wasn't the impenetrable vault I liked to imagine I was. "Fair assessment," I said. "Come on in."

"It's a nice night," she said. "Thought we could sit on the porch."

"I'll get some glasses."

I filled a bowl with ice, got down two tumblers and found a brass bottle opener that I had gotten as a gift years ago. I think it came with a flask; the sort of hipster drinking set I had no use for even when I did imbibe. I followed her outside and we settled into the black porch chairs I would soon have to bring inside, before the weather got wet and miserable. I pulled up the WFMU stream and plugged it into my little speakers. October Project warbled "Deep As You Go" as I poured us a pair of drinks and we toasted with a muted cheer. I took a small sip. "That's strong," I said. "The good stuff."

"You don't think I'd show up here with anything less, did you?"

"Of course not." This was what I really missed about drinking. The quiet camaraderie, the easy flow of conversation, the end of the day when I could loosen my tie and let all my defenses down. I always told myself that if I had one hour left to live, I'd treat myself to one last taste of good bourbon, smoke a cigarette and listen to records. A Lucky Strike and *The Queen is Dead*, specifically, or maybe *Imperial Bedroom*. A perfect evening for the end of the world.

But I also knew that Valerie didn't come here just to sit in silence with her boss, especially not after a long late night in the car together and a full day of work. "Something you want to ask me?" I said. "Go ahead, spit it out."

She grinned like she knew she'd been made. "I want you to tell me about Ron and Janie," she said, rattling the ice in her glass. "All of it."

"All of it, huh?" I should have known I couldn't keep a secret from her forever. "Why don't you tell me what you already know, and I'll fill in the rest."

"I know that Ron was your guitar player," she said. "And I know he's had some trouble in the past. DUIs, domestics, a couple of possession charges. And I know that Janie is studying violin at Raines under a different name."

"What name?"

"Janie Lovette."

She was a better sleuth than I gave her credit for. "Her mother's maiden name," I said. I should have thought of that. Still didn't explain why she was using "Archwood" in my office. Amy Rigby's "20 Questions" was playing tinny from the tiny speakers. Appropriate for this little interrogation. "Ron and his wife, Sharon Lovette, had a daughter, Janie," I began. "Sharon was a folk singer, nice gal, Janie was a cute kid, born just before *Fait Accompli* came out. I'd go over there with Cecelia, Ron and I would play,

Janie would dance around in her nightgown, and after her mom put her to bed, we'd drink a couple bottles of wine, listen to records. Then Ron, Cecelia and I started using, and Sharon got really into cocaine, and, well... I guess you can figure out the rest."

She took another sip like she was waiting for me to continue. I obliged her. Even if I'd wanted to, I couldn't stop. My meeting had left me in a confessional mood. "I knew there was something familiar about her when she walked into the office," I said. "But I couldn't place it. Or maybe it was wishful thinking. Either way, guess it turned out to be true."

For years, I'd wondered what had become of Janie, if she'd gotten out safely or if she fell into the same traps her parents did. And now I knew. It was a relief I didn't deserve. Not after what I'd put her through. Not after all the apologies I owed her.

The radio ambled into a pledge drive. I reached over and turned down the volume. "Ron used to call me up and play me some music," I continued. "And only about a quarter of it was an unlistenable mess. He was a genius, even when he was tanked. We lost touch after I got out of rehab and moved to Minneapolis, and I would have been fine to keep it that way." That wasn't entirely true. I thought about Ron and Sharon a lot, wished it all could have been different, wished we could have come through our hells together. But only the men made it out alive, it seemed.

"So what are you going to do?"

I finished my drink and set down the glass. "I'm going to give her back her deposit," I said. "And close the case. I'm glad she's doing well and I hope she'll be able to sort things out with Ron on her own, but I can't be involved. It's too personal, opens too many old wounds."

"I think that's a good idea," she said. "Besides, it's distracting you from your passion for divorce work. Lot of loose spouses running around. I need you on your game."

I let her have the laugh she was looking for, some assurance that I could hold it together.

"Right," I said. "Thanks for the drink. It's exactly what I needed."

"Any time." She glanced at her phone. "But call if you need anything. I mean it."

"I don't need you to be my sponsor, Valerie," I said. "I just need you to be my assistant."

I didn't intend for that to hurt, but there was a momentary flicker of insult across her face. She shuffled her feet a little and forced a smile. "That's fair," she said. "Good night, Martin."

I felt like a jackass. "Good night, Valerie," I mumbled. "I'll see you in the morning."

I picked up the glasses as she drove away. I dumped out the ice and put away the bottle opener. I rinsed out the bottles and put them in the recycling bins, a quiet domestic scene not unlike the hundreds that were probably playing just like it all over Perrine.

If you offered me a drink I would politely decline. If you put a needle and a spoon down in front of me, I could walk away easily. But there are some things a man is just powerless against. Money. Sex. Revenge.

Or a voice from the past.

The Vanguard Hotel was one of the first buildings in Perrine I really got to know. I did some surveillance there, found a junior partner screwing his neighbor and billing the company for her "consulting services." It was tawdry work, but it paid the bills. I hadn't been back since, although I'd heard the restaurant at the top was one of the best in town. I didn't have anyone to take, didn't have any reason to drop a couple hundred bucks on dinner, and didn't have the money to spare if I wanted to.

I got Ron's room number from the clerk and took the elevator to the fourth floor. I knocked before I could talk myself into making a better decision. I heard the news click off and he answered the door a beat and a half later. "Martin," he said. "Didn't expect to see you here."

Looking at him now, you wouldn't have been able to guess he was one of the great rock-and-roll hellions. He'd gotten softer, his shaggy brown hair now close cropped and thin at the crown, a map of lines on his face that told plenty of stories of loud nights and wild days. But I wasn't a bellhop or a waiter. I knew who he used to be. It's impossible to forget the face of a man who has been to the heights of heaven and the depths of hell alongside you, no matter how much you may have come to finally despise him.

"Didn't expect to be here," I said. "Guess I just had to see you for myself. I… I'm sorry about earlier."

"Come on in," he said, opening the door a little wider. "You want a nine-dollar Coke? I've got a fully stocked mini-bar here."

I let myself smile. "I'll take a six-dollar seltzer, if you've got it."

In the early days of touring, we'd stay up writing in one of our rooms after everyone else went to bed, drinking what we'd never be caught dead ordering in public, a Jack and Coke for me, canned Bud Light for him. We'd share the same ashtray because Ron always wanted a clean one to steal as a souvenir, and fuel ourselves with Twix bars and KitKats and half-stale pretzels. Drinks with the band were a good way to wind down after a show, but I always looked forward to the mini-bar raid most of all, like a small heist. And our management hated it, which made it that much more fun.

He got me a seltzer and took a Diet Coke for himself. As though we were sharing the same memory, he added, "There's a Twix in here too, if you want it."

I hadn't eaten dinner, but I wasn't hungry. Time and age had dulled my sweet tooth. He gestured for me to sit on the couch and he settled into a chair nearby. "So you're a PI now," he said. "Wouldn't have expected that."

"I'm not on the case," I said quietly. "I just... wanted to see you."

He let that settle between us. "You still play?"

"I'll work out a tune every so often, but nothing new," I replied. "Nothing of ours. Not since..."

"Shame," he said. "A waste of talent."

"What about you?" I asked. "You still get into the studio?" A smarter man would have already known the answer to that question. A smarter man would have done his research, come in with all the answers. But that man wasn't me, not tonight.

"Session gigs mostly," he said. "Did some music for a cop show that got cancelled after one season, a couple soundtracks. Working man's stuff."

"So what brings you to town?"

The minute the words came out of my mouth I regretted them. He narrowed his eyes for just a moment before he answered. "When Sharon was dying, one of the blessings we had was that the past didn't matter. The bad parts, anyways. Janie came out when she could; I made us dinner, we all watched TV together, I helped Sharon with her medicines and took care of her when she was too weak to do much for herself. We were a family, at least for a little while. And that was all I ever wanted. Even if I was the one who wrecked it all."

I almost believed him. But even if he had spent time with his dying wife and his estranged daughter, I couldn't let myself believe that there wasn't an ulterior motive – like the drugs in a dying woman's toolkit.

"I know what you're thinking," he said. "And yes, I was tempted. I'd be lying if I said I wasn't. Sharon was on morphine and there were plenty of times I thought, 'Hey, she'll never miss a couple drops in a ginger ale.' But I didn't. Never once. Because my baby girl needed me. My wife needed me. I've been sober four years, Martin. I completed rehab, just like you. I go to meetings. It took me a long time to get here, and there were plenty of slip-ups in-between, but I own those. These past four years aren't much, but they're mine."

Ron was always the best among us at pretending to be sober. He had that easy, effortless charm that lured you in like a carnival barker. You'd give him your last dollar, your last baggie, without ever considering the consequences.

"Janie was worried you wanted money," I said.

He snorted. "Don't know where she got that idea," he said. "I mean, it's not like the old days, but I'm comfortable. Hell, if anything, I could give *her* money. She's a student, after all, and she left a bunch of scholarships behind to take care of her mother. What twenty-four year-old couldn't use a couple extra twenty-dollar bills in a birthday card?"

"Like your dad always sent you in college," I said.

"'Don't spend it all on beer,'" he recited. "Which is good advice – I mean, you had to save some for cigarettes."

I let myself laugh, but only for a moment. "Did she ever ask you to stop contacting her?"

"Only in the last few weeks," he admitted. "But I think that had more to do with Nora than anything."

"Nora?"

"You remember Nora Archwood, right? She was Sharon's friend."

Guess I knew where Janie took her pseudonym surname from. "Sure," I said. "The violinist, right?"

"Correct." He rolled the empty tumbler between his palms. "She took guardianship of Janie when she was in her teens so that she could focus on her violin," he said. "Truth is, I think Sharon just wanted to give Janie some stability. Janie's been with Nora ever since, and when she got accepted into Raines, Nora followed her up here to teach. Janie's a grad student. She's very good."

"Of course she is," I said. "Her parents were brilliant."

He didn't smile. "Good thing she got that trait," he said. "Instead of how fucked up we both were."

Silence. "I'm sorry about Sharon," I said after a minute. "If I had known..."

He waved me off. "She wouldn't have wanted you to see her like that," he said. "It was ugly and painful, and you know how vain she was."

I kept waiting for him to ask about Cecelia. I was glad he didn't. That whole chapter was an ugly piece of our lives. Of Janie's too. After all, she was the one who found me. Some memories just need to stay in the past. We exchanged numbers and said our goodnights. It wasn't until I turned onto Lido Avenue that all the sadness settled on me. It was a hurt I knew well, a scar that ran down the center of my chest that reopened so quickly I hadn't felt it until I took a breath. I parked the car and fought back tears until I was sure I could make it to the front door without falling to pieces.

It was nearing midnight. I went inside and rifled through my records. There are some sorrows so deep that sleep or pills or company cannot fix them. For those times, there is Elvis Costello.

7

VALERIE

There was something familiar about the tune Martin was playing on the upright piano when I got into the office, a melody with a title on the tip of my tongue. "Is that...?" I breathed. "Is that Elvis Costello?"

He didn't stop playing. " 'Man Out of Time,' to be specific," he said without looking at me. "I got a little lonesome last night."

I put on the kettle to boil water for coffee. "You could have called," I said. "I would have come back over."

"It wasn't anything *Blood and Chocolate* couldn't fix," he said. "And *King of America*. And *Imperial Bedroom*." He finished out the tune. "OK, maybe I got *really* lonely."

"And Elvis Costello cheers you up?"

He gave me a weak smile neither of us was buying. "It was a fine idea at the time," he said.

Now it's a brilliant mistake, I heard in my head. I'd only gotten into Elvis Costello because Martin played him constantly the first few months I was here; I'd tried to listen to him on and off throughout the years, but it didn't click until I had someone to share it with, like a secret language I had finally learned to speak.

The kettle boiled. I measured out a double-strength pot of coffee into the French press. "Should I be worried about you?"

He shook his head. "A minor annoyance," he said. "It'll pass in a few days. I'm just indulging my inner sad-sack. Feels good every so often." He plunked out a few bars of "Watching the Detectives" like a goddamn joke.

I didn't feel like laughing. "Something happen after I left?" I asked.

"Guess the day just caught up with me," he said. "It'll pass, I promise. I've had longer nights."

I pressed down the plunger and it didn't go easily. A harbinger, perhaps, of what the day was to bring? The buzzer jolted us both. "That must be Janie," he said. "Show her in."

The walk to the door felt like a million miles. The door weighed two hundred pounds in my hand as I pulled it open. Today she hid her hair under a vintage turban with a long sleeve shirt and a maxi skirt like a traveling queen. She looked tired and frazzled, clutching the strap of her bag like she was using it to swing over a chasm.

"Thank you for coming in, Ms Archwood," Martin said, standing. "Coffee?"

"No thank you."

"Right this way."

He did not invite me to join them. I took my coffee and went back to my desk to close out Janie's file. I didn't feel right doing so. It all felt unfinished, too much unspoken, not enough spelled out. Divorce cases were clear-cut. He or she cheats, we catch them in the act, the end. *Make the check out to the Wade Agency, thank you for your business.* We can both walk away clean, wash our hands of the whole mess. Not this one. It should have been easy. A phone call, that was all. But we should have known that nothing easy in this business is worth trusting. And it didn't take a black-and-white matinee or a paperback to tell me that a young woman with a lie on her lips was always trouble, even long after she walked out that door.

My phone buzzed. A text from an unknown number: *It's Dott, from Topsy's. Deacon gave me your number. Hope you don't mind.*

Of course I didn't. *How was the show?* I asked.

Pretty fucking stellar, came the reply. *Joyride was just on fire. Really high energy. Gives us a lot to live up to.*

I'm sure you'll have no problem replicating it.

Let's have coffee soon. I want to ask your opinion about a couple of tattoos.

I swooned across my desk.

8

MARTIN

I made the motion of flipping through Janie's file while she arranged herself in the chair. I could see it now. She had her father's eyes, her mother's mouth and nose and pale skin. "I spoke with Mr Chesterfield," I said, glancing up at her. "Or, should I say, Ron Carlock."

She let out a small sigh. "You figured me out," she murmured. "Guess I should have seen that coming."

"So why did you lie to me?"

"I was afraid you wouldn't take the case," she said. "You and my dad were best friends. I thought you wouldn't believe me."

"But you must have known I would recognize him."

"I didn't really think it was you," she said. "I tried to go to the police, but they said unless there was a specific threat, there wasn't really a whole lot they could do. Someone suggested I hire a PI, and I found your listing. I thought it was just a coincidence... until I saw you. And then I thought, well, maybe you'll just call him, tell him to back off without telling him who you were."

"I did call him," I said. "And I gave him your message. He said he'll back off, but that's as far as I can go with this." I knew better than to tell her I'd seen him. Didn't want to muddy this case any more than I already had. It was a stupid impulse to go over there, one I was already regretting.

"I'm sorry I lied to you," she said.

"It's not just that," I said. "You asked me to get involved in a case I've got a personal history with, and that's not right or fair, Janie." I reached into her folder and took out a slim envelope, sliding it across the desk to her. "Your deposit. It's all there. It doesn't seem right to take it."

She didn't touch the money. "When I was little, I used to imagine you'd come back for me," she said, like she had sand in her throat. "That you'd rescue me and take me to wherever you'd run off to and raise me as your own. Just like I rescued you. Remember?"

She couldn't have hurt me more if she pulled a gun out of her purse and shot me through the heart. The overdose. She was the one who found me on the floor of her bedroom, foam in my throat, a few minutes from a fatality. The overdose that landed me in rehab, the first domino in a falling chain that led to police suspicions and a suicide attempt, the breakup of my band and my retreat from LA, all the way up to her standing here in my dusty little office.

"I'm sorry I never came through," I said. And I was, suddenly more sorry than I'd ever been about anything in my whole life. Recovery is all about making up to those you've hurt, but at the time, I brushed it all off, believing she'd be too young to even remember me as anything more than a shadow, a face in a photograph with a name that meant nothing. "But Julliard, now Raines, first chair… you've done beautifully for yourself. I'm proud of you." I wouldn't have been able to give her that even if I had managed somehow to take her with me, and no state agency was going to just give a child to a recovering addict living a thousand miles away in his sister's guest room.

"Nora has been good to me," she said. "She's really provided for me. Paid my tuition, always kept a roof over my head. I owe her everything. I think that's what my dad doesn't understand. I can't just up and leave her. Not for someone, let's be real, that I barely know."

It made sense. Part of the journey of sobriety is realizing that things can't just go back to how they were instantly. The addict is always anxious to fix it all, but it goes so much deeper. It takes time we're terrified we don't have. And more often than not, that makes it worse.

"What made you choose violin?" I asked. "Other than teenage rebellion?"

That made her laugh. When she was little, she laughed constantly, loved to be tickled and teased. I was relieved to see that a tough childhood hadn't driven her joy completely out of her. "My granddad played it," she said. "I have his violin now; the one that his father built to play in restaurants when he first got to America."

"The Carlock concerto legacy," I said. "I've heard the stories, some from your grandfather himself. Glad someone can keep up the family tradition."

"Yeah, well, I got a little burned out on Joni Mitchell and the Stooges," she said. "Orchestra rehearsed after school, so it was one more reason not to go home."

Music never had to save me. I came from a good family, I had parents who supported me even when they didn't especially love the decisions I made, a sister who opened her home to help me stay clean, a niece who didn't hate visiting me. Hell, everyone in my band was just a suburban punk; one could make the argument that music was what destroyed us. But Janie found her salvation there, she found a safe place when her own home life was intolerable and built it up into a fortress.

"You look like you're doing well," she said. "Is that your daughter in the other room?"

Now it was my turn to laugh a little. "Valerie? No, just my assistant." When I hit fifty, I had a few nights of melancholy, lamenting that I had never settled down and had a family of my own. I loved doting on Janie when she was little, sitting her on my lap during rehearsals and playing the *Sesame Street* theme for her on the keyboard. Sometimes I would let her play a few keys, create a loop of the melody and play it over a riff from Ron, make up some silly lyrics and sing it back to her, tell her she was part of the band now. Vic and Kurt always seemed annoyed by her toddling presence, but I couldn't get enough of it. I think I would have liked being a father.

Her phone buzzed in her purse. She took it out and glanced at it briefly. Her whole expression changed like a storm had swept in.

"Everything OK?" I asked.

"Sure," she said, shoving her phone back in her bag. "I've just got to get to rehearsal. I've got a recital this weekend. Nora keeps me busy getting my name out there. Thanks for handling everything with my dad."

"Of course," I said. "I hope it all works out."

I wasn't sure if I should hug her or shake her hand or do nothing at all. She made my choice for me. She dashed out of the office, calling back whoever was on the other line. I heard a faint "I'm sorry" in a frantic tone I didn't like. But it was no longer my business. She was no longer my client. An old friend, a warm memory. Maybe we'd get lunch and catch up more before her father left town. Or maybe we'd just see each other around town, smile and wave and keep moving.

"What do you want me to do with her file?" Valerie asked.

"Mark it as closed," I replied. "No payment needed."

9

VALERIE

Saturday morning Aunt Gina invited me over for breakfast. She had lived in the apartment above Topsy's since she got custody of us; Hank and Lena had been renting it to college students, but the day the semester was over, it was ours. Her aesthetic had eased a bit as we all aged; show posters were now artfully framed, the records were stored in a cabinet instead of milk crates with the "Theft of this Case is a Crime" warnings prominently displayed. The Goddess Shrine, a road-worn gift from the members of Icebox, stood majestically next to the record player in the corner of the room.

The Goddess Shrine had traveled from Icebox's earliest days in clubs, evolving from a decoupage cigar box to a small jewelry cabinet, decorated with pictures of their rock idols – Patti Smith and Aretha Franklin, Debbie Harry and Wendy O. Williams. It was placed in the green room with a tealight candle for good luck; Mia, the drummer, would even leave a small portion of their dinner on a plate in case the Mother Goddesses – women like Janis Joplin and Etta James and Billie Holiday – were hungry. One time, in Tampa, they arrived so late there wasn't time to set up the shrine and they played one of their worst shows, so from there on out, they took the shrine with them on the first load in. The back was graffitied with signatures of other women they admired: Shirley Manson in silver glitter marker; a long-faded lip print from Courtney Love; a floating heart drawn by Tori Amos; Carrie Brownstein's scrawl, dated just days before Gina had to come home to bury her brother and raise his kids. Whenever any of us were having a bad day, we were encouraged to go to the drawer and pull out a quote, song lyrics written on small slips of paper like fortune cookies. More often than not, it was exactly what we needed to hear.

Burt Bacharach was playing on the turntable when I let myself in. The whole place smelled of sizzle and coffee. Gina was in the kitchen, wearing an apron she'd made out of old T-shirts. "Just put on a fresh pot," she said, pointing to the mini coffee maker. "Help yourself."

"Is this some of the Icebox Terrible Coffee Club coffee?" I asked.

"Yep," she said. "Maple Bacon. It's not as terrible as Lacy led us to believe. Doesn't mean she'll see mercy – I found Banana Split coffee at TJ Maxx. I can't imagine that won't be disgusting."

Not all bands fell apart like the French Letters. Some bands sent each other boxes of noxiously flavored coffee as an ongoing prank. Mia and Lacy and Denise acted as surrogate aunts after Gina left; they stayed with us when they came through town, got us backstage passes and showered us with merch and let us eat their green-room snacks, which, as a kid, was my favorite part. Mia was now a producer in Los Angeles, Lacy ran a record shop in Portland, Oregon and Denise got married and settled down with a family in Keyport, New Jersey.

I made a small cup and took a taste. It had a chemical aftertaste that could only be washed away with a second sip. I must have made a face because Gina laughed. "There's real coffee in the thermos," she said. "It's from Wegman's, I promise. You want some eggs?"

"I won't say no." Breakfast lately had been a cup of coffee in a travel mug; the stakeout was still taking its toll and by the end of the day I was too tired to go grocery shopping. "Should we wait for Deacon?"

"No, just us this morning," she said, cracking eggs into a bowl. "I wanted to talk with you about something."

I couldn't imagine anything good was going to come at the end of that sentence. I'd had a lot of heart-to-hearts in this space, sitting on the counter while my aunt cooked and walked me through The Talk and teenage heartbreak and college anxieties. But for the first time, she seemed nervous, focusing intently on the scrambled eggs. "Out with it," I finally said. "You're making it worse."

She stopped. She sighed. "You got a letter," she said. "From Memphis."

I was glad Deacon wasn't there. I didn't even like that Aunt Gina was there and it was her house. I didn't want anyone to know anything about what happened with Katy Memphis, didn't want to think about it, didn't even want to acknowledge the city's existence. *It could be anything,* I told myself. A final paycheck from the paper. Junk mail. A birthday card sent unaware and forwarded until the post office found me here. But that meant it could also be a police report, a trial summons, a suicide note. Nothing good was ever going to come out of Memphis. Not these days anyways.

"You know you can talk to me," she said. "I'm here to listen."

"I don't want to," I snapped. I wasn't even hungry anymore. I just wanted to go home and pull the covers back over my head and pretend this day never even started.

She didn't push it further. "It's on the sideboard if you want to take it with you," she said. "But for right now, let's eat."

There was no return address, but the handwriting was unmistakably Katy's. I had a handful of options. I could open it, I could throw it in the garbage or the shredder in Martin's office, I could mark it *Return to Sender* and drop it in the box on the corner. Every single option seemed crueler than the last. The skin around my scar burned like a fever I couldn't sweat out. I couldn't even remember the last time I got mail; my bills were all online, I could go days without opening my mailbox and still find nothing inside when I finally did. The small saving grace was that the sender hadn't tracked me to my home address or the Wade Agency, instead using Aunt Gina as a clearing house for whatever location unknown I might be hiding in. But whatever was inside was important enough that it needed to be mailed. An email can be deleted without a second thought. A phone call can be hung up on or never answered, a voicemail left unheard, a number blocked for all eternity.

It wasn't important enough, however, to be opened today.

10

MARTIN

The weekend felt like it went on forever. I had lunch with my friend Malee at Flower House; we traded case notes over spring rolls and Pad Thai. Sandwiched between a nudie joint, a liquor store, a leather shop and a topless bar in Perrine's east end, Flower House was an oasis in the center of vice. But Malee did more than just food – she posted bail bonds, tracked fugitives as a licensed bounty hunter and ran a sort of sawbones operation out of the back, everything from taping a dancer's sprained ankle to pulling out a bullet to getting her hands on prescription-strength meds and antibiotics for people who couldn't afford a trip to the doctor. Not to mention the folk remedies, salves and tinctures and teas. Malee was a one-stop shop.

Ron left a message that I wasn't in the mood to return. I thought about calling Valerie to see if she wanted to get lunch on Sunday afternoon, but never picked up the phone. I finished Terry Teachout's biography of Duke Ellington. I did the *New York Times* Sunday crossword puzzle and checked in with Rex Parker's blog and considered leaving a comment about the D14 clue but decided against it. No sense starting an argument with strangers.

There were three days' worth of messages when I got to the office on Monday: a granddaughter who had stolen a necklace, a couple requests for background checks, the follow-up from

Dr Russell. The rest was just junk. Valerie sorted the mail while I returned all the calls. *Bring a photo, we'll ask at the pawn shops. 10:30 tomorrow works fine. Happy to run those background checks, please send over the information at your earliest convenience.* When all that was finished, I sat down at the piano and plunked out Men at Work's "It's a Mistake" because I woke up with it stuck in my head. Valerie sang along from her desk. That lifted my mood. Things felt normal again. *I* felt normal again.

A car door slammed in front of our building like a shot fired in the night. Valerie glanced out the window. "Cops," she muttered. "Roland and Rue."

I wondered if Dr Russell had shot her cheating husband at the lake house, if the granddaughter had been caught taking more jewelry, if whatever Valerie left behind in Memphis had finally caught up with her. "I will handle this," I said. That did little to erase the worry from her face or my mind. Cops like Roland and Rue don't make social calls.

The hard knock came about thirty seconds later. "Police," came Roland's bark. "Let us in, Martin."

I answered the door, leaving the chain on. "Good morning, detectives," I said. "Do you have a warrant?"

"Relax, Martin," said Rue. "It's just a friendly chat."

There was nothing friendly about those two. Roland had the bitter world-weariness of a lifelong civil servant whose pension was shrinking at the same rate as his hairline, but Rue was the one you had to watch out for. He had a face like Gilbert Godfrey's voice and a sadistic streak as long as his nasty little nose. If Roland had been tasked with keeping him in line, he'd long since grown tired of the chore. There's a pair like this in every precinct in America. "Forgive me if I don't put on the coffee," I said.

"Just let us in," Roland said. "If you make us get a warrant, we'll come back and tear the place apart just on principle."

I lifted the chain and let them both in. I couldn't take the risk that their threat to get a warrant was based on a solid tip;

not just because they'd find Valerie's paperweight, but because I didn't want to get the reputation of a man who'd let the cops toss his place. That was hard to live down. "Only because my cleaning service doesn't come until Thursday," I said. "Touch anything and Chief Hollander is my next call."

Roland pulled an evidence bag out of his coat pocket. Inside was my water-wrinkled card. "What kind of work were you doing for Janie Lovette?"

"Ask her," I said.

"That's going to be difficult," said Rue. "Seeing as how we pulled her body out of the Leslie River at about four this morning."

Time cracked in half. Everything in the room stopped. Valerie gasped, somewhere in another dimension. "Janie…" I sputtered. "Janie's dead?"

When Janie was a toddler, I pulled her out of Ron and Sharon's swimming pool after she'd accidentally fallen in. I'd felt her heart pound against my chest as she clutched me, coughing pool water and terror on my already soaked shirt. I'd saved her once. But no one was there to save her this time.

"We didn't ticket her for swimming," Roland said. "Now tell us about the work you did for her."

When Cecelia went missing, I kept thinking I'd wake up from the nightmare and she'd be safe next to me, over and over for what felt like forever. But the news of Janie's death felt like the end of a campfire story, the kind where the boy goes to a gravesite and finds his letter jacket draped over the headstone of the beautiful hitchhiker he'd driven home the night before. Maybe she was always a bad dream, a ghost haunting our office for a few hours. This couldn't be real. There was no goddamn reason for any of it to be real.

"Wednesday and Thursday," I said, straightening a tie that was already as straight as a field sobriety test. "She hired me for a few hours to look into something for her."

"Care to elaborate on what?"

"You'll have to get a warrant for that," I said. "Client confidentiality."

This wasn't the answer Roland wanted. "Make this easy on us, Martin," he grumbled.

"My tax dollars at work."

"Jesus Christ, we just spent the whole goddamn morning pulling a girl's body out of the river," Rue snapped. "So, forgive us if we're not feeling especially warm and fuzzy."

"And that girl was my client," I said. "She deserves the same respect I'd give anyone. I've got a reputation to uphold."

"Your reputation," Roland sneered. "You wreck marriages for a living. You're a window-peeping creep. You're a joke, Martin, a bus-bench private dick who cashes in on the worst expectations of people. Get off your damn soapbox and give us the fucking file."

Even if I had a note, a signed confession, video footage of the whole thing and a witness to back it all up, I wouldn't have given it to them after that insult. "If there's nothing else I can help you with, door's that way," I said. "I'm happy to send over all of my case notes on Ms Lovette if Jack sends over a warrant. Until then, I'm afraid I'm not going to be much help."

Roland turned his margarine gaze on Valerie. "What are you going to tell us about Janie, sweetheart?"

"Not a goddamn thing," she snapped. "You heard him. Get a warrant."

"She's not going to be any help," Rue said. "Pretty girl working here, I'd bet he's already got his hooks in her hard." He grabbed her chin with a mean, meaty claw. "Let's just hope he doesn't have a spike in her too."

I snapped. Forget decorum, forget the law, forget all of it. I seized Rue's shoulder and pulled him off her. "Touch her again and I will break your jaw," I said, crumpling up his cheap lapel in a tight fist before shoving him away. "You got your answer. Now get out of my office."

"That's assaulting a cop," Roland said, reaching for his handcuffs. "That's time, Martin."

I laughed. None of this was funny, but it had all the makings of some twisted cosmic joke. "I can get Chief Hollander on the phone, tell him you're here without a warrant, harassing my staff and making threats." I picked up a business card and flicked it into Roland's big barrel chest. "He'll have you two back to the midnight shift, writing drunk-and-disorderlies for college students until your sorry little retirement kicks in."

Roland put away his handcuffs. Rue gave us both a glare that should have spilled blood. "Come back with a warrant if you think you've got something," I added. "And I'll have my lawyer here to pick apart every word of it."

The slam of the door got Valerie like a shotgun. She crumpled against her desk and I grabbed her up, easing us both down to the floor. Maybe on a normal day, I could have shaken it off, but today was not a normal day. Janie was dead and it might have been our fault and the cops had us in a corner I wasn't anywhere near comfortable with. "I shouldn't have let them in," I murmured. "Are you all right?"

"I'm fine," she said, squaring her shoulders. "I'm fine."

We both knew *that* was a lie. But there wasn't anything either of us could do to fix it. She clung to me like a shipwreck. I could feel my heart pounding hard against her shoulder. That much I wasn't going to fight, not when the whole world threatened to swallow us whole if she let go of my lapels. I fought back the image of Janie cold and alone in the river, struggling against the very real sensation of my own lungs filling tight with fluid.

Valerie started to sob, an ugly cry filled with snot and rage and salt. I pulled her in closer, held her tight against me, not caring if I was overstepping some imaginary line of decorum. She was hurting, I was hurting, and we might be the only thing either of us had that could close this wound.

I was going to have to call Ron. I was sure he already knew; Nora would have gotten the call; Nora would have told him. I toyed with the idea of going down to the crime scene myself, driving along the river until I saw police tape, trying my hand at figuring out how it came to this. I dismissed it just as quickly. In a few days they would have the cause of death, homicide or suicide, accident or overdose. For right now, I just had to hold us both together.

After a few minutes, Valerie had cried all her tears. I took a shaking breath and she disentangled herself from me and we both laughed a little in that way that you do when you're embarrassed by any outpouring of emotion, any show that you're human. "I think we should close up for the day," I said, forcing a smile that hurt both of us. "I'm not exactly in the mood to go trawling pawn shops."

"Are you sure?" she asked. "I can stay, if you need me."

I didn't really want her to leave. I didn't want to be alone, not with the dark thoughts that were already beginning to form like storm clouds in my head. But I couldn't make her stay, couldn't ask her to be some sort of emotional cushion for me to fall apart on. I shook my head. "Go on," I said. "I'll be all right."

I went into my office. I locked the door behind me. I put on Cocteau Twins, "Pitch The Baby," tasting the words in my throat. I'd made Janie a mix tape when she was born, this song and "B-A-B-Y" and "Kimberly," rock-and-roll lullabies for my best friend's baby girl. I never worried that she'd take him away from touring, from partying, from being my partner. I'd welcomed her in like she was a new composition, I held her in the hospital and the swell of love I felt right there was a high I'd never been able to replicate. That beautiful little girl was gone now, drenched and drowned and left on a cold slab in the coroner's office.

I put my head in my hands and I sobbed.

11

VALERIE

The cops called Janie's death an accident. So did the papers. People on Facebook said it was suicide, a drug overdose, a mafia hit. The *Perrine Courier* didn't have too many details; water in her lungs, a pending tox screen, quotes from Nora and a few friends at Raines. Then it was onto the next headline, as though she never existed.

Janie's funeral was held Wednesday evening. It had been a while since I'd been to one, but I knew all too well the taste of funeral parlors, the suffocating-sweet smell of lilies, of wax and plastic fillers designed to polish death into a presentable facade, paint over the ugliness and package up mourning into an acceptable public spectacle. My parents, buried side-by-side, classmates lost to suicide and accidents and overdoses. I had never been to a funeral where the guest of honor had died peacefully at a comfortable age. They were always gone too soon.

The funeral was closed casket and the service was packed. Martin and I sat together, near the back. Neither of us said anything. He wiped his wet eyes on a white handkerchief pulled from an inside coat pocket. I used a handful of tissues and hoped my mascara wasn't running down my face. Her mentor, Nora, gave the eulogy. Streaks of gray hair were bound up among fading bottle black in a tight bun, and between her dress and her scarves, it was hard to know what was human underneath, like a Victorian ghost weaving among the living.

Two of Janie's classmates, Laurel Price and Proctor Monroe, performed a duet for voice and violin. Proctor was a cold blonde with wet blue eyes, playing sharply and without love, and Laurel, equally cold, looked like she was somewhere else entirely.

The reception was held at Raines College. Martin stayed close to Ron. I got a drink and hung around the fringes, trying not to get lost in the sea of strangers.

"Valerie?" I turned around and there was Dott, almost unrecognizable with her pink braids pulled back into a ballerina bun and covered with a swath of black lace. "I didn't know you knew Jo– Janie."

What name was she about to say? I chalked it up to funeral stress, a dry throat, a long day. But I wondered how she knew Janie. Friends at Raines, perhaps? "I'm sorry for your loss," I said, almost automatically. "I didn't know her well. I'm here to support another friend."

She put her hand on my arm. I almost dropped my drink. "Can we talk?" she asked. "Someplace more private?"

Out of the corner of my eye, I saw Martin embracing Nora. His back was to me. "Sure," I said, motioning her towards the coat room.

We ducked inside and pressed ourselves against the back window, close enough that I could smell rose oil on her neck. "Gina told me you were a detective," she said. "I thought maybe you could help us out."

Gina and her big mouth. "I work for a private investigator, sure," I said. "But I'm not licensed or anything."

Dott took a sip of her drink. "I don't think this was an accident," she said. "Or a suicide. I think Janie was murdered."

My stomach dropped like the Tower of Terror. I had barely begun to process that one of our clients had died; the concrete thought of murder hadn't even crossed my mind. "Who would want to kill her?" I asked before I could stop myself.

"That's what I'm hoping you'll figure out," she said. "I just need to know the truth. She was my friend. I can pay you; we can figure out something..."

"It's not that," I said. "It's just... I'm not licensed, I wouldn't even know where to begin..." I sounded like Martin and I hated it, but this was too much pressure. This wasn't a cheating spouse or lost dog or a fraudulent Workers' Comp. This was best left to the professionals, the cops, someone with access to labs and databases we could only dream of.

"Please," she begged. "She was in real trouble before she died. Someone hurt her. Badly."

Why hadn't Janie told us any of this when she was in our office? Why was I hearing it only now, at her funeral, when she could have told us something more than a muddled story about her dad? There was so much we could have helped her with, if she'd just spoken up. But lies were the currency of our career – if people told each other the truth, there would be no need for the Wade Agency. "Any idea who?"

Dott glanced around. "I can't talk about this here," she said. "Call me later. I'll get everyone together and we'll tell you all of it."

She ducked out of the closet and by the time I got back to the main room, she was gone. Out of the corner of my eye I spotted Martin leaving. I shouldered past other mourners, muttering *sorry* when I could, and caught up with him on the steps. "Wait up," I called. "Where are you going?"

"I told Ron I'd give him a lift back to his hotel," he said.

I didn't want Ron in our lives one more second than he had to be. I didn't like him, didn't trust him, didn't want him around. "Can we meet back at the office?" I asked. "Think someone has a case for us."

"I'm really not in the mood," he said. "And anyways, it's after hours. It can wait until tomorrow."

I grabbed the sleeve of his dark gray overcoat. "I don't think it can," I said. If Janie *was* murdered, the trail was already getting cold. I lowered my voice and moved in so close that our shoulders were practically touching. "Janie's friend Dott has some information about her death that she wants to share."

Martin took a step back like I'd shoved him. "Absolutely not," he said. "If she has evidence that a crime was committed, she needs to go to the police."

"It can't hurt to hear her out..."

"I'm asking, as a friend, for you to drop it," he said. "And I'm ordering you, as an employee of the Wade Agency, to cease and desist. This is not the kind of case we handle."

The heat rose up in my face. "No, it isn't," I spat. "No, the kind of case *you* handle is wrecking rich people's marriages. You're more concerned with cashing a check from someone who can't keep his wife faithful or making sure some corporate stooge doesn't have to pay one goddamn cent more to someone who snapped his back falling off scaffolding. That's the kind of case *you* handle."

His face got as dark as a storm warning. My nerves were all tied in knots. But before either of us could say anything more, Ron appeared behind me, gripping the railing, his coat draped over his arm. "Thank you for coming," he muttered as he walked past me, down to Martin. Martin put his hand on his back to steady him, gave me one last hollow glance and turned towards the parking lot. I went back inside, but Dott was gone.

I went home and put on my pajamas even though it was just barely seven. I put on the Tragically Hip's *In Between Evolution* and moped around. I played through half of Tori Amos's *Boys for Pele*, but even that didn't match my dark mood. I thought about going to the gym and taking out my frustrations on the heavy bag, but getting dressed again felt like effort I didn't have in me. I made myself some pesto and opened up my laptop and flipped around on Netflix until I'd exhausted all the possibilities. Too many shows about dead girls. Too many dead girls in real life.

Life expects a lot of a woman – be pretty, be patient, don't bother the men, don't get hurt and if you do, don't cry. Because you must never cry over something that you could have prevented, and you must always be ready to prevent everything: rape, a closed fist, an earthquake, a tsunami. But life expects too much of dead girls too. Be a gorgeous corpse. Be a symbol of something, even of tragedy. A dead girl must never rest.

But that meant that neither should the living.

12

MARTIN

Valerie's parting words rattled around in my skull as I drove Ron back to the Vanguard. Is that what she really thought of me? Is that what I had become, or was I always like this? I picked up a criminal justice major in college because I thought I might become a court advocate, work with my fellow addicts to get them help and treatment instead of sixty days in County. I had fallen into PI work when a classmate introduced me to his cousin Phillip, who helped me get my license and set me up at his firm in New York. It was never as glamorous as pulp novels made it out to be; no fedoras, no murders or stolen Brasher Doubloons; there were a couple of long-legged girls at the office, but none of them wore garter stockings – that I knew of – or double-crossed their men with the derringers in their handbags. The work was methodical, a little like songwriting, in a way, putting all the pieces together in a way that made sense. When people asked for my help, I gave it to them. That was, perhaps, what Valerie didn't understand.

Ron hummed along with "Bobcaygeon" on my playlist. Valerie had gotten me into the Tragically Hip; she told me she had a high school pen-pal in Newfoundland who sent her their albums on burned CDs. I tried not to think about her, tried not to play over what she had said to me, resisted the urge to switch to something less loaded. I held my breath until the song faded into the Sons, "Too Much of a Good Thing." That I could handle.

"This song was wasted on *Dumb and Dumber,*" Ron said.

"No kidding," I said. We all saw that movie together on an off-night between shows, a one-screen movie theater with smuggled beers and cheap popcorn; groaning and rolling our eyes and knowing it beat watching TV in the motel room. But we all paid attention to every song cue; Kurt bought the soundtrack the next day and we played it in the van's tape deck from Kansas to Nevada, over and over, until we had every chord etched on our hearts.

"That should have been us," he said. "No reason we couldn't have gotten that Farrelly Brothers soundtrack money. We were way better than that Green Jelly shit they included instead."

I snorted, but I couldn't help but smile a little. Even in sorrow there was something comforting about having him beside me in the passenger seat. Late nights driving between clubs, or home from the studio. Only thing missing was some gas station coffee and a couple of Luckies. I was craving a smoke the way a teenage boy might crave his friend's older sister.

We pulled into the parking lot, but he didn't get out immediately. "I don't want to be alone right now," he said. "Let's get a drink."

I'd never had an affair, but the first sip of my Manhattan tasted like everything I imagined one would be. Delectable and sinful and fiery; I savored every delicious note. I only had this one, after all, a pricey selection from a cocktail menu to keep me slow, keep me focused.

I hadn't had a drink in eighteen years, not since a slip-up with a bottle of Cordon Rouge on the one-year anniversary of Cecelia's disappearance. I had no intentions of repeating that miserable night, but I didn't want Ron to drink alone. It might be too easy to drift into old habits. Better to model moderate behavior and close the tab myself.

The hotel bar was filled with loud corporate types, already drunk on generous per diems, flirting with their married coworkers. We managed to find two low-slung leather chairs in a quiet back corner, as far away from the bar as we could get. The waitress would take her time getting to us. One long drink and then I would go home and tomorrow everything would go back to normal. Normal except for this little piece of my heart that was gone forever.

"I can't believe she's really dead," Ron said. "My little girl. First Sharon and now Janie. It's not right."

"No it's not," I said. What else could I say? I was sitting across from a man who had lost everything. I at least still had my sister, my niece, Valerie, and the hope that Cecelia was still out there. Ron had lost the last piece of his family. *I couldn't even begin to imagine the bottomless hollow of hurt inside of him.*

Ron deflated deeper into his chair. "You know what the worst part is?" he said. "This is my fault."

"You can't blame yourself…" Blame a curse placed on her cradle at birth. Blame a river witch come to collect her cruel due. Or better yet, blame the bastard who went behind her back when all she needed me to do was protect her. I'd managed to absolve myself of a lot of sins over the years, but this one was going to sting for a long, long time.

"I was a shitty father," he continued. "I was a lousy husband and a bad friend."

"You made some bad choices," I countered. "We all did."

"Yeah, but I never made amends," he said. "I thought maybe Janie wouldn't remember the really rough times, that I could pretend it never happened. But she always was a smart girl. Too smart. She remembered all of it – especially the stuff I had forgotten. And now she's gone, and I'm never going to get to apologize. My little girl."

What do you say to a man who's lost everything, not once, but twice? I knew loss; Cecelia, my father felled by a heart attack, my mother from cancer two years in December. But

Ron had lost a child, a hurt I couldn't even begin to fathom. And yet, despite all of it, I was glad I could be here with him. I hadn't let him be with me after Cecelia left; he was too far gone and I was newly sober, it would have been another disaster, just like the one that landed me in rehab in the first place. Amazing how life can come together and fall apart at the same time.

His glass was empty. Mine was too. He gestured for two more. I let him.

13

VALERIE

Dott told me to meet her over at her place, a small house not far from my apartment, two blocks past the Giant grocery store with the cardboard sign that read *WE NOW SELL BEER AT 8AM,* turn left at the burned-out husk of Thom's Pub, then a right on Graydon Street. Her neighborhood was slightly nicer than my side of town, rental houses instead of apartment buildings, but still with the weathered fatigue of out-of-town landlords and overworked managers. A few of them one of them had sheets hung up as curtains, a couple of lawns were dotted with abandoned kids' toys.

She wasn't alone. She introduced Gordon, his black spikes flattened for the funeral, and Melanie, in a slim black suit with her dark hair pulled back in a ballerina bun. There was one drink left in a bottle of red wine on the table and an array of photographs laid out. I picked one up. The girl had spikes and a nose ring on a chain that connected to her earlobe. Her breasts were bare, nipples covered by Xs of black electrical tape, a waist-trainer corset and black vinyl leggings, white stiletto buckle boots and a purple Mohawk. But all of that couldn't disguise who I recognized her as.

Janie Lovette.

Dott poured me that last glass of wine. "How do you guys know Janie?" I asked.

"We know her as Joyride," Dott replied. "We're all in

Machine Gun Snatch. We played at your aunt's bar a couple of times, surprised we never saw you there."

If I had seen them on Tuesday night, I might have been able to put this case together, how the violinist who had visited our office could have possibly been the punk in the photographs. *Joyride*. "You said you didn't think this was a suicide," I said. "What makes you think it was something else?"

"Everything," Gordon said. "Joyride wouldn't do that. Not to us."

Everyone who'd lost someone to suicide said the same thing. "It could have been an accident," I offered.

"Joyride wasn't the type to party at the riverfront," Melanie said. "I can't think of a reason she'd be down there that late at night."

"Who do you think would want her dead?" I asked.

Dott glanced at Gordon. "Go on," she said. "Tell her what you saw."

He pulled out a pack of cigarettes. Dott rolled her eyes but nodded and he lit up and took a drag before he answered. "I think Joyride was being blackmailed," he finally said. "I saw her fighting with some guy outside of Topsy's, said he was there to take photos even after she asked him not to. He came back about halfway through Strict Nine's set, and she fucking lost it. Deacon had to throw him out.

So that *had* been Janie arguing with the man with the *BOMB SQUAD* bag. I hadn't been crazy thinking I had recognized her voice. "And what would someone have on her to blackmail her?"

"Exactly," Dott piped up. "I mean, yeah, he was being an asshole, but no one's going to get killed over a couple of photos."

"Women have been killed for less, Dott," Melanie said. "He was probably pissed that she rejected his *art*."

Dott rolled her eyes. "I don't think it was that," she said. "I think someone from her past showed up."

"Like who?"

"Her father," she said.

"Dott, c'mon–"

"I'm serious!" she said. "Guy shows up out of nowhere and three days later she's dead? Tell me that isn't suspicious."

"Not everything is *Law & Order*," Melanie said.

Dott let out an audible huff and stormed into the bathroom. Gordon muttered, "Christ, Melanie," under his breath. I hadn't considered Ron – hadn't considered much of anything, really – but he was as valid a suspect as anyone. What if he had come here with nefarious intentions, lashed out when his daughter didn't respond to him the way he wanted? I wondered if Martin was still with him, if he was safe, if he might be able to pry anything out of the grieving father or if they'd be pulling Ron out of the Leslie next.

Dott returned. Some of her eyeliner was smudged, as though she'd wiped away tears with toilet paper.

"Maybe you should ask her boyfriend," Melanie said.

"What boyfriend?" Dott and Gordon asked in unison.

There might have been a smug smile underneath that mournful mask. "There was this guy," she said. "I don't know anything about him, but I overheard her talking to someone on the phone, sounded like she was planning to meet him later. She sounded kind of frustrated, but, like, that way that girls get when some guy just won't listen."

So maybe Melanie knew as much about Janie as she did about Joyride. Dott, at least, seemed surprised. "What does that have to do with anything?" she said.

"You know how she always showed up in show clothes?" Melanie said. "It's not because she was 24/7. It's because she got changed someplace else and came like that, then left and changed before she went home. Probably didn't want her trust-fund friends to see her in all her vinyl finery."

"Did you know about this second life?" she asked Gordon.

He stubbed out his cigarette. "Yeah," he said. "It's not that big of a deal. I mean, it's not like she can go to a job with her titties hanging out. We all gotta exist during the day, you know?"

Oh, but it might be. Who would Janie – a grown-ass woman – have to hide from? Certainly not her dad, who was stage-diving in ripped jeans before she was born. But a boyfriend – or a stalker like *BOMB SQUAD* who might feel that her body belonged to him – would be a perfect suspect. "Tell me more about the boyfriend," I said.

Melanie shrugged. "I don't know anything about him. I thought I heard her talking to some guy on the phone, you know the way you talk to a guy you're fucking when you don't want anybody to know."

Ah yes, the hushed and blushed tones of lovers. Or the feverish whispers and apologies when you're trying to bury your shame. They weren't always easy to tell apart. "When was this?" I asked.

"Saturday morning. At practice, before the two of you showed up," she said, glancing over at Gordon and Dott. "She hung up and told me not to say anything. Guess it doesn't matter now."

"So maybe it's tied in with our blackmail theory," Gordon said. "That camera guy at Topsy's threatened to show this guy the photos..."

"No," Dott insisted. "Then that leads us back to suicide."

Unless the BOMB SQUAD *guy showed the boyfriend the photos and he flipped out,* I thought. It wasn't entirely implausible; if thirty-two years on this earth had taught me anything, it was that there was no level too low for a man to sink. But I needed to know how she died. The papers reported that she drowned, but that wasn't enough. Why drag her to the river and drown her when there were far more convenient ways to kill a person? It seemed awfully risky, too many witnesses. There had to be more to the story. There always was.

Dott reached over and rubbed Gordon's back. Melanie finished her drink. My mind was racing with thoughts that wouldn't connect into anything resembling sense. A potential stalker, a mysterious boyfriend, the sudden arrival of a deadbeat dad and a mishandled case. That was enough to intrigue me. But I couldn't commit, not without Martin's approval. I'd have to apologize for what I said at the funeral, hope that maybe he would hear me out now that I had the thinnest threads of evidence. "Let me talk to my boss," I said. "And I'll see what I can do."

14

MARTIN

We abandoned the hotel bar and went upstairs when a very drunk woman in a very loud dress tried to join us. Ron had a bottle of Maker's Mark in his room with the wax still intact and tasked me with finding the ice machine. I stared at the vending machine for a few minutes, wondering if I should get us a couple of bags of chips. Only crudités at the repast. I knew better than to drink on an empty stomach.

My phone rang. I liked the picture of Valerie that I had assigned to her number, snapped one afternoon while we were hanging around the park on a mission from an anxious mom to trail her new nanny. Valerie was smiling in the picture, the sunlight hitting her face just right. I always wanted to tell her how pretty she was, but maybe that was crossing a line. I smiled as I took her call. "Hello Valerie."

She didn't sound as happy. "Where are you?" she asked. "I drove by your place and you weren't home. I wanted to talk with you. It's kinda urgent."

"Ron and I are having a drink," I said. "At his hotel. We can talk in the morning."

There was a slow pause on the other end of the line. "Martin," she said. "You don't drink."

I was suddenly overcome with shame. She was right. I'd told myself one, had two, and was on my way to a third. In my head, I wanted to tell her to meet me here, and that we'd go to Flower House so I could eat my way back towards sobriety. I leaned my forehead against the vending machine, the electrical hum loud in my ears.

But what came out was exactly the opposite. "I think tonight's a fine exception," I spat. "So, mind your own goddamn business."

I hung up on her. My hands were shaking. I filled the ice bucket and went back to Ron's room. He poured a couple of heavy measures. "What'd you get lost?" he asked.

"My assistant called," I said.

"Big case?"

I shook my head. "Just checking in on me," I said. I had everything under control. Just this last drink and then I'd go home. Might have to call a cab, though. My lips were starting to feel numb. My tolerance was not what it was used to be.

"She's cute," Ron said.

"She's smart," I snapped. "Too smart."

"Like Janie," he said, lifting his glass. "Here's to girls too damn smart for their own good."

We tapped our glasses and I killed my drink in one swallow. Ron got up from the couch and opened his laptop and put on our debut album, *Sidewinder*. I hadn't listened to any of my own music in two decades, but I immediately melted into "Fifty Below" like a hot bath. I had written this one on my old piano while snowed in at my parent's place in Duluth on my first Christmas home from college, just after I'd met Ron, still nursing the breakup that had me drunkenly calling into the campus radio station demanding to hear the bitterest breakup songs the DJ had. Sandy and my mom baked while my father and I shoveled; the crunch of the snow became Vic Van Owen's snare work, the steady rhythm of the shovels reflected in Kurt Rich's bassline, the icicles forming into lyrics. I had called Ron long distance like a lonesome lover, played him what I had, and by the time we got back to school, he had retrofitted it for guitar and we were a band. Five months later it would become our second single, topping the Billboard charts for six weeks, and although we lost the Grammy to Don Henley – I still get pissed when I hear "Boys of Summer" – we got considerable college rock airplay, a music video on MTV and a tour across Europe. The first of the last of the really happy times. *There's a lyric for you,* I thought to no one. Maybe I still had a little songwriting talent left after all.

"We were geniuses," Ron said. "Listen to that chord progression! Sublime. Just pure magic."

"*Were*?" I asked. "Speak for yourself. I'm still a genius."

He laughed. "Yeah? When was the last time you wrote anything?"

He had me there. *Bullets for Breakfast* had been widely derided by critics as an unlistenable mess, mostly because it was. It was one of my lowest points, just six months before I got clean, unable to tour, unable to write anything that wasn't a knock-off of better acts. The first year after rehab, just sitting down at the piano gave me a panic attack. After a while, those faded, but so did the urge to play anything new. "We can't all be TV composers," I cracked.

"Hey pal, the theme to *Murder by Law* is paying your bar tab," he said, refilling my drink.

"And when they make a TV show out of my practice, you can compose that theme too," I said.

"Deal."

I settled back into the armchair. This felt right. Good music and good bourbon, just like old times. Valerie couldn't understand this, the intimacy of men, a necessity in times of sorrow. After nineteen years, I was back with the man who knew me better than anyone, even if it took a tragedy to put us back into each other's lives. I felt strangely whole again. Warm. Complete. Or maybe that was just the bourbon.

Ron looked at me and tried to smile, but started to cry instead. And before I could stop myself, I was sobbing too. It wasn't fair. Janie had so much promise and so much hurt, and

I couldn't be entirely sure that I hadn't caused some of it. I was the one who left her behind, defenseless and scared; I was the one who got involved in her case and tipped my hand when all I should have done was collect her fee and kept my mouth shut, let Ron go back to LA and send us all back to our lonely little lives. None of this would have happened if I hadn't pried us all open like raw oysters.

A knock at the door interrupted our grief. "I called for room service," Ron said, sniffling. "Why don't you let him in?"

My blood went as cold as the ice in my glass. *Room service.* I'd heard him use that term before and it was never for dinner plates. I should have called Valerie back and begged her forgiveness. I should have gone downstairs and told the front desk to call me a cab and had the bartender make me a cup of coffee while I waited. But what did any of it matter? Not a goddamn thing. Janie was dead. I was drunk and I was angry and I hated myself for every little failure that had brought me here.

I opened the door.

15

VALERIE

After my parents died, I used to skip school to wander out to the stretch of back road where the accident happened. For a time, there was a cross, a cheap roadside memorial Deacon and I constructed and kept up with plastic flowers. I would walk the space when the coast was clear, as if somehow I could figure out *exactly* what went wrong, stop time and correct it. But I couldn't go back and melt that patch of ice any more than I could raise them from the dead. No crime was committed, no one would pay. There was some insurance money, for a time, and flowers sent yearly from the man who was driving the other car. I met him once, about five years after the accident, and he was nice enough, apologetic to the point of fresh tears, but it didn't change a goddamn thing. The flowers stopped after that.

But maybe Janie's death could be solved, could be fixed, could be made right. My insides were tangled up like an abandoned Slinky. I needed to establish a timeline of who she was with and what she was doing in the hours before her body went into the river, figure out if she went in as Janie or Joyride. Maybe I could pull some strings, FOIA some crime scene photos, talk to the medical examiner and the coroner.

From Dott's place I drove over to Topsy's. I had to capture this momentum before I slept on it and got swept back up in the background checks that dotted my days at the Wade Agency. If anyone would know about a stalker, it would be Gina.

There was a small memorial laid out for Joyride in front of the bar. A photo, some guttering jar candles, wilting flowers. In another day or two, it would all be gone. In six months, she might be forgotten entirely. Looking at the pile, I found myself wondering if I was trying to solve this case for Janie or if I was doing it for Katy. Would solving one murder absolve me of the one I might have committed? I don't remember enough about that night to know for sure that I didn't kill her. It was all a blur of kitchen steel and blood and sirens and florescent lights. For all I know, I slit her throat. For all I know, the cops fired on her when she wouldn't drop the knife. For all I knew, all my days here in Perrine were numbered, time-stamped until the hour the cops finally caught up with me and took me in for a crime I couldn't recall.

Elvis Costello's "Blue Chair" was playing when I arrived. Elvis Costello was the last thing I wanted to hear. I didn't want to think about Martin. He clearly wasn't thinking about me, so there was no fucking reason I should give him another flicker of my synapses. My first stop was the jukebox to put on something else, anything else. But my mind was whirring like a blender; all I could do was hit shuffle. The Housemartins, "Happy Hour." Nope. The Replacements, "I Don't Know." Damn Aunt Gina and her college rock tastes. I hit the button one last time and finally landed on Electronic, "Getting Away with It." That much I could stand.

"Was wondering when you would show up," Gina said. "I'm guessing you talked to Dott?"

"I did," I said dryly, sliding onto a barstool. "Why did you tell her I could help?"

"You wouldn't be here if you couldn't."

She had me there. "Melanie said Janie – Joyride – had a stalker," I said. "Any truth to that?"

She thought for a minute. "She told me someone was bothering her," she said. "Kept trying to take her picture, even after she asked him to stop."

Now I was getting somewhere, even if I didn't know where that was. "Do you know who he is?"

"Not a clue," she said. "But Deacon would. I know Deacon tossed a guy last time Machine Gun Snatch played."

"Tell me a little more about Joyride," I asked. "Maybe something that seemed just a little out of the ordinary? Something she said that didn't seem right to you?"

"She always arrived fully dressed," she said. "Makeup, spikes up, everything. But she always left in plain clothes, washed out her hair in the green room and covered it up with a hat. Most of the bands hang out after the shows, but not her. She performed and then left. Not even a drink with Dott. I figured she had a job early in the morning."

That lined up with what Melanie had told me. I wished I had a pad to write this all down on. I grabbed a napkin instead; made some notes I knew I wouldn't be able to read in the morning. "Thanks for this," I told her.

"Sure thing," she said. "I didn't know Joyride very well outside of the club, but I liked her whenever she came in. If this is something that needs looking into, I know you'll see it through."

I didn't usually feel pride in my job. I enjoyed it, I enjoyed Martin when he wasn't being an asshole, but it wasn't something I ever thought to be proud of. I was just an assistant. But maybe I could be more tonight.

"One more thing," she said as I got up to leave, like Columbo. She leaned on the bar and I leaned in to hear her. "Why not see if the Goddesses have some advice for you?"

I snorted. "I don't think Kathy Valentine is going to have much to help me out with a dead body."

"You never know," she said. "Can't hurt to ask."

I went upstairs and let myself into her apartment. The Goddess Shrine was in the corner of the living room, on a shelf above the turntable. I closed my eyes and reached into the drawer. I plucked one like a daisy petal and opened it. The chorus from The Pretenders, "I'll Stand by You."

So much for going home to work on my case. I knew, even if Martin didn't want me nagging him, he needed me, a knight in Dr Martens, to slay the dragon that'd lain slumbering for nineteen years, now breathing hints of fire on the back of his neck.

On my way to the car, I tried calling him again. I was surprised he picked up. But he didn't say anything. There was a moment of music, loud and messy like a high school band, then nothing. He hung up on me. That bastard.

For a mean moment I considered giving up. He was a grown man, he could get plastered post-funeral with an old friend if that's what he needed to do, give in to one temptation if it would keep him from another. But the stone in my heart wasn't worried about a few too many emptied glasses.

At the intersection of Holland and Byrne I had to make a choice. Go right and head home, make my notes and go to bed to pick this all up in the morning, in the office, when all our heads were clear again. Or I could go left and make my way across town to the Vanguard in hopes that I might be able to persuade him home in whatever condition he might be in. It wasn't in my job description to babysit my boss. But maybe Gina was right, maybe he needed me and he didn't even know it.

The light turned green. The car behind me honked hard. I hit the left turn signal and hoped I was doing the right thing.

I found Martin's car in the parking lot of the Vanguard. I knocked on Ron's door, hoping that what I had heard in the background was just music from turned-up speakers. No answer. I searched his car in case there might be ticket stubs, a program, anything that might give me a hint of where he could be, but Martin knew all too well how to stay hidden.

I sat in the driver's seat and tried not to cry. I just wanted to know he was safe, that was all. He didn't need to accept my apology. Hell, I'd let him fire me if I could just know that he was going to bed with clean veins.

Through my tears I saw neon, the flashing sign that advertised Mr Jones, a Hard Rock Café knock-off that tried to capitalize on the city's music scene by selling sixteen-dollar cheeseburgers and watered-down drinks to parents staying at the Vanguard ahead of their kids' senior recital. Shitty bands and shittier food, the kind of place that Martin always rolled his eyes at.

Oh fuck.

16

MARTIN

I tried to count backwards. Two Manhattans? Not including the two at the hotel bar. The bottle in Ron's room didn't count. No telling how many drinks were in there. Hard to hold stemware in shaking hands. Put it all in a rock tumbler, bartender. Easier to make a fist.

The band was putting me to sleep. Twenty-dollar cover charge for watered-down blues and watered-down whiskey. Two at the minimum. Two on top of the two I already had? Have to start at the beginning. Better order one more, just to be sure.

I touched the small plastic bag in my jacket pocket. Had to be careful I hadn't dreamed it, had to know I still had it together. Ron went to the bathroom more than once, came back wiping his nose in short, quick motions. But I wasn't going to waste it. Not in this shithole. I'd waited too long for this.

I kept calling the waitress Valerie. Valerie was the last person I wanted to think about, and yet I kept saying her name out loud. The waitress didn't bother to correct me. Maybe if her nametag wasn't so goddamn blurry. I closed my eyes and opened them again.

And then it really was Valerie.

I sat up straighter. "What are you doing here?"

"Looking for you," she said.

"Well, you found us," Ron said. "So stay, have a drink."

"I think you've had enough for all three of us," she said. "C'mon, Martin, let's get out of here."

I picked up my glass like it weighed a thousand pounds. "Go home, Valerie," I said. "Take tomorrow off, but just... go home."

She grabbed my elbow and squeezed. "Do *not* make me make a scene," she hissed. "I've been driving all over town. My feet are killing me, I haven't eaten since the funeral and I just spent my last twenty bucks bribing the door girl to let me in here, so I am in *no mood* for your bullshit."

So I owed her twenty bucks. I dried the bottom of my glass and crawled around for a few minutes, exploring the glaciers. Ron snickered. I took a brief nap on a twist of orange peel and snapped back to life when I heard her voice.

"Please," she said. "Martin, please."

She was right. It beat a cab; it beat sleeping on Ron's couch. Besides, I had big plans. Guests to attend to. I had to order my feet to cooperate. At least someone listened to me, even if they weren't good at following directions. Valerie took my arm and guided me through the tables. "Wait," I said, trying to turn back. "The tab."

She tugged so hard I nearly toppled over. "Let Ron get it," she said. "It's the least he can do."

We took Valerie's car. I wasn't sure where mine was. I don't remember much about the ride home except she had a Steely Dan tape she wouldn't play even though I was sure I asked her to. What was it Vic always said? You either die a hero or live long enough to become the joke of a Becker/Fagen composition. Fifty-three seemed like as good an age as any. Maybe I was "Black Cow." Maybe I was "Time Out of Mind."

I must have fallen asleep, because I woke up to her opening the passenger-side door. She offered me her hand, but I swatted it away. I didn't need her to carry me. It was a hundred miles of broken fault line to get to my front door, but I made it. I didn't realize Valerie was under my arm until I had to take my hand back to retrieve my keys.

She took off her boots and threw them in a corner. She vanished through the dining room and came back what felt like a couple hours later with a bottle of seltzer and two glasses filled with ice. Not the drink I was hoping for. Probably the one I needed.

My pockets were too heavy. I got tangled in my jacket. Valerie came to my rescue, just like always, guided my coat down my arms, set my watch and my keys on my table, loosened the patterned noose around my neck. Before I could stop her, she patted down my pockets. She found half a pack of Lucky Strikes I didn't remember smoking and a crumpled cocktail napkin. She pulled out my phone and a hotel keycard from the Vanguard. She pulled out the plastic bag, the glass pipe and the foil, a pink lighter she left on the table.

"Martin," she breathed. "What is this?"

"That," I said, reaching for the seltzer, "is *exactly* what it looks like."

17

VALERIE

I felt like a mom in an Eighties after-school special. "Martin," I managed to choke out. "Did you?"

He picked up the cigarettes. He stuck one between his lips and fumbled with a plastic lighter that wouldn't spark. "*No,*" he insisted with a mean little sneer. "No, I was waiting until I got good and drunk. Now would be perfect."

I didn't know how much longer my valiant effort to hold back tears was going to last. Nineteen years. Nineteen goddamn years down the drain for a girl he hadn't seen since she had Barbies. All the sadness I had over Janie's death was replaced with rage. My first instinct was to hit him, ball up all my fury into fists and blood, knock him around until he felt the way I felt inside. My second instinct was to leave him there, get in my car and drive to another state. But I was out of family, out of places to hide. All that was left was a stand-off.

Without another word, I gathered up the whole kit and took it into the upstairs bathroom. He didn't try to stop me. I flushed the powder down the toilet, rinsed the bag of residue and threw it in the garbage. I snapped the glass tube in half and tore the foil into confetti just for spite. My face was hot and my chest was tight. The last time I'd done anything like this, I got carved up for my troubles. The jones will always want to keep up with you.

So maybe this was a futile gesture. Maybe tomorrow morning he'd go looking for more. Hell, maybe when I got back to the living room he'd be waiting with a kitchen knife in hand, wanting revenge for ripping him off. I was angry. I was exhausted. That was all that was left of me to take and he was welcome to it. I no longer gave a shit.

By the time I got back to the living room, Martin had his head in his hands, the cigarette unlit and forgotten in his lap. "I'm sorry," he said, wiping his wet eyes with his shirt cuff. "I just… I thought…"

From the earliest days I'd known him, my instinct had always been to protect Martin. Following him for my article revealed that while he had plenty of associates who greeted him fondly, he didn't seem to have a lot of friends, people he could go to or rely on. He, like me, was running from a past, and to serve him up to a hungry editor who would strip him for parts and sell him to the world seemed too cruel. So I buried my story and lost my job, absorbed a blow so he could escape without a scratch.

Now I knew what Goddess Chrissie had been trying to tell me. I sat next to him on the couch and folded him into my arms. He felt so small, so fragile, his skinny shoulders shaking. "I'm here," I murmured. "You're all right." That was a lie and both of us knew it, but I had to say something.

"She was just a kid," he sobbed. "A kid with so much promise. She had a rough go her whole life and I didn't do a damn thing about it. I was so wrapped up in my own… my own *bullshit* that it never occurred to me to do something about this sweet little girl growing up in a house with two junkie parents. I could have done so much more, but I'm just one more person who failed her, right to the goddamn end. I shouldn't have taken the case, and now she's dead, and some of that is on me. Can you blame me for wanting to check out for a while?"

I felt even worse about my parting words to him this afternoon. This was how I would make it up to him. I tilted his chin up so that I was staring into his hurricane eyes. "And can you blame me for wanting to stop you?" I murmured, smoothing the hair along his temples.

He swallowed hard. He took my face between his warm hands, kissed my forehead with dry lips and nestled against my shoulder, gripping me tight. He smelled like cigarettes and bourbon and misery. "You're my little angel," he murmured. "I don't deserve you."

Angel. For a time, I used to think that I had died in Memphis and everyone was just too polite to tell me. I felt invisible to everyone, a lonesome spirit wandering through the wasteland of Perrine. But then I met Martin, and he saw me, perhaps, because he was a ghost too.

I'd held Katy like this on a lot of fucked-up nights, trying to calm her enough to put her to bed. But this was different, somehow. This was love from some long-frozen part of my heart, a secret chamber I had never let anyone else inside. It all locked into place, like two halves of a cheap heart necklace, and for a few seconds, I felt an unfamiliar wholeness that blossomed from my gut up into my ribcage, down my arms and into his veins, binding us to an invisible bloodline.

He took a shaking breath and sat up and I hated to let him go. He took a sip of seltzer, the clatter of the ice cubes louder than a drum solo. "Thank you," he finally choked out. "For all of this. You saved my goddamn life, Valerie."

The ugly part of me wanted to burn this all down. I wanted to fight him, snark about the gas it took me to get back and forth across town, lay out an invoice for the cover charge. Sincerity wasn't my best skill set – sincerity made you a target – but for once I knew better than to crack a perfect moment in half. So I kept my damn mouth shut. I had to just let it sit between us.

I guided him back against the throw pillows. I fought the urge to lie against him, cling to him like a life preserver, my head against his back to listen for the rhythm of his breath, the time signature of his heartbeat. But it wouldn't be right of me to take advantage of him like that, to use his tragedy as a bolster for my battered self-esteem. "Why don't you get some sleep?" I said, forcing myself to stand up. "I'll check in on you in the morning."

He grabbed for my hand and missed. He got a handful of my dress instead. "Stay here," he insisted. "It's late. There's a guest bedroom in the back. I'll make us breakfast. Please don't leave me. Please."

I doubted he was going to be in shape to do anything during any sort of breakfast hour. But a real bed did sound inviting, and I didn't want to run the risk that he might try to chase in the middle of the night. "I'll stay," I assured him.

That seemed to satisfy him. He closed his eyes. I got him a blanket and tucked him in and waited on the edge of the couch until he was snoring softly before I went to the guest room, got undressed, crawled under the cool gray sheets, and cried myself to sleep.

18

MARTIN

I woke up with a headache that seemed to start in the middle of my chest. I lay absolutely still, my face stuffed into a throw pillow, hoping the hurt might pass over me like a predator, like the Angel of Death, if I just kept quiet. I tried to tell myself it was a migraine, that it was anything but what I knew it was. No goddamn mystery to solve here. I was being punished. The question would come down to what my crimes were.

I turned over onto my back. The room was spinning and I waited for it to stop so I could piece together the clues. I was home, but *how*? I sure as hell didn't drive. Jesus, I *hope* I didn't drive. When it was safe to open my eyes again, I took stock of my surroundings – a blanket, my jacket, my wallet, my phone with eleven percent battery life. Hell of a lot more than I had. A half-smoked pack of Lucky Strikes, a cheap lighter, a crumpled cocktail napkin with the words *THE POOL* printed on it. I had no idea what it referred to, but it must have been important at one time. My tie, my shoes, my father's watch, a gift from my sister for my first year of sobriety. 6:29am. Too early to call her and offer to send it back.

But something else was missing. I didn't know what, but I knew I was short something I had come home with. There was a pair of rose-patterned Docs in the corner. Who did those belong to? Whoever she was, she was still in the house. I'd find her soon enough. Maybe she had what I was looking for. Maybe she *was* what I was looking for.

I pulled myself to my feet and closed the curtains. Valerie's car in the driveway. Now I remembered. The scene at the bar. Steely Dan in the car. Valerie sitting with me on the couch, my head against her chest, our faces close. Did I kiss her? Did I want to have kissed her? And did those shoes belong to her? Would I find other clothes scattered elsewhere?

The worst part of the morning after a long night was never the pounding headache or the sour stomach. It was the apologies, the begging, the slow dawning recollection of bad behavior. Surely she would quit, and I'd deserve to lose her. But where *was* she?

I went to the kitchen. There was a note on the fridge: *Coffee, Basil, Chicken Thighs, Bread Crumbs.* I had meant to go to the store two days ago and that meant I was out of coffee. This morning was getting worse by the goddamn minute.

The guest room door was slightly ajar. I peeked in and there was Valerie, curled up on her side, her back to me, tights and a dress and a cardigan thrown on the chair, one tattooed arm bare over the blankets. I knew she had ink because she told me, what felt like a thousand years ago, back when she was writing for *High Wire* and I was her half-unwilling subject, but this was the first time I'd seen any of it. She had full sleeves; on her left shoulder and bicep was a triceratops in a rose garden, more whimsical than I would have pegged her for. There was a long scar that cut from her elbow through the windowsill scene of her forearm, as white as a country church. She looked like a fresh kill. I felt like a monster.

But she'd stayed. I'd begged her to stay and she hadn't left me. That, at least, was some sort of sickening relief. Still, I needed a detailed itinerary of my behavior, just so I covered all my bases when I apologized. And I was going to apologize. Hell, I might never *stop* apologizing.

I went upstairs and got undressed and got in the shower. The water hurt. I soaped up twice like I could wash away my sins, but it wasn't until I got out and toweled off and was shaving that I noticed what was in the garbage can – foil like discarded confetti, a broken glass pipe, an empty glassine bag. I gripped the edge of the sink to stay upright. Had I? It was bad enough I'd crawled to the bottom of a bottle. But this… this kind of relapse was nineteen years in the making. I'd been so good. I'd been so strong. Not even a taste since my cleaning lady found me slumped in my bathtub, a half-rambling suicide note in one hand, a needle in the other, a bottle of pills in the soap dish and a fifth of bourbon in the sink.

No, I told myself. *No, Valerie wouldn't let this happen…* but when did she arrive, what state did she find me in? I couldn't remember, couldn't tell what was fear and what was reality. I leaned back against the wall and sank to the floor. I put my head in my hands and leaned back against the cold tiles. *Goddamn it, Martin,* I sneered at myself. *Goddamn it, you selfish bastard.*

After a minute of gasping I was finally able to get a deep breath into my lungs. I got dressed. I retrieved my phone and mistyped *Perrine NA meeting* four times before my shaking hands got it right.

There was an 8am at the Baptist church. I'd have to walk, but if I hurried, I could make it. I found my sunglasses in my desk. I took what was left of the seltzer. The walk would either do me good or kill me. I welcomed either option.

I was standing in front of the church before I realized I left my phone on the charger. Couldn't even text Valerie to tell her where I was. She'd be worried and I'd already put her through hell. Stack it on top of the list of apologies I owed her.

19

VALERIE

When I woke up in the guest room, it was 9:17am and Martin was gone. My heart jumped immediately into my throat. How did I not hear him slip out? Where was he, how long had he been out, was he OK? I should have searched the house before I let him go to bed, made sure there wasn't some other secret stash.

I knew this feeling and I hated it. I had spent too much of my life worrying about Katy; getting us a car home, explaining to the neighbors that yes, we would be quiet, please don't call the cops, shrinking and silencing myself so as not to disturb her while she slept off a three-day bender. I'd flushed baggies and lied convincingly that she'd smoked it all last night. In the end, we were gaslighting each other.

There was nothing stopping me from leaving. It was my car in the driveway, after all. I could go home, shower, go back to bed. There was nothing in my job description about being a sponsor or a clean-living coach, nowhere did it say I was responsible for dumping drugs or putting my boss to bed. The morning after had cooled my affections, as it all too often did.

The skin around my scar throbbed. All that was waiting for me at home was that unopened letter that could be anything. A police report, a ransom note. Staying here a little longer was one more way to protect myself. But from what?

The sound of keys in the door sent my heart into my throat. Did I hide, did I stand my ground, did I even know who was coming in? Katy had a habit of handing off her keys to random partygoers looking for a place to crash; I never knew who I was going to find passed out on my couch when I got up in the morning.

"You're awake," Martin said as he came inside. "I got us some coffee. And coconut water. And aspirin. Christ, I haven't had a hangover this wretched in almost two decades. How'd you sleep?"

I was so happy to see him I could have kissed him right on the mouth. "Not long enough," I admitted, stifling a yawn that came up on me like a mugger. "You?"

"Out like a light," he said, handing me a large bodega coffee cup. "Too bad I woke up at 6:30am with the sun in my eyes. It took me a few minutes; why I was sleeping on the couch, whose shoes were in the corner, where my car was and how I got home." He sighed. "I'm really sorry," he added. "I'm completely mortified, if that's any consolation."

It wasn't. I didn't want his embarrassment or his apologies, I wanted him to promise me that he wouldn't pull this shit again. I had enough to worry about without wondering when he was going to fall to pieces. "Just tell me the truth," I said, remembering what I had found in his pocket. "Did you take anything else?"

He shook his head like it hurt to do so. "Just the bourbon," he said. "Told myself I could stop at one, but I should have known better. And when you called, well, I was more embarrassed than anything. I shouldn't have snapped at you." He lowered himself into a dining room chair and rubbed his temples. "Ron called a dealer and I... I got tired of fighting myself. I told myself it would help with the hangover, just once, just to hold off feeling this agony for a few more hours. Ron offered me a bump, but I declined. I wanted to wait until I was home. The plan was to put on some music, smoke up and nod off. Just like the old days."

It almost sounded romantic, the way he spoke of his drug use. Too bad it was anything but. "I should have come right after you hung up on me," I said. "I knew you were in trouble, I just..."

He waved me off. "My bad behavior is not your responsibility," he said. "As it is, you've gone above and beyond as an assistant. I want you to mark all of this on your time sheet, by the way. It's the least I can do."

Time sheet. I'd let him in close to me, closer than I'd let anyone else since things got bad in Memphis. I'd held him while he sobbed. I'd let him see me tender and he just brushed it aside as a transaction. Did he think I only came back because I needed to boost my paycheck? That I was trying to cash in on his heartbreak? The dark hours had made us both vulnerable and stupid. Maybe he was right to shrug it all off as a late-night mistake and not assign any emotion to it.

He took a slow sip of his coffee. "That was some good detective work, tracking me down," he said. "I never told you where I was – not that I can remember anything after the funeral – and you still managed to find me."

"Janie said the calls came from the Vanguard and you told me you were at the hotel with Ron," I said. "When I called the second time, I heard music for a few seconds before you hung up on me."

"You could hear that?" he asked. "Didn't realize it was up that loud. Surprised no one at the hotel complained."

"You weren't at the hotel," I corrected. "I found the two of you in a cozy booth at Mr Jones. I left him there to pick up the check."

He groaned and put his head down on the table. "Please tell me you're kidding," he said.

"Wish I could."

"Now I'm really embarrassed," he said. "Probably best that I don't remember *any* of that." He sat up and gave me a rueful smile and drank a little more of his coffee. "But I do remember promising you breakfast. If you want to get a shower, we can go to the Red Top."

"I was just going to go home," I said. "Catch up on some sleep." That wasn't entirely true. I wanted to follow up a little more on the stalker angle, see what Deacon could tell me about the man he had to toss a few nights before Janie died. If I could present Martin with a little more evidence, he might give a second thought to taking Janie's case. But he wasn't in any shape to take on a murder investigation today. Truth was, neither was I, but one of us had to before the trail got cold, and I wasn't the one nursing a vicious hangover and a tenuous grasp on sobriety. He needed to get his head right before I could ask any more of him.

He looked hurt. "OK," he said, trying to mask it behind the last long swig from his coffee cup. "That's completely fine. You've more than earned the day off. I'll just go into the office, get some work done."

"Martin, go back to bed," I suggested. "Sleep this off. You've had a rough few days."

"Can't," he said. "It's Thursday; I've still got to do those background checks, and make a couple calls around to the pawn shops. Find that missing necklace. Cops sure as hell aren't going to."

Couldn't he, just for once, take my advice? "Maybe you should go to a meeting," I said. "Last night was a pretty close call."

"Already ahead of you," he said. "There was a morning meeting up the street. Shared and everything. It won't happen again, I promise. But I need to keep moving, keep busy. I know myself and it's just what I have to do."

That was a relief, at least. But there was a canyon between what he said and what I knew was squeezing him. "How about this," I offered. "Let me shower and we'll get breakfast. We'll work a half day; I'll check the pawn shops and you can do the background checks. We'll call it early, deal?" That would still give me some time to look into what I had on Janie while keeping him comfortable. He needed a friend, and for now, I was the only one he had. Ron didn't count. Ron was going to be on my shit list for the foreseeable future.

He brightened just a little around his bloodshot eyes. "Deal," he said. "After breakfast, we can go find my car. No clue where I left it. Christ, I'm such an asshole."

"It's at the Vanguard," I said. "Don't worry. I locked it up after I searched it."

"What did I ever do to deserve you?"

I left him pondering that question in the living room while I went upstairs to get a shower. I could still smell his cigarettes in my hair as I undressed and the scent sent me straight back to Memphis. Now wasn't the fucking time; I'd spent enough of my energy on Katy and I didn't have any to spare. I turned on the water as hot as I could stand and stood underneath the stream for a minute, letting it wash away all the night's tensions. I washed my hair with his shampoo and let the conditioner sink in for a full two minutes before I toweled off with a soft, oversized white towel. The shower made me feel a little more human, a little less like a discarded deli bag.

Joan took a lot of pity on Martin. She seated us at the back table where we'd have a little quiet, kept the coffee coming, kept his water glass refilled, gave him a series of small, sweet smiles. I think she could tell he was embarrassed by his sorry state.

We were halfway through our meals when I glanced up to see two familiar jack-offs coming in the door. "Do *not* look behind you," I hissed.

Of course he did, and both Roland and Rue caught his eye. He groaned and slumped forward, trying to shrink into the corner. But they came over, Roland clamping his meaty hand on his shoulder and Rue sliding in next to me. "You don't look so good," Roland taunted. "Long night?"

"Leave us alone," I said.

Martin didn't look at them. "Got that warrant yet?" he asked.

"Talked to Papa Ron the other day," said Rue. "Said you called him, told him to stay away from his daughter. Sound about like the work you did?"

"You'd have all the answers you needed if you filed that paperwork," he said. "And anyways, her death was ruled an accident. Nothing I can give you is going to change that."

His hands were shaking as he lifted the coffee cup to his pale lips. I couldn't tell if it was his hangover or nerves. Everyone in the diner seemed to have the same tight-wire tension between them. Nobody in this town liked cops. If you got lucky, maybe you knew a couple honest ones, but just because you went to school with a guy or your wife invited her cousin for the Fourth of July barbeque didn't mean you wanted them hanging around your diner. Because even if they were harassing someone else today, tomorrow it could be you, and it didn't matter if what they said was truth or just a lot of fiberglass fluff. Cops had a way of leaving a thousand little cuts that got septic before you even knew you were shredded.

"Any reason we saw you coming out of the Baptist church this morning?" Rue asked.

"None that should concern you."

"That's where the junkies hold their little meet-and-greets," Roland said, as though he was trying to educate Rue. "So either you were tracking someone or..." He leaned in close. "Or you're on the spike yourself."

"Might explain those bloodshot eyes," Rue said. "What's the matter, Martin, stuff stronger than you're used to? They mix it with elephant tranqs now. It'll really fuck you up."

I fought a sick feeling in my stomach that maybe he *was* holding, that his NA meeting had been a cover for fixing up and that a pat-down of his jacket would reveal a needle, a pipe, a bag of powder to be snorted off the kitchen counter. But that's what they wanted. To get me to blurt out that he had scored, even if he hadn't used, that there was far more to Janie's case than we were letting on. I stuffed my mouth full of waffles. They weren't going to pry an answer out of me that easily. "Is there a point to this whole performance?" I said when I swallowed. "Last I checked, it wasn't illegal to go to a church."

Rue looked at me like I was the centerfold of a porno mag. "Maybe his assistant does more than keep the books," he said. "No one would suspect a girl with good teeth and nice legs of running a couple errands to the bad part of town."

In an instant, he recoiled, shrinking up and howling, reaching down to rub his shin. "Sorry," Martin snapped. "Leg cramps. Spasms. You get them when you're dehydrated."

"You're never going to learn, are you?" said Roland.

"Probably not," he said. "Look, my assistant and I are just trying to have breakfast. You have nothing on me, no warrant, no evidence that I did anything illegal. You want to shake down Ron, be my guest. But unless you're picking up our check, you have no reason to be crowding our goddamn table."

Before the argument could progress further, Joan came over with a pitcher of water. "Let me get you a refill," she said. She topped off my glass and then picked up Martin's, pouring just a little before dumping the rest of the pitcher, ice and all, into Rue's lap. "I'm so sorry!" she squeaked. "Look at me, so clumsy. Let me get you some napkins, clean that up."

The tension was broken. The whole restaurant laughed. Well, everyone but Rue and Roland. "You did that on purpose, you bitch!" he hollered.

The laughter immediately fell silent. Martin shoved him out of the booth and onto the floor. I reached for the roll of nickels in my purse. But we weren't the only ones to react. Two men in Carhardt jackets and trucker hats stood up from the front table and surrounded Rue. "What did you just call Joan?" said the first.

"Don't do anything stupid," Roland said, easing out of his seat and showing his badge. "We're cops."

"And this is my diner," said Joan, holding out a stack of napkins. "You have no right to come in here and bother my customers. Get out and don't come back. Don't make me call the police."

More snickering. I never knew Joan was such a badass, but I shouldn't have been surprised. Rue got to his feet and snatched the napkins out of her hand. They both stormed out and slammed the door behind them. Martin stood up, his right leg soaked from the splash. Joan brought him a dry towel and he mopped off like it took the last energy he had. "Thank you," he said. "Sorry for the trouble."

"Sorry I didn't get to you sooner," she said. "My first thought was to get a frying pan and bash them both upside the head with it."

He looked at her with love in his weary eyes. "You did great," he said. "My guess this isn't your first time with a rowdy client."

"Not by a long shot," she said. "Take the booth up front, I'll bring you new plates. On the house." To the truckers, she said, "You too. Gentleman's discount."

We got resettled and new coffee was poured. "You know what?" Martin said. "Screw it. Let's take the whole day off."

"That," I said, lifting my cup for a toast, "is the best idea you've had in a while."

20

MARTIN

Breakfast helped, with one notable exception. The bourbon had managed to block out Janie's death for a few hours, but with my head slowly clearing, I had no choice but to face the sorrow lying in wait.

In the days after Cecelia disappeared, the most comfort I got was a quick hug from the other patients at the rehab clinic, a pat on the shoulder and an insincere offer to talk if I needed it, recycled words from a counselor who had a lot of other patients to deal with that day. I was alone in my fear and mourning and withdrawal, sobbing into a pillow, afternoons at the pay phone to call my sister Sandy and the detective assigned to my fiancée's case, hitting the treadmill in the gym like I could outrun all of my monsters. That anxious waiting, just a few days sober, was the hardest thing I'd ever done in my life. But it wasn't oblivion I really craved. All I wanted was some human contact, a piece of quiet intimacy to know that I wasn't completely alone when the woman I loved was somewhere I couldn't find her.

And it was that same need, shortsighted and clouded with heartache, that put me in Ron's room last night. I knew I was weak and I let myself give in. That was on me. And worse, I should not have piled that all on Valerie, not without warning, but I'd be lying to myself if I pretended she wasn't exactly what I was looking for. When all my walls had come down, when my soul was ugly and raw and hungry, she was the one who cared enough to hold me together. Addiction had burned a lot of bridges; it had been a long time since I'd let anyone in like that. Tomorrow I was going to tell her everything. She deserved to have all the facts. Not knowing Janie's whole story had landed us in this mess. It was just truth from now on.

But despite what I told her when she dropped me off, I still went into the office. Being home would just aggravate me. I could catch a nap on my couch if I needed it, and I was going to need it.

The office felt too empty without Valerie. My head hurt too much to put on music, let alone play. I made my calls on the background check. I played a couple rounds of solitaire with a deck of cards I kept in my drawer. I was just about to go home when the buzzer cut through my skull like a table saw. I swore my eyes filled with blood; I blinked them clear before I got up and answered.

There was Nora, looking pale and weak and fragile, like the consumption-addled heroine in a Merchant Ivory set piece. "I didn't mean to disturb you," she said. "The police told me you had an office here. I didn't even know you were in town until I saw you at the funeral."

Goddamn cops. "I've been here about five years," I said.

She let herself inside and I didn't have the energy to stop her. "They told me you were a private investigator," she said. "And that you had done some work for Janie."

"She came by," I said. "About a week before her death."

"What did she want?" she asked.

I didn't feel like doing this waltz, not when I was already dizzy. "Just to catch up, I guess," I lied. "What brings you here?"

"I'm looking for Ron," she said. "I've called his phone and his hotel room and he isn't answering. I thought he might be with you."

"I don't know where he is," I admitted.

"Aren't you worried about him?" she asked.

"I am," I said. "He's relapsed and so have I. So you'll understand why I can't be around him. My sobriety has to come first."

"Janie's death has been hard on all of us," she said. "But Ron is our friend. He needs us."

I wasn't in the mood for the guilt trip, but I might be able to leverage it into some questions I needed answered, for my own sake. "What was he doing in town?" I asked.

"I didn't even know he was in town," she said. "Apparently, he's been here a few days."

"Did you two keep in touch?"

"I saw him when I went out to say my goodbyes to Sharon," she said.

"Janie didn't mention he was here?"

"She didn't," she said.

"Did she mention Ron at all?"

"Not much," she said. "But I hadn't seen much of her in the days before her death. She was practicing for her recital. I hate to think that it was her last performance. It wasn't her best, but certainly not worth..."

She didn't finish that sentence. That was fine. I didn't want to hear it anyway. "Did you tell her Ron might want money from her?"

She took a tissue from the box on my desk and dabbed her eyes. "I'm sorry," she said. "This is just all so hard. I can't believe she's gone."

My head couldn't handle her sobbing right now.

"If you're worried about Ron, you can call in a welfare check on him," I said. "But more than likely, he's still sleeping off our little bender. I appreciate you coming by, but I need to get back to work."

She glanced around my shabby little office like she was trying to catch me in a lie more obvious than the hangover I'd gotten tired of hiding. "If you hear from him, tell him I'd like to see him," she said.

If I don't see Ron for the rest of my life it'll be too soon, I thought. "I will," I assured her.

"Let's have dinner sometime," she said. "It would be good to catch up with you."

That was the last thing I wanted to do. I had never cared much for Nora; she had a habit of getting drunk at parties and making a melodramatic scene, complete with tears and the occasional thrown bowl or wine glass. The first thing Cecelia and I would do when we got in the car to leave would be to let out all the laughter we'd been holding in all evening; Cecelia used to do an impersonation of her that would leave me doubled over the steering wheel with tears in my eyes. It wasn't so funny these days. Janie was dead and Ron was a mess and I wanted to wash my dirty hands of all of it. In a few days this would pass. In a few days things would go back to normal. All I had to do was get through today.

I gave her the usual line and let her take a card off Valerie's desk. We said our goodbyes and I closed and locked the door behind her. I waited until I was sure she was gone to get my coat, go home and put myself to bed for the rest of the afternoon.

21

VALERIE

Janie had lived in an art deco building on the college edge of the Leslie River. The name on the buzzer said *N. Archwood,* no mention of Janie. I knocked on her apartment door first and when nobody answered, I used a credit card to let myself in. Katy taught me that trick.

The apartment was tastefully decorated, with high ceilings and crown molding. Behind the velveteen sofa was a large abstract painting in blues and reds, and next to a low-slung leather chair was a twisted brass sculpture of a bird, maybe a foot tall and a fist wide, so freshly polished I could see my warped reflection. It looked like a fancy dildo. Maybe I was just never going to get art. There was no carpeting, not even an IKEA throw rug, leaving the room with an unfinished feel.

I went into the bathroom and studied everything in the cabinet. Toothpaste, two toothbrushes, a dentist's sample of dental floss, a couple orange pharmaceutical bottles in Nora's name. I turned all the labels facing out and photographed each one with my phone. Xanax, Zyrtec, Erythromycin. Two of the three were past their expiration date.

Across from the bathroom were two bedrooms, one with the door closed. I went into the open one and found some of Janie's mail on the desk. The cops had likely already gone through everything, so I didn't feel bad about poking around.

Her purse was in a white plastic police bag on her desk. The black leather was unblemished; it had not gone into the river with her. I rifled through the contents of the purse; I took her phone and her keys and left her wallet. Either she didn't carry cash or whoever found her was nice enough to leave the credit cards and her student ID when they took the easy stuff.

There were clothes in her hamper, a bookcase full of sheet music, her laptop. There was a lock on her closet door and I tried a few of her keys until I found the one that fit. I expected to find her Joyride life in there, stashed away from Nora's prying eyes. Instead, there was a series of plain dresses and long skirts and one dress suit, all hung on padded hangers. It wasn't until I glanced a little further up that I saw why she locked the door.

On the top shelf were four foam heads, each mounted with a chestnut wig – an updo, a French twist, the braid she'd worn to the office. I wasn't going to shame her for wearing wigs, but it seemed strange that they were kept under lock and key. Surely Nora wouldn't try to steal a couple of hairpieces?

Unless Nora didn't know about Joyride.

There were no traces of Joyride in her bedroom. No Manic Panic jars, no torn jeans, not even a bottle of black nail polish stashed between her sweaters. Melanie was right. She kept her secret life elsewhere – but where? Had she really managed to hide a completely different identity from everyone? I guess I could relate. Martin probably could too. But *why*? It was one thing to reinvent yourself to escape your parents' image, but something else entirely to create a whole other persona. And if she had a boyfriend, as Melanie suspected, there was no evidence; no love letters, no framed photographs, no jewelry that might indicate romance. Janie, it seemed, lived a life as stark as one of her Styrofoam heads; blank until someone projected a life onto it.

In addition to her life as Joyride, her violin was also missing. I wondered if her dad had gotten ahold of it or if she had taken it to the bottom of the Leslie with her. If she took it with her, there went the accident angle. Maybe it was a suicide like Melanie had feared, a farewell to an ugly world with the one thing that brought her joy, the only piece of her anyone wanted.

My eyes filled up with tears. What could she have done to hurt someone so badly that they killed her for it? Ron didn't seem like the violent type, but maybe the drinking and the drugs were a mask for something sinister, something he wanted to forget. That was the piece I was missing, and the pathway to finding it seemed like a thousand miles of rocks and desert sun. But it was a path I was determined to walk. I had to know why she died and who was responsible. I owed her friends that much.

I found a photo album at the bottom of the drawer. It spanned about ten years; underexposed candids from a disposable camera showing teens in matching blue polos laughing on lush lawns, Polaroids and pixilated 3x5s. One of them was Gordon, hair soft and shaggy, holding a guitar. He hadn't mentioned knowing her as long as he did. Maybe he was the secret boyfriend.

Later on in the album were a few stiff portfolio pictures of Janie in a long black dress with her violin. If I found her secret hiding spot, would I find a whole other set of shots from punk clubs and parties, a scrapbook of posters and patches?

Tucked in the back of the book were a few loose photos from earlier years. A birthday party, back when Ron was thinner and had more hair. Janie looked just like her mother, the two of them smiling in the garden in front of the house. Normal photos from a childhood that, from what Martin told me, was anything but.

And it didn't take me any time at all to recognize Martin in the last photo.

He was dressed in a skinny blue suit with no tie and the two buttons of his striped shirt undone. Ron stood behind him in a Blasters T-shirt and Janie was in the lap of a woman who wasn't Sharon. The woman was beautiful, with curls the color of coffee crème, rhinestones around her slim neck, curvy in a sequined blue cocktail dress. She was seated next to Martin on the couch with her head on his shoulder. There were empty champagne glasses on the table. On the back was written *New Year's Eve, 1993.*

I heard keys in the door. I heard Nora call out, "Is someone there?" I wrestled open the window and climbed out onto the fire escape. I slammed it closed behind me and climbed down two floors and lay flat against the brick, trying to catch my breath, trying to remember if I had left any doors or drawers or the window open. And it wasn't until I was steady again that I realized I still had Janie's photo album, clutched tight against my chest.

22

MARTIN

I wished someone had told me that hangovers got harder to shake as you got older. I still felt like death when I went into the office on Friday morning. I apologized again to Valerie, muted and humiliated, the way drunks always do. I'd made those apologies a thousand times before. I never planned on making one again.

We spent the morning driving around pawn shops looking for the lost necklace. We found it at Charlie's Pawn, unsurprisingly. "They're not even real rubies," he told us as he handed it over. "But the girl who sold it to me was in bad shape. I figured the cops would come looking for it eventually. I gave her twenty dollars just so she'd get out of my store."

It was a good grift Charlie had going. He handed over the cheap stuff to me and a couple of cops – stolen silver, costume jewelry, small electronics – and we all pretended we didn't notice the diamonds and the video game systems that fell off the back of a truck. Not when he gave the kind of tips he did. Despite my better judgment, I liked Charlie. He'd never given me any trouble.

Back at the office Valerie called the client, Mrs Orthwine, and wrote up the file. Maybe Roland and Rue thought what I did was sleazy, but neither of them would have taken her case. The report would have ended up buried in some file cabinet, her necklace around the throat of some other woman. My work would never make the headlines. I was OK with that. All that mattered was solving what my clients needed me to solve, even if it rarely fixed the real problem. I'd be back at Charlie's looking for more of Mrs Orthwine's costume jewelry next month. In another two years I'd be peeping in the new Mrs Russell's windows. But being able to do one good thing helped my headache. Being able to solve one small case made me feel less like a cigarette butt left drowned in the gutter. And it took my mind off Ron for a minute. That was the biggest relief of all.

I had lunch with Barry, my old sponsor. We talked about the weather. I had never quite connected with Barry the way I had with my first sponsor, Todd, back in Minneapolis during that first long year of sobriety. Todd began using after his daughter died in a car accident, started with painkillers, same as me. We had loss in common. Barry was a matter of routine, someone I connected with when I first moved to Perrine, just so I knew someone was there in case I fell to pieces. Barry was exactly what I needed in the moment – warm, a little dull; a familiar, quiet comfort.

Valerie was still away at lunch when I got back. The office had the eerie quiet of lingering ghosts. But ghosts eventually dispel. There would be other cases, real cases. I tried not to think about what Valerie had said to me outside the funeral home. It, like the rest of my hangover, would fade in time. But until then, I felt sick to my stomach every time I heard her echo rattle around my skull. Because I knew at the core of it, she was right. Not about the murder – she had no proof of that – but that I had failed Janie. I had to find a way within myself to reconcile that.

Janie's folder was still on Valerie's desk. I swore I had told her to shred it. Her desk drawer was open just slightly and I went to push it closed. There was a photo album tucked inside and a photo face-down on her desk blotter. I picked it up and turned it over.

And there, staring back at me, was Cecelia.

23

VALERIE

Martin wasn't the only one with contacts who skirted the law. I took Janie's phone to Lyca, who managed a cell phone store on Crestmont, a few blocks down from my brother's tattoo shop. In the early Nineties, during a brief period of the city's revival, the area was known as Antique Row; now many of the stores had dust on their shelves as old as some of their wares. But the rents were cheap and there were just enough businesses that the place hadn't become a stroll for the nighttime crowd just yet, so a few stores – like Arc Tattoo and MetroCell – hung in there.

Today Lyca was wearing their pink wig. I hadn't seen them in a while, but they gave me a hug and we caught up briefly and they showed me their new tattoo: a chibi Godzilla stomping through a city made of cookies and milkshakes. They asked if I had any new ink. I told them no.

"I got locked out of my cell phone," I told them when we were all caught up. "Roommate thought it would be funny to change the password, you know how it is."

"I know how it is," they said.

Burner phones and accessories kept the store front clean, but everyone in the know knew that Lyca's real business was breaking into phones likely obtained through less-than-legal means. After all, they could claim they didn't know, that they just helped someone who told them the phone was hers and if they couldn't trust their customers, who could they trust?

Martin wasn't going to be happy when he learned I'd lifted evidence, but he didn't have to know, and he'd thank me when I broke this case. Who knew what might be hiding behind that passcode?

"I'm a little backed up right now," they said. "Might be a few days."

"No real rush," I said. "But I've got some work stuff in there, so if you get some time to bump it up, I would appreciate it."

"That costs extra, so you know."

I'd sell my plasma to make it work, or let Lyca bank a favor in case they ever needed it. "Whatever it takes," I said. "Just text me when it's done."

I took a quick trip down to the riverfront, tried to match up the crime scene to the photo in the paper now that the yellow tape had come down. There wasn't anything left to paw over. The autopsy listed her cause of death as an accidental drowning, another Ophelia, young and angry and beautiful. But Janie was no Ophelia. She was no Virginia Woolf with stones in her pocket. Did that make it better or worse? Add that to the list of questions I didn't have an answer to. Put it on the tab of what I might never know.

I spotted Gordon a few paces down, sitting on a busted park bench, staring at the water. I stuffed my hands in my pockets against the cold-water wind and went to him. "So, this is it, huh?" he said. "This is where it happened."

"Guess so," I said.

"Feels like we should put up a little shrine," he said. "But the junkies would just kick it over."

"There's one over at Topsy's," I said. "And Gina's going to put her photo up on the wall."

"The Pitt too," he added. "People loved her. She could be a pain in the ass, but I'm really going to miss her." He wiped his eyes on a torn blue flannel cuff. "I can't really believe she's gone."

I let the silence settle for a few moments. "When did you see her last?" I finally said.

He took a pack of cigarettes out of the pocket of his flannel shirt and lit up. "Saturday morning," he said. "Rehearsal. There's a guy who owns a space in the warehouse district; he rents it to bands."

"How'd she seem?"

He took a drag. He stayed silent, wouldn't look at me. "Gordon…" I said. "If you want me to solve this…"

"I know, I know, it's just that…" Another drag. "I'm sure it's nothing."

"How about you let me decide that?"

He flicked ash onto the sand. "When I pulled up that Saturday, Janie and Melanie were inside and screaming at each other," he said. "You could hear it through the open windows. I couldn't exactly make out what they were saying – I did hear Melanie call her a 'spoiled little bitch' – but they shut up as soon as I got in the door."

That put a new spin on why Melanie didn't want her death looked into. But there's a big difference between calling someone a bitch and dumping their body in the river. "They always fight like that?"

"Yeah," he admitted. "Constantly."

"What about?"

"A lot of things," he said. "Set lists, the direction of the band; hell, Melanie once called her outfit 'Hot Topic clearance-chic.' She thought Janie was a poser living off her dad's fumes. I guess he was some hot shit for a minute in the Eighties."

"Early Nineties," I corrected. I immediately felt like a jerk. "But from what I heard, she hated her dad."

He shook his head. "It wasn't that easy," he said. "I mean, a lot of people hate their dads, but not Janie. I think she really loved him, but he was just a sad junkie, and I think that hurt more. There's only so many times you can forgive a person before you gotta guard your heart, you know?" He tapped his chest with the two fingers holding his lit cigarette, and I held my breath in case he caught himself on fire.

"Our senior year, he 'surprised' her at her recital," he continued. "He had completed rehab and had two years of sobriety under his belt, so she invited him out to see her. They had a couple of good days together – she was happier than I'd ever seen her, honestly – but when he arrived at the recital, he was completely trashed. He and Nora had gone out for lunch and, well, I think you can guess. Nora acted all horrified, but seeing as how she was the one who drove him there in that condition, I think she did it on purpose, like she was trying to prove to Janie that she was the better parent. It was absolute bullshit."

There was a lot to unpack there. I'd start with the basics. "You two went to school together?" I asked.

"It's how we met," he said. "My mom is Sylvia Rettenbouer, the soprano. I got my dad's singing voice, unfortunately, but I was a really good viola player, so they shipped me off to Interlochen. I met Janie there, we got into punk and hardcore together. It was the furthest thing from what we were playing, especially me. I hadn't grown up with that in my house, so Janie became my teacher. Best education I ever got."

I had a lot more questions – about the band, about Melanie and Ron and whether or not Janie followed in her father's drug-addled footsteps – but my lunch hour was ticking close to over and I needed to pick one rabbit hole to dive down. "Tell me about Nora," I said.

He snorted. "You know how Melanie said Janie didn't wear her show clothes outside the venue? I think Nora was the reason for it."

"Nora didn't approve of the punk rock lifestyle?" I said. "How very 'Satanic Panic.'"

"She didn't approve of it because she didn't know about it," he said. "It was like Joyride was living two completely different lives. That's why she freaked out about the photos – she didn't want anyone to know about Machine Gun Snatch."

Goddamn it. Why hadn't we started with that? I felt like a therapist, trying to coax more out of him without shading the answers. "And what did you think about that?"

He shrugged. "I mean, at first, I was pissed," he said. "We've talked about starting this band our whole lives and then we're in a place to do it and she's hiding us in shadows? That hurt. But as long as Nora was paying her tuition, she felt like she was in debt to her. I could wait for her to make the decision between her violin and our band, but maybe Melanie couldn't."

"So what do you think happened that night?"

He stood. He threw down his cigarette and buried it in sand with the graffiti-covered tip of a Converse sneaker. "I honestly don't know," he said. "But I do know that Melanie didn't answer her phone on Saturday night."

I let him walk back to his car and drive away before I went back to the parking lot. I had a lot to think about. Three people to question and only one with a motive I could chew on, a history of rage and a blank Saturday night. Or maybe I just hadn't landed on motives for Nora or Ron yet.

Pulling into my parking space, I forced myself to take a few calming breaths. *One step at a time,* I told myself. Martin always told me that you didn't solve a puzzle with the first couple of pieces. It was a process, more like a series of tightrope steps, one foot in front of the other until you found yourself safely on the other side. Gordon had told me plenty, likely more than he intended to. I could come back to the riverfront after dark, see if maybe one of the regulars saw anything they might not be willing to tell a cop. But the riverfront at night was always risky. I would need someone to go with. At some point I was going to have to bring Martin in on this. I just had to decide when that point would be.

I got upstairs and saw Martin sitting at my desk, Janie's open file in front of him, the New Year's Eve photograph in his hand.

And just like that, someone cut my tightrope line.

24

MARTIN

There are plenty of ways a man can be betrayed. His wife could bring someone else into their bed, his children could empty his bank accounts, he could get laid off from the job he worked his whole life a day before retirement or his best friend could put a bullet in his gut.

This, somehow, was worse.

I pushed the photo across the desk to her, face down. I couldn't bear to see my fiancée's face right now. "Where did you get this?" I asked.

The whole room had a black patina over it, like I was trying to see through smoke. Valerie looked like she wanted to jump out of a window. My jaw was clenched so tight I thought I might crack a molar. To her credit, she didn't try to bullshit me. "I found it," she said. "In Janie's apartment."

"What were you doing in Janie's apartment?"

"Investigating her death," she said. Her words came out in a rush, like she was trying to get everything out before I cut her off. "Martin, this might not have been an accident. I just have to prove it. I've been interviewing her bandmates; I searched her apartment..."

I couldn't even look at her. I walked over to the windowsill, leaning so hard into the frame that paint flecks came off in my hands. "Do you have *any* idea how *wrong* all of this is?" I hissed. "There are *laws*, there are systems and protocols in place. You can't just walk all over them because you get a wild theory."

"I was just trying to help," she said. "Her friend asked me to look into her death. There was blackmail, she had people who wanted to hurt her." She picked up the notepad and flipped to the second page. "I've got leads we can follow up on. There's a trail here, Martin, we owe it to her to follow it."

"You are not a detective!" I hollered. "You are my *assistant.* You have no license, no right to snoop around. You went behind my back, you opened a case I did not want opened. This isn't a game, this is my *profession,* Valerie. This is my life, and ever since she walked into this office all of that has been hanging by a goddamn thread. And *still,* after *everything* I've been through, everything I've asked you *not* to do, you keep pushing."

This wasn't about my profession. This wasn't about who was licensed and who wasn't. I didn't even know what it was about except that I had let her in close enough that she could stick a knife between my ribs. She had no right. No goddamn right at all.

I didn't need to look at her to know she was crying. "Martin, please," she begged. "We can work through this. Please, just hear me out..."

I couldn't listen anymore. I went into my office and slammed the door and sat against my desk until I didn't hear her sobbing. The front office was empty. She hadn't slammed the front door to tell me she left. She didn't even close it all the way. It hung half-open, a bridge between the worlds. After a minute, I shut that too.

Around 2pm the last lingering traces of my hangover disappeared. Too bad I didn't feel any better. If anything, I felt worse. Valerie didn't come back. Didn't text, didn't call, gave me no indication that she had any plans to return. I couldn't blame her.

I let myself look at the photograph again. New Year's Eve, 1993. The French Letters had played the first set at the Bastone Ballroom, the perfect proportions of music and beer to create the illusion of hope and goodwill. The girls all danced. The band sounded fantastic. And Cecelia... even now I could see her as I had seen her then, standing in the pit in that vintage dress and her mom's rhinestones, her hands clasped over her heart, beaming at me. I was only singing for her; the music sounded real because it was reaching her ears. I could have stared at her all night, awestruck. But there was dancing to be done, and after our set we listened to one more band before heading home so we could ring in the new year with just the five of us. We were so goddamn happy then. What happened? The migraines happened. The Percocet happened. The heroin happened and ripped us all apart. From this photograph to her disappearance was just over three years. A small lifetime.

There were new notes on Valerie's notepad. Before I could stop myself, I was sitting at her desk reading through all of them. I never would have guessed that the trembling girl who sat in my office drinking black coffee was a hardcore punk singer, but if what her bandmates had told Valerie was true, then there was more to this situation than even Janie had let on. Blackmail, for starters. That alone was enough to open a case, but the details about the fights with her bass player – I knew how nasty those could be – gave us one more suspect, and the boyfriend no one could identify added a third. Never mind her father's sudden arrival and a life hidden from a strict mentor. It was starting to look exactly like anything but an accident.

I put in a call to Captain Hollander and made a fresh pot of coffee and lay down on the couch until he rang the buzzer just after three. He came upstairs with a thick file in hand. He'd grown out his beard a little longer than when I saw him last. I couldn't decide if it worked for him or not.

"Long time no see," I said as we sat. "Saw a couple of your boys the other day, though."

Hollander rolled his eyes so hard I thought he might fall out of his chair. "Jesus Christ, those two," he said. "Hope they didn't rough you up too badly."

"I can handle them," I said. "But tell them if they come near my assistant again, my next call is my attorney. Vinny just finished a weekend production of *The Elephant Man* at the Thorington Playhouse. He's in the mood to grandstand and the courtroom is his favorite stage."

I was acting like I still *had* an assistant. If Valerie didn't come back, I wouldn't blame her. *You sure know how to ruin a good thing,* I sneered at myself. *First one life and then another.* But there wasn't time for self-pity. Not when my synapses were finally all firing again.

Hollander glanced at me. "I'll remind them to keep their distance," he said. "But you didn't call me down here to snark about my cops."

"No, I did not," I said. "Come into my office."

We got settled and he passed me the folder. "It's a pretty cut-and-dry accident," he said. "No other marks, no signs of a struggle, water in her lungs. Time of death is around 2am. No reason a Raines girl should be in that section of the riverfront at 2am."

I was no longer convinced it was merely an accident. "Not a suicide?" I offered. A late-night culmination of a lifetime of unhappiness was as likely a possibility as anything, given everything she had been through. I'd heard that same urgent whisper in dark hours, that sweet promise that all that pain could end in just a few short steps, and I'd let that whisper grow into a scream until I tried to silence it myself. I was lucky, though. I survived. Too few of us do.

Hollander brought me back around to the task at hand. "No note," he said. "They don't always leave notes, though."

"Tox screen?"

Hollander swung his left ankle over his knee, revealing hamburger socks. "You're not going to like it," he said.

"A girl is dead," I snapped. "What would there be to like?"

Hollander sighed. "Xanax," he said. "And alcohol. They found vomit in her lungs, but that wasn't what killed her."

"Any possibility she choked and someone dumped her in the river?"

Hollander looked at me funny. "What's your angle on this, Martin?" he said.

"She's a family friend," I said. "I just want to make sure every option's been explored."

"I wish I could tell you something different," Hollander said. "But it looks like she was intoxicated, passed out on the shore, got swept up in the tide and drowned. She's not the first body we've found like that down there. I know that makes it worse for the family, but that's the truth of it."

"She's dead," I said. "It can't *be* any worse."

Hollander let that sit between us. I closed the folder without looking at the photos from the crime scene. We said our goodbyes and I put on Paul Westerberg's *Eventually* and paced the office, sneaking an occasional glance at the folder on my desk, like a dirty magazine, like a Dear John letter. After a few false starts, I couldn't avoid it any longer.

There's something haunting about a drowned woman. A drowned man is sad, maybe a little pathetic, a real head-shaker while you try to figure out how much he had to drink before he went beneath the waves. But a woman in the water is a lonely island, a siren silenced.

The girl in the photos didn't look like Janie. Her long wet dress twisted around her like cling wrap. She had a stripe of dark hair and nothing else on her shaved head. So she was wearing a wig when she came into the office. But why? Was she in disguise, and for what reason?

I cross-referenced Valerie's notes. And there it was. As Joyride, she played Friday night at the Pitt. Sure enough, a printout photo tucked inside her notes showed a girl with a purple Mohawk, screaming into a microphone. So she did take after her dad, in all the best ways. I let myself smile. Nora would have hated that. Good.

Then there was the blackmail theory. Someone had taken photos she didn't want taken; someone had followed her to Topsy's last week. Blackmail was always an ugly business but it was easy to follow; the men with the dirty cameras didn't usually cover their tracks particularly well. But a blackmailer has to want something and that something has to be equal to the cost of a human life if it was going to be murder. And human life is, to some, all too cheap.

I rolled my shoulders to try to stretch out the tight feeling in my chest. A damp cold chill had settled under my skin, seeping into my bones. There was something so hatefully familiar about these photos, her soaked body stretched on the rocks. We'd been here before and it took me a few minutes to place it.

The pool.

It hit me like a speeding car. The note, the words I had scribbled on a cocktail napkin in some forgotten piece of yesterday's relapse. It was the single smart thing I did that night, a reminder to a future sober self to investigate further.

June 1994. Janie was two. "Storm Before the Calm," our first single off *God Machine*, had just made the Billboard charts and we were celebrating in their backyard. It happened so fast. One minute Janie was playing with dolls underneath the table, the next, Sharon was screaming that she was in the water. Ron and I both dove in but I got to her first, carrying her to the surface and laying her on the cement and pushing the water out of her lungs until she gasped awake into my arms. They drained the pool the next day.

Goddamn it.

Valerie was right.

25

VALERIE

Fuck Martin.

Fuck his Elvis Costello playlists. Fuck his gorgeous suits. Fuck his sheet music and his pocket squares and his French press, fuck his piano and his name on the door of his stupid, dingy little office.

I'd done my crying in the car and now I was left with the sort of empty, hollow rage you can only take out on the heavy bag. I hadn't been to the gym in a few weeks, giving in to the temptations of dinner in front of my laptop, but it wasn't even a choice between home and the gym. A couple of girls from the boxing team invited me to get in the ring alongside them. I declined. I was feeling too mean to go against someone I might actually hurt. The bag was a loyal listener. The bag would be there to take my blows.

Gina was the one who insisted I take up boxing. It started as a protective measure, but when I showed a talent for it – honed from schoolyard fights – she got me on the team. Coach Craig had the old-school toughness of a man who didn't like the idea of having to teach girls, thinking that if he talked to us the way he talked to his boys, all of us would quit. *None of you powder-puffs are pretty enough to get a husband if your nose gets broken,* he'd tell us as a way of teaching us to block.

But we didn't quit. We even bested some of his boys,

and by the end of his tenure as coach, he was training girls almost exclusively in a program he jokingly called "Charm School," complete with a logo his wife Dolores made. He took in girls with bad home lives, girls with dim futures, girls who just needed someone in their corner, and he taught us all to stand up for ourselves. Monica Smith, his first trainee, went on to become a professional MMA fighter, and when the camera panned to the audience, you could always see Coach Craig right in front, beaming with pride. When he died in 2012, Monica contacted all of us and we each chipped in for an arrangement. All of us attended the funeral, outnumbering his boys two-to-one, and more than a couple of my teammates said at the reception he had either attended their weddings or sent lovely gifts, all with the same cheeky inscription in the card – *Don't mess with this powder-puff, or you'll rue the day!* It was all that training, the blocks and the parries, the slips and counters, that saved my life back in Memphis.

The bag was spinning. My head was spinning. I grabbed it hard and I held on and let my heart come down a bit. It wasn't that I was out of a job; I could always go back to Topsy's and tend bar. I was angry that I'd let myself get sold on a fantasy that what Martin did was noble and good, that he was misunderstood, that he helped people. What hurt was how easily he'd been able to dispose of me, dump me out of his office like a record with a long scratch across the grooves. Where was the man who bailed me out of lockup when I went in search of Jenny Rees at the Glass Factory rave, when the cops rounded me up with all the other party people? Where was the man who trusted me to solve the cold case, literally, of a girl found in the Wegman's snowbank? Maybe the man I let drench my dress with his tears was the stranger, and all those other variants had just been for show. Maybe that's what I get for believing he was actually my friend and not just the guy who signed my paycheck. He could always get another assistant.

So maybe Rue and Roland were right about him – that he was just another window-peeper, not to be trusted to do the right thing unless money was involved. Janie needed him and he had let her down, time and time again.

But I didn't have to.

I knew how detective work was done. I knew what records I could request. Just because I didn't have a license, didn't mean I couldn't ask questions of the people who knew her. And when I proved this was murder, I'd go ahead and apply for my own license, open my own shop, show Martin that I didn't need him. Seriously, fuck him.

Arc Tattoo was closed for the night, but from the parking lot across the street I could still see my brother at the register. Crossing the street, I could hear Swans at a volume that should have rattled the windows, the only acceptable volume for Swans. There were no neighbors to complain, after all.

I knocked on the door and he let me in. "Little late to start some ink," he joked. "Even for my little sister."

"Aww, come on," I joked. "It's not the first time you've tattooed me after hours."

"It won't be the last time, I'm sure," he said. "But I'm burnt. You want to go over to Topsy's? You look like you could use a drink."

I was about to give an automatic *yes*, but instead of the word on my tongue, I could taste the bourbon on Martin's breath when we were only atoms apart. I didn't want anything to dull my rage, but that meant I might have to spill what was on my mind without a truth serum. "Not tonight," I said. "Thought we could just hang out here for a minute."

"Sure," he said. "There's water in the fridge, if you want. Might be some iced teas in there too, if you're feeling fancy."

I got us both bottles of water and flopped on the couch. When I was younger, I used to hang out in the shop all the time. Couldn't hang out at Topsy's, after all, and being alone in the apartment triggered too much anxiety. After my parents died, I lived with a near-constant fear that I would lose Aunt Gina and Deacon too, waking up in the middle of the night to check if they were breathing in their beds. It was a fear that persisted well into high school, so on days when Katy couldn't hang out, I'd come here and read magazines and admire his work on the skin of sorority girls and hipster dads and sex workers and new couples, planning the artwork I would get when I was old enough. That fear had passed – reversed, even, where now the thought of sharing a space with someone was what terrified me – until the other night. I wouldn't have gone to find Martin if I hadn't been afraid that I might lose him.

No, I reminded myself. *Martin can go fuck himself.* He had turned me inside out, brought every single one of my fears to the surface and then shoved me out the door. I wasn't going to think about him, tonight or ever again.

"Something you want to talk about?" Deacon asked. "Or you just get a craving for a too-soft couch and bottled water?"

Right. I had come here for a reason. "Dott asked me to look into Janie – Joyride's – death," I said.

"Heard it was an accident," he replied. "Or maybe a suicide."

"Her bandmates don't think so," I said.

He grinned. "Most people just ask their crush on a date," he said. "Not try to solve a killing to impress them."

Leave it to my brother to tease me when I just needed an answer out of him. I doubted romance was on Dott's mind, even if it had been for a fraction of a second in the dim light of Topsy's. "Deacon, this is serious," I insisted. "I heard she had a stalker; someone she told to leave her alone outside of the bar the last time they played there. Did she say anything to you?"

He stopped piling up receipts and thought for a minute. "There was a guy," he said. "Think his name is Rodney, he writes the *Capital Numbers* 'zine."

"People still make 'zines?" I said. "I knew the Nineties were coming back but I thought that was, like, just crop tops and mom jeans."

"I didn't say he was successful," he joked. "He does have a pretty good Instagram page, though, you should check it out. He photographed all the bands, but Joyride, for whatever reason, didn't want to be photographed. She asked me to bounce him, and I did. He was pissed, but I'm not gonna let some goon harass the bands. It's bad business."

I pulled out my phone. For a second, I hoped I'd find a message from Martin, apologizing for being such a dick. No such luck. But I did find the *Capital Numbers* page on Instagram. I recognized a couple of the performers, including a gorgeous photo of Dott behind her kit, braids and drumsticks wild, her face slick with sweat, playing with The Chirmps. I'd never seen anyone more gorgeous. If there were any photos of Joyride, they were buried down at the bottom. "Thanks," I said. "This could be the break I need."

Deacon finished his water and tossed the bottle into the recycling bin. "Glad to be of assistance to justice," he said. "Is there something *else* you want to talk about?"

Not tonight. Not right now. Maybe not ever. "Why does everyone keep asking me that?"

"Because you look pissed," he said. "Because it's 8pm and you're here instead of home watching TV. Because you got a letter from Memphis and for the last six months you've been walking around with a pretty significant injury you won't talk about."

"Jesus Christ, Aunt Gina told you about that?"

"Of course," he said. "We're worried about you, kid."

I should feel safe talking to him and Aunt Gina. But it wasn't about the confession as much as it was about not wanting to put words to what I might have done. It was one thing to punch a frat boy who was giving you shit outside a bar. It was something entirely different to admit that you might have carved up your best friend, even if she attacked you first, to put words to the cowardice that had you running for home like a bullied child on a playground. If I didn't say it out loud, maybe it never happened.

I put my unfinished water bottle in my bag. "Thanks for the tip," I repeated, getting up.

"I mean it, Valerie," he said. "You can talk to me."

"I will," I assured him. "Just not tonight."

26

MARTIN

The diner was empty except for Joan and one of the cooks, talking behind the counter. She turned and saw me and pasted on a smile like an alibi. "Little late for you, Martin," she said. "Didn't feel like cooking?"

"I feel bad about the other day," I said. "Wanted to come in and apologize for the trouble."

The cook went back into the kitchen. Joan brushed off my remark like she was shooing away a fruit fly. "Sit," she commanded. "I was going to make myself a milkshake. Do you want one?"

I couldn't even remember the last time I'd had a milkshake. "Sure," I said.

"Vanilla or chocolate?"

"Vanilla."

"Whipped cream?"

"Why not?"

She made a chocolate shake for herself. She gave us both a cherry and a red straw. I took a sip that tasted like a first date. "People don't order these as often as they should," she said. "But one of my core beliefs is that you cannot be sad while drinking a milkshake."

I was certainly testing that theory. But it did help a little, gave me one small thing to feel good about. "I wanted to thank you," I said. The shake was so thick I could hardly work my straw around it. "For the other day. You didn't have to do that."

"I wasn't going to let those two harass you," she said. "One day it's you, the next it's the college kids or the guys who panhandled a buck for a cup of coffee."

So, I wasn't special. I was an example. What was one more blow to my ego? "Besides," she said, pausing to take a pretty little sip, "the two of you looked like you needed someone to stand up for you, for once."

The two of us. I waited for her to ask where Valerie was. "Yeah," I finally said. "It's been a rough week."

She folded her arms and leaned on the counter. "I hear you," she said. "You want to go first or should I?"

I just wasn't ready to put all my sins into words, wasn't ready to reveal myself ugly and raw to someone so lovely and kind. I didn't deserve Joan. I had barely deserved Cecelia and I certainly didn't deserve Valerie. "Ladies first," I offered.

"My ex-husband wants to move his girlfriend into our home," she said. "Wants me to move into the mother-in-law suite. Never mind that he's gone half the week, never mind that he's the one who left me. It's never going to hold up in court, but he knows I don't have the time or money to fight him, so he's going to make my life miserable until I give in."

"Vinny O'Neil," I said before I could stop myself. "My lawyer. He'll help you out. Nothing will get him in front of a judge faster than a damsel in distress. Tell him I sent you. He'll take care of you."

"I'm hardly a damsel," she joked. "But thanks for the suggestion. I'll call him in the morning."

"Happy to help."

"Your turn."

The combination of her perfume and the shake and the quiet of the empty diner lowered my guard like a stiff drink. "I screwed up," I admitted. "Royally. I sabotaged nineteen years of sobriety, I botched a case, my friend's daughter died and…" I looked up into her face, her faded red lipstick and her smudged eyeliner. She was beautiful. She was perfect. And she was going to hate me for what I was going to say next. "And I really hurt Valerie. That's the worst part of it. She was with me through everything and I turned around and... hurt her. Like it was all nothing."

My chest hurt. I was a blink away from tears falling. Joan put her hand on mine. Her fingertips were cold from the glass. I took it one step further and laced my fingers with hers and gripped her tighter than I probably meant to. I didn't deserve her kindness, but at the core of it all, I was selfish and I was needy and I wasn't going to let go until she released me. I needed one moment of my day to go right so I could remember what right looked like.

"I'm sorry," she murmured. "About your friend. About all of it, really."

Now that I was talking, I couldn't stop. "I just wish I knew how to repair it all," I lamented. "I met with my sponsor, but I can't go back in time and fix my case. At the end of the day, this girl is still dead. It all just feels so... broken."

Joan took one last loud sip of her shake and untangled her fingers from mine and patted my hand. "There's one thing you can do," she said.

"And that is?"

"You can go apologize to Valerie."

Easier said than done. "And if she won't hear me?"

"She will," she said. "Trust me. And once you apologize to her, everything else will fall into place."

She was right, the way women are always right. Here I was trying to wind circles around the one thing that needed to be done and she cut right to it. I stood and reached for my wallet and she shook her head. "My treat," she said.

"Joan..."

"You helped me find a lawyer," she said. "That's worth a hell of a lot more than a milkshake. Besides..." She cleared away our glasses. "It was good to have the company."

"Yes, it was," I admitted. "Just what I needed."

27

VALERIE

Martin was waiting on my doorstep like a lost dog when I pulled into my driveway. He had a folder in his hands. I didn't need to take my gloves inside but I pulled them out of the trunk just so he knew I wasn't going to fuck around with him. "What are you doing here?" I demanded.

"I came to apologize," he said. "For this afternoon. I was out of line."

He didn't stand. I wondered if it was a subtle power move, an unspoken way of proving whether or not he could break me. I didn't sit. We faced off like gunfighters, like cops and robbers, like betrayed lovers.

"I was wrong about a lot of things," he said, finally rising to his feet. "But the first was treating you like you didn't matter. You're not just my assistant… you're…" He stumbled over the words, working them around his mouth like a rock tumbler. "You're my friend, Valerie. Probably the only one I really have."

After a minute I climbed up the stairs. We both sat. He stared at the skyline like he was trying to pick out a few stars through the city lights. "Ron was always my closest friend," he began. "We thought alike. We heard music the same way. And he was a goddamn genius – he would play a chord that looked so easy on paper, but when you heard him play it… it was like the echo of stars. Like it could align the planets."

I didn't want to hear about Ron. Not after the hurt he'd inflicted on Janie, not after what happened at the Vanguard. But Martin wasn't finished. "Heroin took all that," he said. "From both of us. It made him into someone I didn't recognize and it made me into someone I hated. I was able to pull myself back, but Ron… Ron just doesn't always have that in him. Not right now, anyways. Some people don't."

I knew all too well how quickly someone you loved could turn into a monster, how deep that pain could be, burrowing into your cells until that betrayal becomes part of your DNA. I slipped my arm through his and put my head on his shoulder. I needed to know he was really there, that this wasn't just a dream. He wrapped his hand around mine. "My best friend tried to kill me," I finally said. "So I get it."

"Memphis?"

I nodded and sat up and he let me. I lifted my left arm and pushed up my sleeve and ran my finger along the white line that ran along the outside muscle. "I don't know if it was meth or mental issues, but she started telling me she could hear God. Then she *was* God. And then I woke up with her standing over my bed with a knife and a Bible. I fought her off, but no matter how quick you are to block a knife, you can still get cut. My biggest worry is that I may have hurt her too – or that she hurt herself. It's all kind of a blur."

He traced his finger along the scar, cool and dry and feather-light. That wasn't the only one, there was another, just below my collarbone, above my left breast, one I wasn't going to show anyone. I had the urge to undress in front of him, strip bare until I was nothing but skin and ink. I wanted – no, needed – for him to see me raw, some cosmic leveling of the scores.

There was traffic on the freeway in the distance. I could hear the TV in apartment 1A, turned up too loud on the hell-and-damnation station. Somewhere in the city there were fights being fought, cigarettes being lit, drinks being poured.

Couples might be kissing or fucking or saying absent-minded goodnights, someone was going to sleep for the last time. On the steps of 57 Fenton Boulevard, two lost souls sat silently as the secrets between them became part of the ether.

There's a difference between what you bury deep and what hasn't yet been discovered, a willful withholding of truth verses a story that you just haven't been sparked into telling. There was a lot I didn't know about Martin. There was plenty he didn't know about me. But all of that would come in time. What mattered was that I felt safe with him, a sensation I was wholly unused to. It was hard to feel safe when your parents were taken from you by a winter night, when the one you always tried to protect was the one who betrayed you in the end. But Martin was close enough that I could smell vanilla and a little sweat, laundry detergent and the last remnants of sandalwood aftershave. There was nothing left to hide. There was no point even trying.

After a few minutes of quiet, he picked up the folder at his feet and opened it. "I did some digging after you left," he said. "Talked to Hollander, got the labs and the ME's report. But I'm sure we both know some things they don't – her secret life, this fight she had the day she died. And that means that I can't close this case without what's in your head. So what do you say? Partners?"

Partners. I liked the sound of that. Better than *friend*. A friend could betray you. We both knew that. A partner had your back, saw you as equal. I stood and offered my hand. "C'mon upstairs," I said. "I'll make us some dinner and we'll get back to work."

28

MARTIN

Valerie's apartment was a bachelor studio with a foldout couch and a kitchenette and a coffee table, a small shelf of books and an IKEA crate filled with blankets and pillows. No art on the walls, no TV. I doubted the walls would support one and there wasn't room enough for a cabinet. I wondered if I was paying her enough. Probably not, if she was living in this neighborhood. But she didn't seem to mind, didn't seem embarrassed having me there. Didn't mean she wasn't getting a raise at the end of it. She was earning every penny of it.

I sat on her couch, still waiting for her to change her mind and throw me out, while she made a couple of grilled cheese sandwiches. It wasn't until I smelled the sizzling butter in the pan that I realized I hadn't eaten since lunch. A milkshake was hardly dinner, no matter how delicious it was.

She put a playlist on shuffle and brought us a pair of sandwiches. "Sorry it's not vinyl," she said, sitting down across from me on the couch. "Not enough room in here to store records."

"As long as there's music, I won't complain."

Steely Dan's "Midnite Cruiser." Appropriate. I came too close to losing her and I was not going to let it happen again. I savored the fractured memory of my head against her shoulder, her weight against mine, human contact I hadn't had in what felt like decades. It reminded me of the early days of touring, being crammed in the back of our van, waking up along some empty stretch of highway and catching myself leaning on Ron or Vic or Kurt, a comfortable reminder of camaraderie.

"First things first," she asked. "What was the official cause of death?"

"Drowning," I said, flipping to the ME's report. "Autopsy showed water in her lungs, a little vomit too. At some point, she must have aspirated some of it, but that wasn't what killed her."

"Drugs or alcohol?"

"Both," I said. "Xanax and alcohol."

She took out her phone. "Found Xanax in her apartment," she said, flipping through some photos to show me. "It's in Nora's name, though. Not that it means a damn thing."

My habit had started with prescriptions – Percocet for recurring headaches I got even now – but by the end, not one pill I took was ever in my name. "It means Nora might be able to shed some light on whether or not she knew Janie was raiding her cabinet," I said. "Looks like two Xanax and a couple of drinks. Blood alcohol content was .09 drunk but not plastered. Might make her loopy, but I don't think it would be enough to knock her out or make her sick."

"So she's a lightweight," Valerie countered. "She's partying down on the river's edge, get a little giddy, decides to go swimming. Happens every so often. One time the cops arrested the whole high school wrestling team down there. They were drinking Four Loko and wearing diapers. Some sort of hazing ritual."

Charming. "I'd be surprised if that was the case here," I said. "There's no sand or debris in her lungs, so she wasn't on the beach when she vomited."

She chewed that over with a bite of her sandwich. "So someone brought her there – possibly unconscious – and dumped her."

"Possibly," I finished. "Which makes it, at the very least, criminally negligent homicide. She was alive when she went into the water, but someone left her there in a vulnerable state."

"Her bandmate Gordon said she had some problems with their bass player, Melanie," she said. "Drugging someone in public is just the kind of prank a mean girl might pull."

I took a bite of my sandwich and licked a little grease off my thumb. "Walk me through it," I said. "Pretend this is the aria of a cop show, tell me exactly how she might do it."

She leaned back against the arm of the couch. "Melanie doesn't intend to kill her," she began. "Just embarrass her. Maybe Janie's straight-edge, got that holier-than-thou vibe going on, and Melanie wants to prove she's not so perfect. She gives her a couple Xanax, maybe she tells her it's OTC, maybe she dissolves it in her drink. But Janie has a bad reaction, vomits and passes out. Melanie panics and dumps her at the beach. She might have already thought she was dead, or that someone would find her and call the cops. But instead, Janie wades into the water, falls or passes out again, and drowns."

I was suddenly sick at the thought of her drowning, cold and lonely. I had no memory of my own overdose, only memories cobbled together from other nightmares. The miserable sick, the sweet relief, the Chinese box, the bedroom carpet against my cheek. But what was clearer, what was real, was the moment the police hauled me in and demanded to know where I'd hidden Cecelia's body. Those hours were all still real to me, the hot lights and the shakes and the spittle that hit my cheeks whenever the detective wound out another impossible scenario. I didn't know what happened in those hours between when I went to Ron's and when I came home from the hospital, but I know I didn't kill her. In the end, my overdose was my alibi, so I went home and did it again in hopes of giving myself a permanent alibi. Luckily, I failed, forced myself to get clean so she might have someone safe to come home to. Except she never came home.

Valerie's voice, saying my name, her hand on my knee. I snapped back to myself sharply. "I wrote this down sometime the other night," I sputtered, reaching to the back of the folder for the cocktail napkin I'd scrawled on. "Although I can't for the life of me remember when. But Ron didn't think what happened to Janie was an accident either."

She picked it up and read it. "The pool?"

"Apparently, Janie was terrified of water," I said. "She almost drowned in her parents' pool when she was a kid; Ron and I rescued her but, the way he tells it, she never went near open water again. So if this was a prank gone wrong, it was an especially cruel one."

"What's your theory?" she asked. "Now that I've given you mine."

"I don't have one yet," I admitted. "I'm open to suggestions. File says that a sex worker named James Light reported seeing the body in the water. Cops tried to locate him for an interview, but were unsuccessful. I say we go down to the waterfront and try to locate him."

"Martin, that's a needle in a haystack," she said. "Emphasis on needle. Even if we do find this witness, they won't hold up on the stand when we *do* find her killer."

"We won't need them to," I said. "All we need is a starting point. The rest will fall into place. Or it won't and we've wasted an evening. What have we got to lose but a couple more hours of sleep?"

She sighed. She smiled. "Let me get my coat."

Janie's body had washed ashore in the Music Box district of the city, the river divide between the factories that once made drive-in theater radios and the decaying cinemas and music halls. Every so often some well-meaning not-for-profit tried to restore the old Perrine Theatre, but never finished the project. The buildings that weren't boarded up were repurposed as strip clubs and dive bars, vape shops and all-night bodegas.

By midnight, the waterfront itself was poorly lit and well occupied. Near the end of the month, pigs like Roland and Rue would pad out their quotas by raiding the beaches for sex workers and addicts, steal wigs and needles and maybe cop a few feels, but that was still a few weeks off. For tonight, it was just us and the johns.

I bought a couple packs of cigarettes and an economy-sized box of condoms. We split up; I would talk to the junkies, Valerie would chat with the dates. I doled out smokes like Halloween candy, lit them with an old silver Zippo I found in the glove box. I almost took one myself, just to blend in, but I knew better. If I gave in to one vice, I might give in to another. I settled for savoring the secondhand smoke.

None of them knew where James was. Most of them thanked for me the cigarettes, almost apologetic for my offer, sorry they couldn't help. One of them recognized Joyride from the club scene, talked about how much he loved music and played in a band he'd get back to, one day, when he kicked the habit. My heart hurt. He asked me for twenty bucks and I gave it to him. I've been dope-sick. I wouldn't damn that on anyone.

Valerie came jogging up to me. "Got a line on James," she said. "One of our girls saw him a couple days ago. Said he's in bad shape."

I followed her up the shore to where a woman in a pink wig was sitting on a half-busted park bench. "This is Roxanne," she said. "Roxanne, this is Martin."

She was missing one of her fake nails, but she had a good firm handshake. I could smell the alcoholic sting of her drugstore perfume over the garbage stench of the river. "You said you saw James?"

"JoJo? Sure. Couple days ago," she said. She held out a cigarette and I lit it like a gentleman. "He was a mess. We all like to party, but he was starting to look like the other side of a teen idol."

"Did he give a reason why he went off the rails?"

"More like on the rails," she joked. "Told my friend Sugarcane he saw the drowned girl." She took a long drag and blew a smoke ring. The whole scene had the neon vice of a Ralph Bakshi cartoon. "That would fuck anybody up."

"Any idea where he might be now?" Valerie asked.

Another smoke ring. "Where we all go when we need a vacation," she said. "The Islands."

29

VALERIE

Old postcards in the Perrine Historical Society show the Islands as a thriving resort, with poolside drink service and a glittering ballroom with a crystal chandelier, air conditioning and color TVs. But time and bad management and bankruptcy had turned it into the kind of dump the state sent ex-convicts and homeless people to. At least the owner finally drained the pool; it only took the cops pulling two dead bodies out of there. Now the empty pit was filled with broken furniture and stained mattresses. Anyone who would stay at the Islands was of a particularly desperate breed.

A couple of Martin's twenty-dollar bills to the night manager got us the number of a room for a client matching JoJo's description. There was the sound of a game show coming from 203, but no human voices, even after I knocked twice. "He could be hurt in there," I said. "And normally I'd knock down the door, but…"

Martin got my message loud and clear. He studied the door for a second, then aimed for the weakest point and kicked it open. The chain snapped like an old rubber band and a banshee wail came out of the bathroom.

JoJo was huddled in the bone-dry bathtub, shrieking and shivering. Every muscle in my body twisted up. This was what Katy was like in the last few days I saw her, pacing the floor with her eyes bloodshot and wild, reciting old song lyrics like feverish prayers, talking to and about people who didn't exist. Three days without sleep. That's when she broke. And if JoJo was about to similarly snap, I didn't have my cutting board shield to defend myself. I glanced around the room to see what I could use if he attacked me. A lamp, maybe, or I could bash his brains in on the sink. I had enough scars and I was not going to get one more. Not tonight.

Martin recognized my fear and took the lead. "It's OK," he said, wedging himself past me in the bathroom door. "Roxanne sent us. You know Roxanne, right? Sugarcane's friend, got the pink hair? She's worried about you."

"You're not Roxanne," he said. "You are *not* Roxanne. You're the cops. You're the fucking *cops*!"

Martin turned back to me. "Look at his pupils," he said. "Whatever he's on, he's on a lot of it. Go get the duvet."

He got in the bathtub next to him. "It's OK," he said, putting his hands on James's skinny shoulders. "You're all right. Just... take a breath. Deep breath, you'll be OK."

I always thought of Martin as a little aloof when it came to working the streets. He had the professional connections, the sophisticated mannerisms, but what I never realized was that there was a piece of him that would always be a shivering addict, bombed out someplace cold and alone. Maybe he had been junk-sick in high-rise hotels, but junk-sick was still sick. He was able to understand this kid in a way I could never relate to, speak to him in a language I had no way of learning. I was helpless to do anything but fetch a cum-stained duvet.

He wrapped JoJo up tight enough to calm him down a little. "The girl," JoJo said, clenching up to half his size in the corner of the tub. "The girl in the river. She's following me. I saw her. She's waiting in the parking lot. You led her right to me."

There was no one in the parking lot when we pulled in. Martin thought fast. "You're right," he said. "That's why we came. You're not safe here. We're here to take you someplace safe, someplace she won't find you."

JoJo's eyes were flying around the room like he was watching for shooting stars. "You won't give me to her?" he asked.

"Of course not," said Martin. "We won't leave your side. Not this time. We'll get you to a safehouse, get you something to eat. You must be starving."

JoJo shook his head. Martin squeezed his shoulders just slightly and got to his feet, knocking his head a little on the low curtain rod. "Go get the car," he said, handing me his keys. "I'll stay in here with him."

"Be careful," I said. "You don't know what he's capable of in that state."

"I do know," he said. "Which is why I'm not stupid enough to leave him with you. I'm twice his size, I'll be all right. But hurry. We need to get him out of here."

I didn't feel much safer crossing the parking lot. Someone was retching loudly near the dumpsters. A pimp winked at me as he lit up a joint between tattooed fingers, silently offering me a hit like we were at a college party. I pretended I hadn't seen him. In the distance, I heard sirens. It didn't seem to bother the pimp.

I called Martin when I had the car at the bottom of the stairs and a moment later, he appeared half-dragging, half-carrying JoJo, who was crashing fast, still muttering about the girl in the river. We got him stretched out in the back seat and then he was asleep. "We need to take him somewhere safe," Martin said as I handed him back his keys. "Somewhere he can sober up."

"I know just the place."

Deacon met us at the back door of Arc Tattoo. "Aww, shit, you didn't tell me it was JoJo," he said as he opened the car door.

"You know him?" Martin asked.

"I did his tattoos," he said. "He's got a rose on his left shoulder with six fallen petals. One for each month of sobriety. What happened?"

"He saw Janie in the river," I said. "We found him at the Islands; he was screaming that she was following him around."

"That would send anyone back to the pipe," he admitted. "C'mon. Let's get him inside."

I knew I'd made the right decision to call my brother; he had made it his mission to care for all the street kids who came through his door. He knew all the names of the bums and the slingers and the sex workers in the neighborhood; when Tonya saved up enough for her bottom surgery, Deacon gave her a small tattoo of a pink dove, a blossoming symbol of change, on her left wrist, free of charge. When someone was trying to kick a habit, he would order a pizza and let them hang out in the back until the need passed. He taught me not to judge, to serve the streets with an open and generous heart. But that's what had gotten me in trouble with Katy, thinking I could save her, thinking all she needed was me to take care of her until she came around. Maybe I should have brought her here. Maybe I just didn't love her enough, didn't have as big a heart as Deacon or Gina. Or maybe JoJo would prove them all wrong; trash the place and rip off the register.

Martin carried JoJo inside to the back room. Deacon had prepared it with a pillow and a bottle of water and a trash can for when he got sick. JoJo was shivering so hard it sounded like his bones would rattle apart. His lips were cracked; he smelled like burnt plastic and unwashed skin. I wondered when the last time he'd had a shower, a meal, a clean drink. "Maybe we should get him to a hospital," I said.

"He'll come around," Martin said, all but swaddling him in the waffle-weave cotton blanket Deacon had provided. There was three times as much blanket as there was JoJo. "A good night's sleep won't fix him, but it'll be a start."

"I'll keep an eye on him," Deacon assured me. "It's not the first time he's slept here. Just hope it's the last."

"Call me when he's awake," Martin said.

It was 2am when we left Arc Tattoo. The drive back to my apartment was quiet except for the radio and Martin chewing his lip. Lester Fritz, the overnight DJ, came on as the tune wound to a close. "That was R.E.M.'s, 'So. Central Rain,'" he said in his cool-uncle drawl. "Here's a long-lost tune for you nightflyers, this is 'Sidewinder' by the French Let–"

Martin turned off the radio.

30

MARTIN

Deacon would call Valerie's cell phone if he had word about JoJo, so I took the morning to visit Nora. The first thing that struck me about Nora's apartment was the painting above her velveteen, eggplant-colored couch. It was almost the size of the couch itself, a wide blue swath with short, sharp cuts of orange and red, possibly flowers, maybe a sunset, maybe hellfire depending on your mood.

And it was one of Cecelia's.

"I did manage to see Ron," she said, setting a cup of coffee down on the marble-topped table in front of me. "He's not doing well. I'm very worried about him."

You and me both, I thought. "I'll try to stop over, see if I can't get him to go to a meeting." *Or ask what he was doing Saturday night,* I thought. Valerie and I hadn't named any suspects, but we hadn't ruled anyone out either. Right now, it was just about figuring out where Janie was the night she died, narrowing down a timeline between when she was last seen and when she went into the river. That, and trying not to look at that painting. Any longer and I might go mad.

"I'm glad to hear that," she said. "He needs a friend, and you two were always so close. He was heartbroken when you left."

"It wasn't easy on either of us." I took a sip of my coffee to give myself something else to focus on. It was weak and bitter, likely pissed from a plastic pod. "How are you holding up?" I asked. "I meant to ask you the other day but I was... in a fog."

"We all are," she said. "Teaching keeps me distracted, but it seems like every piece I conduct just sounds like Janie. The music department is hosting a charity concert; I'm in the process of putting together a scholarship fund." She leaned forward and put her hand on my knee and I had to fight not to recoil. "I'd love it if you would play."

"We'll see," I said, tossing off her suggestion like a discarded cigarette. "But that's not why I'm here."

"What is it that brings you by?"

"Ron had an insurance policy on Janie," I said. "It's not uncommon; he bought one for himself and for Sharon too. Sharon's went to Janie after her death, so he forgot that he had one on Janie until the company called after the funeral. Problem is, they won't pay if it's a suicide, so I've been asked, in a professional capacity, to follow up."

Lying was a skill I had honed as an addict. Heroin melted all of my inherent shyness and loaded me up with what I mistook as charm, giving me the confidence and the ability to spin a story to get what I needed – money, drugs, a second, third, ninth chance. But it was a valuable skill to have as a detective, to know when to push that half-concerned smile, when to lower my eyes and lift them on cue so that whoever I was talking to absolutely believed I was on their side.

"I thought the cops declared her death an accident," she said.

"You know how insurance companies are," I said. "They always want their own investigation. I'll try to make it as painless as possible."

"It seems crude to try and squeeze money out of her now," she countered.

"Crude, yes," I said. "And he'd kill me for telling you this, but I think he wants to pay you back for raising his daughter, cover some of her... last expenses."

It worked. She softened. "That isn't necessary," she said. "I loved Janie."

"I know you did," I said. I reached out and put my hand on hers. Her fingers were cold. "And you did a beautiful job raising her. But you know Ron and his pride. I'm doing this as a favor to him, that's all. Just walk me through the weekend, and take as much time as you need. I know it's hard."

She stood. "I could use a drink," I said. "What about you?"

Oh, she was good. She brought me right back to the edge, kicked my knees out from under me, laying an easy, rose-petal path to temptation. I wanted a drink very, very badly. I wanted a drink because I knew how much better it would make me feel, how much easier this conversation would come if I could just lubricate it a little bit. Three days. Three days sober and I was determined to make it four, make it seven, a month and a year and a decade and beyond. "It's a little early," I said. "I'm fine with the coffee."

She got up and went into the kitchen. I pulled out my phone and took a picture of the painting. I had seen it recently, but I couldn't place where. It had been so long since I'd looked at one of her paintings that for a second I thought I might be losing my mind.

Nora came back with a vodka tonic in a heavy glass tumbler, lime wedge and all. She settled back into her chair and I began again. "When was the last time you saw Janie?" I asked.

"Saturday night," she said. "We had a concert in Ithaca."

"How did she seem at the show?"

"Fine," she said. "She played beautifully, but, of course, she always did."

"And afterwards?"

"She was supposed to come back here," Nora said. "I stayed in Ithaca for the weekend."

"Who did you stay with?"

A sip. "A friend."

"I'll need a name, just to verify."

A longer sip. "It's not important."

"The insurance company..."

"To hell with the insurance company!" she snapped. "I don't like where this is going, Martin."

Neither did I. I hadn't gotten one truth out of her since I sat down. I took another swallow of my coffee and stood up. "May I?" I asked.

"Down the hall."

I ducked into the bathroom and opened the medicine cabinet. Sure enough, the Xanax were exactly where Valerie had photographed them. I flushed the toilet for show and ran the water long enough to count how many were in the bottle. Nineteen of a thirty-day supply. If I wanted a drink badly, I wanted one of these worse. I had a terrifying flash that she might not even notice two of them missing. Just enough to calm my nerves about that goddamn painting. That dark part of me would always be desperate, hungry for the taste of oblivion Valerie had saved me from taking.

I put them back in the cabinet. I went back to the living room and sat back down on the couch. I changed direction. "Did Janie ever say why she was avoiding Ron?"

"He wanted money from her," she said. "Sharon didn't leave much in her estate, but Ron and Janie were still listed as the beneficiaries. I guess Ron blew through his portion."

So much for the *he needs us* line. Tongues always turned bitter where money was concerned. "Did you speak with him before Janie died?"

"Briefly," she said. "He called me when he got to town, said we should get dinner, but if he was trying to wring his daughter for what little she had, he was likely attempting the same with me."

I wouldn't put it past him, but that wasn't my concern right now. Especially since it varied from what she had told me before, about him trying to get a job at Raines. "Do you know for sure that Janie came back here?"

She remembered her drink. I felt sick just watching her slurp it down. I tasted the lime on the tip of my tongue. "Her bed didn't look slept in," she said. "I have to assume she didn't make it back here."

Assumptions don't make a case, but they're a starting point. "Did Janie have a history with drugs?" I asked.

"She wouldn't touch them," she said. "We usually have a champagne toast at intermission, but she rarely even finished a glass. It makes sense, of course, given how her parents struggled..."

Quite a sneer for a woman who thought cocktail hour started at 11:30am. "Did she have any friends you didn't approve of?" I asked.

"She was a grown woman, she was allowed to have friends regardless of how I felt about them," she said. "But she was very shy; she really didn't see anyone outside of classes and rehearsal. And she rehearsed a lot, sometimes until one or two in the morning. She was very dedicated to her craft."

I didn't doubt that. It just sounded like Nora didn't recognize what craft she was dedicated to. I took a last sip of my coffee and got to my feet. I straightened my tie and buttoned my jacket. I didn't want to stay there a minute longer than I had to. "I'll let you know about the insurance," I said. Had to keep the lie going, just for a minute more.

"Let me know if there's anything else you need," she said. "And I hope you'll come to the concert. It would mean a lot to Janie. And it would mean a lot to me."

Janie is dead, I thought bitterly. *There is nothing that can mean anything to her now.* I didn't entirely believe that, though. What would mean something now is if I made sure that whoever was responsible for her death – whether it was the blackmailers or a cruel friend or her own family – was brought to whatever justice I could muster. That was the only vow that mattered.

But there was still a question I needed answered. "One more thing," I asked, turning from the door. "Where did you get this painting?"

"I picked it up at an antique shop in Baltimore years ago," she said. "I find it very calming. Janie loved it too."

That was bullshit. Why lie? Did she not think I would recognize my own fiancée's work? "It's beautiful," I said. "Who's the artist?"

"I don't remember," she said.

I left and I tried not to slam the door behind me. In the car I let myself have a couple hard, heaving breaths before I got myself under control. I toyed with the idea of going back upstairs and offering to buy the picture. But I didn't have that kind of cash on hand and it would just wind up in the garage with the rest of Cecelia's art. I didn't know which was worse – being a beautiful lie or being abandoned by the man who was supposed to love you through all of it.

Both felt pretty goddamn terrible to me.

31

VALERIE

A text from Deacon told me that JoJo had woken up long enough for him to get him upstairs into the apartment, where he promptly fell asleep in the guest bedroom without even getting under the covers. Anything we were going to get from our witness would have to wait a little while longer.

I wished Martin had let me go along with him to talk to Nora. I needed to know if what Gordon said was true; that she didn't know about Machine Gun Snatch. If she did know and she disapproved, maybe that was motive. But Martin was playing a game of divide-and-conquer, assessing who knew when and where and what Janie was doing in the hours before her death. It made sense, even if it seemed like neither of us were going in armed with enough bullets to take out a threat.

The *Capital Numbers* Instagram didn't tell me much about Rodney, the founder. All the photos were of the musicians themselves, without even the self-indulgent *I'm with the band* photograph at the end of each series. The seriousness with which he took his work was a real fucking inconvenience.

A photo from two weeks ago showed that he had dropped a stack of 'zines off at Lucca's Records, a record store in the neutral zone between our side of town and the Raines College side of things. I bought all of my favorite CDs there when I was a teenager, and one day, I'd promised myself, I would get a new turntable and get my vinyl there too. I didn't know what was in that envelope still stuffed in the cookbook, but I was pretty sure Katy couldn't fit my records into there.

I sent Martin a text to let him know I was ducking out but that I'd keep my phone close. I offered to get us something to eat. He didn't respond. I resisted the urge to worry, to wonder if he was drinking his lunch in some River Street dive or trolling around kitchens looking for someone with a couple extra Oxycodone conveniently bagged for sale.

After Topsy's and Arc Tattoo, Lucca's Records was my favorite place in Perrine. Peggy, the owner, was a big cheerful blonde who wore brightly patterned swing dresses and loved surf music; she'd seen her father's shop through the decline of vinyl and tapes to the rise of CDs, sold sheet music to Raines College students to keep her afloat when MP3s killed off the chain store in the mall, leaving her primed for the vinyl resurgence. Plus, there was always a shop cat, starting with the original Lucca and now Spike, a black and white polydactyly who lifted his head from where he was asleep in a crate of jazz records when he heard the ring of the jingle bells hung above the door.

Peggy was arranging records in the H section with the Surfrajettes playing overhead. Her dress had flamingos on it. She put the records down and gathered me up in a big hug that smelled like honeysuckle. "Deacon told me you were back in town!" she said. "You stayed away too long, girl."

As a teenager I spent every penny I had here; retreating to the listening booth with a stack from the dollar crate to discover new bands that other people had abandoned, the jazzy Goodbye Girl Friday and the quiet croon of Jason Darling and the curiously-named Trashcan Sinatras. All my CDs were all still boxed up at Aunt Gina's. Might be time to dig them up again; my turntable had been left behind in Memphis, along with all the platters I'd bought at Shangri-La Records. Even if I had managed to grab them all, I wouldn't have had any place to keep them in my tiny apartment.

But today I had a mission more pressing than replacing my lost vinyl. "I have a question only you could answer," I said.

"Shoot," she said.

I picked up an issue of *Capital Numbers* from the stack on the counter. "What can you tell me about the publisher of this?"

"Rodney? Not a whole lot. He brings them by about once a month; he's got a handful of fans who pick them up here. Have you seen his Instagram?"

"I have. He's got a good eye."

"I know he shoots a lot of stuff at your aunt's place," she said. "I recognize the stage from way back when. And I love that he's still doing 'zines. There are some things you just can't replicate online, you know?"

As much as I loved Peggy, I didn't have time to chit-chat about hipster papercraft. "Any chance you have a number for him?" I asked. "Got some friends playing a gig this weekend, thought he could give them a little publicity."

"I just might," she said, turning to her laptop. "He had me order him some GG Allin singles a couple months back; I might still have contact info."

I nuzzled Spike while she looked. "Here it is," she said, writing the number on a slip of paper. "Now I've got a question for you."

"Anything," I said.

"Is it true that your boss was the frontman for the French Letters? I was always a big fan."

I grinned. I gave Spike another nuzzle. "I'd heard that same rumor," I said.

I recognized Rodney as soon as he walked in the door of the office. He had gauges in his ears and a quarter-sized ring through his septum, wearing an awkward black overcoat with fraying cuffs and two mismatched buttons, all weighed down with fading black band patches. He smelled like late nights and cigarettes, and over one shoulder he had an army surplus bag covered with pins, almost obscuring the *BOMB SQUAD* print.

The same guy Joyride was arguing with in the alley behind Topsy's.

I ran through the usual litany – you want coffee, a cup of tea, a bottle of water – but he refused all hospitality. *I* was going to have another cup of coffee. I was still exhausted from last night.

"Tell me about your work," I said.

"I cover all the punk shows in the area," he said. He reached into his bag and pulled out a stack of Xerox-and-staple folds and set them on the corner of my desk before he sat down on the piano bench. "Have been for a few years. What's this about?"

Might as well jump right in. "I saw you fighting with Joyride outside of Topsy's a few days before she died," I said. "You two have problems?"

He slumped forward a little. "Yeah, I fought with Joyride," he said after a minute. "Free press. I'm allowed to be there."

"Legally, Deacon had the right to ask you to leave," I said. "It's a private business. And never mind that it's not good form to harass a woman who doesn't want her photo taken. She has the right to tell you to leave her alone."

Rodney shrugged. "I'm here as a favor," he said. "So maybe get off my dick?"

The night before had worn my patience thin and this guy was on the verge of tearing a hole right through it. "You wouldn't be here if you hadn't seen something," I said. "And if you'd left like you'd been asked to, you'd have nothing to offer. So tell us what happened after Deacon tossed you."

"I went over to the Pitt and took pictures of the metal show," he said. "And her little fit wasn't about what happened that night. It was what happened the week before."

Now I was getting somewhere. He reached into his bag and produced a handful of black-and-white glossies. "These are the photos she got so pissed about," he said. "They were taken at the Pitt a week before she had me tossed out of Topsy's."

I recognized the photos. They were the same set that Dott had on her table when she hired me. "Here's what I don't get," he continued. "Why would her band hire me to take pictures if she didn't want her picture taken?"

That was the real question, wasn't it?

A text message from Deacon confirmed Rodney's account. He even threw in the number of the bouncer at the Pitt, who also confirmed that Rodney was there that night. So much for my big hunch. Now all I had was a question I wasn't sure I was ready to get an answer to. An answer only Dott could provide.

Martin met me at the office just after one, and he did not look happy. "Any luck with Nora?" I asked.

"She told me nothing and everything," he said as he hung up his coat. "The last time she saw Janie was in Ithaca at around 10pm, when she left the Community School of Music and Arts after a performance. Provided she didn't stop for a late-night dinner, that puts Janie back here just after 11pm. We still have no idea where she was between then and when she went into the river. Any word on our witness?"

"Still asleep," I said.

I didn't want to tell him what Rodney told me, not before I had a chance to talk to Dott. I had to believe that she wouldn't ask me to take on her friend's death if it was going to come back that she had a hand in her death, but in this line of work, I could never be sure. Martin once told me about a case involving a judge who asked him to investigate a woman he claimed was his wife, only to find out that she was his partner in a property scheme where a man ended up dead, as though it had never occurred to the judge that he would be implicated.

Before I could say any more, there was a knock on the door. Martin got up to answer it and there was Joan, still in her uniform, with a cream-colored coat and two takeout bags in her hands. "I haven't seen you in a few days, so I thought I'd bring you some lunch," she said. She leaned in a little and smiled at me, then back at Martin. "Good to see you, Valerie."

"You too, Joan."

I couldn't read the look between her and Martin, but whatever it was, I felt like I was peeping in on something intimate. "Thank you," he finally murmured. "My wallet's in my office, let me..."

"On the house," she said.

"Joan, I can't..."

"You can and you will," she chirped, handing him the bags. "No milkshake, though. I didn't have the right to-go cups."

I'd never seen Martin knocked off his feet like Stevie Wonder sang about. It was a welcome change from a week of glowering days, even if it was only going to be for a moment. "I'll just have to come back in," he said.

"That's the idea."

Holy shit. Joan had *game*. I wanted to stand up and applaud, to whistle, to tell him to just go to her and I'd solve our murder case on my own. I liked watching people fall in love.

There was another moment of shy silence between them before a few murmured goodbyes and then she was gone. He watched the door for a moment longer than he might have otherwise before bringing the bags inside. "Something you're not telling me?" I teased.

"There's a *lot* I'm not telling you," he said. "And plenty you're not telling me, but that's for another day. C'mon, let's eat."

He wasn't wrong, but now wasn't the time. We ate in the front office. She'd brought us a veritable feast. A chicken club for him, roast beef for me, chips and pie and little salads. "Nora asked me to play at a benefit for Janie," he said.

"Are you going to?" I asked.

"Not sure yet," he said. "I haven't performed in public in twenty-five years, haven't written anything in longer. I don't even know what I'd play if I *did* say yes, but I'm not sure if I'm comfortable sharing the stage with someone I might suspect, however tangentially, of being involved in the murder of the very person they're fundraising in honor of."

He had a good point. "I've got some time to think it over," he continued. "In the meantime, tell me about Rodney and what he had to say?"

32

MARTIN

So it turns out our blackmail wasn't blackmail. Valerie offered to go over to sort out that whole mess, but I wasn't ready to go home to another long lonely evening. I didn't like how I felt at Nora's, didn't like that temptation was still gnawing on my fresh corpse. There was a meeting at 5:15, but that was another hour from now. Just had to hang on until then.

I'd hired Valerie a year ago, three months after she moved back to Perrine, so that put her exit from Memphis sometime in June. I opened up my laptop and searched newspaper archives, scouring every edition for their police blotter. On June 24, police arrested Katy Morgan, thirty-two, on possession of methamphetamines, resisting arrest, and criminal mischief after a three-hour stand-off situation that only ended when she passed out, the papers alleged, from a combination of the drugs and what they believed were shallow, self-inflicted knife wounds. No one else was at home at the time of her arrest, and she was remanded first to the hospital, then a mental health facility, then to the county jail.

That was a relief. The last thing I wanted was for the US Marshals to come pounding down my door looking for my assistant. It was a fear I'd read on Valerie's face from the moment she showed up in my office with her *High Wire* notepad in hand, a fear I didn't fully understand until just the other night. But it was a fear I knew all too well. Even now I had nightmares that the men with the badges would show up and haul me back to LA, show me photos of Cecelia's bones and tattered clothes and tell the judge I killed her. I'd wake up shaking and cold, and run that same online search on her that I'd run a thousand times since I'd learned how. Dead or alive, she was still missing.

Katy's name appeared just once more, in a feature story about the Shelby County Drug Court. *I'd say drug court saved my life,* she was quoted as saying. *But I still have six months to get through, and every day is a struggle. But they've certainly saved me up to this point, and they'll keep saving me every day I let them.*

I printed both articles and put them in a folder. I imprinted her words on my brain. *Every day I let them.* It was nearing six. I'd made it another day.

My meeting helped, but I was still in a mood when I got home. On the piano, I chewed through a couple of Bill Evans tunes at a pace like a small town with a terrible secret. Every note sounded sour and stale. I switched it up to Steve Nieve's part of "Strict Time." I could practice twelve hours a day for the rest of my life and I was never going to be half the musician he was. I had the tempo, I had the right notes, but there was something missing, some heart, some anger and fragility that I didn't let myself surrender to. *Trust* was a junkie record; pills and coke and nervous breakdowns. Some artists write *Trust* or *Pleased to Meet Me* or *Bad Luck Streak in Dancing School,* some of us write lazy pastiche, the artistic equivalent of stealing spare change from car cup holders. I played a few bars of Billy Joel's "Angry Young Man" to amuse myself. I was not amused.

And still, I sat.

I could have gotten up, made some dinner, watched a movie or read until I couldn't keep my eyes open. But something kept me stuck there. Ten minutes passed. Then another fifteen. *You're a grown man, Martin,* I told myself. *You don't have to wait out an hour on the piano bench like a child.*

And still, I sat.

I finally took a deep breath and stilled my mind. I played a few notes. Then a few more. It was unconscious and pure, a song from a thousand years ago. I was surprised how much of it I remembered. The elaborate, prog-tinged "White Queen," from *Fait Accompli,* was inspired, in part, by the chess games I used to play against my sister Sandy when school was closed for snow. Sandy was a masterful chess player, besting my mother and, all but one time, Cecelia, a fine player in her own right. I preferred to take my blacks and whites in the form of piano keys. If we'd hung on a little longer, we might have been able to do more with that ethereal edge, fit right alongside bands like the Smashing Pumpkins or the Manic Street Preachers, angry and elegant, glamour and distortion.

The music kept coming, pouring out from under my fingers like champagne at a wedding. I played "Sidewinder." I played "Fifty Below." I played "A Caroline Hello," a song we played live but never got around to recording. But when I finished out those, there were still chords I hadn't used. I followed them up and down the keys, letting them fall into place like Tetris pieces. Had I heard this melody in a dream, perhaps, or was it Cecelia's hand at work, my muse returned to her rightful place?

When the notes all found their way home, I summoned them again, and one more time before putting them to bed. It was a wild tune, heavy on the left-hand work, with a light high melody running riverlike over top of it all. I could hear the high-hat in my head, the blossoming guitars and a highway-driving bassline underneath all of it. I felt effervescent. I hadn't composed even a ditty to hum in over a decade. Hell, my sheet music pads remained boxed up in the garage, just as they had in Minneapolis and Brooklyn. I got a piece of paper out of the printer in my office and sketched out just enough to remind me in the morning. At the top I wrote a title.

Joyride.

I couldn't tell if the red around Ron's eyes was from alcohol or crying or lack of sleep or all of it. He looked a little embarrassed to see me, but he still forced a smile. "Come on in," he said, opening his hotel room door a little wider. "You want a drink?"

"Not tonight," I said. "I just wanted to check in and see how you were doing. I left you in pretty rough shape."

"Operative word being *left,*" he said.

"I'm here now, aren't I?"

He opened the door a little wider.

33

VALERIE

Dott was wearing purple lipstick. I'd never seen anyone outside of a Buzzfeed listicle wear purple lipstick, but it looked as natural on her as a slick of clear balm. "What brings you by?" she asked.

I didn't want to be here, not like this. "I wanted to talk with you," I said. "About the case. About Rodney."

She went ashen. I waited for her to tell me to get out, to get fucked, that I was off the case. Instead she invited me in further, gestured for me to sit on the couch and sat next to me. "I was hoping that wouldn't come up," she murmured.

I probably should have been insulted that she distrusted my sleuthing abilities, but I wasn't. I felt bad for her. I knew how necrotic secrets could be. "Why didn't you say anything?" I asked.

"In front of Melanie and Gordon? No way," she said. "Joyride saw the photos on Instagram and she lost her mind. She thought Rodney was stalking her. I tried to explain to her that he was just documenting the scene, but she wouldn't hear it. She confronted him at Topsy's and that was the end of it. He was a dick puppet, sure, but he didn't kill her."

"How do you know?"

"Because I saw him at the Pitt the next night," she said. "He was photographing my other band, The Chirmps, on a triple bill with Strict Nine and the Reach-Arounds. I apologized on Joyride's behalf. Maybe she didn't want her photo taken, but it was good publicity for the rest of us."

So she had an alibi and she verified Rodney's. That made me feel slightly better. My week had been shitty enough without discovering that my new crush was a femme fatale. "The night of her funeral," I said. "You mentioned her father. What makes you suspect him?"

"Nothing concrete," she said. "I just think it's weird that he showed up out of nowhere a week before she died."

Just a sad junkie. "Did she ever talk to you about him?"

"Joyride didn't talk to anyone about anything," she said. "It was like she was born anew every rehearsal. She had no history, no family, no ties to anything except her music. The only person who knew anything about her was Gordon, and he kept that shit locked right down."

I thought about what Aunt Gina had said, that Joyride showed up at the venue in full regalia and washed her spikes down in the sink before she left. "Do you know where she kept her costumes?" I asked.

"No clue," she replied. "I offered to let her keep them here, but I think that might have been too intimate for her. You have to understand, Joyride didn't trust *anybody*. I guess she had a really shitty childhood. Music was the only solid ground she had, and she would do anything to protect that. I just wish she would have let us help her guard it."

She picked up the folder of photos and spread them out on the coffee table. "I wasn't trying to hurt her," she insisted. "I had Rodney take those pictures to remind her that we had something good." She handed one of the five-by-seven glossies to me. "Look how happy she is. Look how happy we *all* are."

Janie was howling into the microphone. Dott was pounding away on the drums, Gordon was hunched over his bass, Melanie was ripping on her guitar. None of them were smiling, but their comfort with each other, their bliss at being on stage together radiated off the page. "I thought she needed a reminder that *we* were her family," she said. "It didn't matter who she used to be or even who she was when she wasn't with us. We loved her, no matter what."

Her fists were balls of frustration in her lap. I wanted to hug her and never let go. For a flash of a moment, I let myself hate Janie for all the razor-blade ripples her death had caused, Martin and Dott and JoJo, Gordon and Melanie and even Ron, bastard that he was. Death did not come in isolation, and it did not leave without destruction. There was a reason anger was one of the stages of grief. I had to let myself feel it, even for just a moment.

"That may be true," I said. "But it sounded like she and Melanie had some issues."

I had to tread carefully here. Gordon had implied Melanie had something to do with Janie's death, but that was a big accusation to make with no evidence to back it up.

"Every band has their drama," she said with a shrug.

That wasn't good enough. Drama was sleeping with the guitar player's boyfriend, drama wasn't drugging a woman and leaving her to drown. Was she covering for Melanie, and why? I wanted to crack her open and shred up all her secrets.

"I'm sorry I'm not more of a help," she said. "I ask you to solve this and then I just drag it all down."

"You might think of something later on," I assured her. "Something that maybe didn't occur to you at first, but seems more significant when you think about it."

She kissed me. Just a little kiss, barely long enough to register, but the way she wrapped her warm hands around my upper arms, it could have gone on much longer and I would have been fine with it. "You're not going to tell Gordon and Melanie about the photos, are you?" she asked.

I felt blackmailed. I felt like I was in love. I felt like if I hadn't seen car lights through the living-room curtains I might have grabbed her and kissed her and never come up for air. I understood why she lied to me. And after that kiss I didn't even care that she had. We all protect something: our friends, our souls, ourselves. I might have done the same in her position. I *had* done the same, for Katy, keeping her secret even though the scars on my forearms screamed pieces of it out loud.

A knock on her door knocked me out of my head. "The rest of The Chirmps are here for practice," she said, letting go of me. "Next time, I'll make you dinner."

I muttered a goodbye I didn't want to give. I walked past the other girls unloading their instruments and muttered a hello. I got into my car and checked the rearview mirror. There was a brush of purple along the corner edge of my mouth. I wiped away the evidence that it had ever been there.

In the car I took out Janie's keys. A car key, two house keys – one for the front door, one for the apartment – and a smaller one that could only fit a padlock. If she did keep her Joyride life hidden, she'd need to do it someplace she could access as needed.

These days, a gym or a high school would be the only place you could have a locker in a public space. Since I doubted Janie wanted to relive her teenage years, that left a handful of gyms. I narrowed my search to ones with late hours that would allow her to change after a show. I found four that fit my parameters, including Fit/24/7, a two-story facility in the heart of downtown, convenient to both college housing and nightlife. No one would think twice about seeing a girl in leather leggings and a tattered jacket down there.

It was after 9pm, late enough when the gym would only be sparsely populated by people who might spot me trying out every lock like a petty thief. I considered texting Martin to tell him what I was doing and then thought better of it. He didn't need to be bothered tonight.

I tried twenty-five lockers before I found the padlock that fit Janie's key. Stashed inside was a fund-drive duffle bag and a couple black dresses hanging from the hooks, three pairs of leggings folded neatly and stacked on the top shelf. I took the bag. The dresses would never fit over my hips; I'd let Dott come and gather them all up when this was all over. Maybe they'd fit Melanie, if she wanted them. I let myself think about Dott's thick thighs for a long couple of seconds before I remembered I was here to gather up a dead girl's evidence. That cooled my ardor quicker than a cold shower.

I waited until I was home to unpack the duffle bag. A half-emptied jar of purple Manic Panic – I opened it just for a hit of that high school smell – the electrical tape she wore as pasties, two composition books filled with lyrics and quick sketches for costumes. The lyrics were all dated, going back a little over a year. She'd been living two separate lives for so long I wondered if she'd known how to live any other way.

The most recent note was dated just two weeks ago, under the title "Razorfuck."

Light me up like Joan of Arc's pyre
you'll hate what you see,
you'll drown your desire

Maybe it sounded better set to music.

My phone buzzed so loudly I almost fell off the couch. *Your phone is ready,* wrote Lyca. *You can pick it up Monday morning.*

34

MARTIN

It didn't look like housekeeping had been by Ron's room in a few days. The trash cans were full of beer cans and bourbon bottles and glassine baggies. I didn't see any needles anywhere; he was either taking pills or snorting his supply.

"What brings you by?" he asked, cracking open a can of Milwaukee's Best. Had we finally gotten that old? Sandy and I used to call it the Official Beer of Dads when our father would bring home a six-pack. Even as teenagers trying to sneak a drink, we wouldn't touch the stuff, as if it might age us instantly.

"I wanted to see how you were holding up," I said. "I'm worried about you."

"You weren't worried the other night," he said. "You and your girlfriend left me with a hefty tab."

There were more important things to do than correct him on calling Valerie my girlfriend. "I am sorry about that," I said. "But she was right to come find me. I was in bad shape."

"We should all be so lucky," he said. "To have someone who gives a shit."

I sighed. I could give him a lecture about recovery, invite him to a meeting, beg him to put down the beer and sober up and get some sleep. I wondered, for a moment, how JoJo was faring. But a man can't be forced to get clean. That much I knew. "How much longer are you in town?" I asked.

"I'm leaving Wednesday," he said. "I'll take Janie's ashes back to LA and bury them next to her mother's. I think she'd want to be there with her."

"I think so too," I said. "She was a really great kid."

"She really was," he said. "I just wish I'd been a better dad."

I couldn't argue with that. I reached into my jacket pocket and pulled out the New Year's Eve photo. "I found this the other day and made a copy. Thought you might like to have it."

He took the photo and another drink. Silent tears rolled down his face. "I had hair back then," he said.

"And I wasn't so goddamn gray," I said.

He was quiet for a moment, tracing his finger around Janie's face. "They're all gone," he murmured. "All the women in this photo. We're the last men left standing."

He wasn't wrong. The women in our lives had all been collateral damage – to our addictions, to our anger, to the brutality of life itself. I let that sit for a minute, didn't correct him on Cecelia. I still had to believe she was out there, even if it meant that I wasn't worth coming back to. "There's a couple of things I wanted to talk with you about," I finally said, tapping the painting in the corner edge of the photo. I knew I had seen it recently. "Do you know what ever happened to the painting Cecelia gave you and Sharon? The one in this photo?"

He looked at me like I'd punched him in the throat. He took another drink to cover for it. "I gave it to Nora," he said softly. "After Cecelia went missing. Sharon couldn't even look at that painting. She used to say it reminded her of a parade, confetti and candy, but she'd wake me up crying, saying the colors were ghosts, said it was blood, said the blues were broken glass. I'd just be thankful she didn't take a knife to it the way she did our wedding photo. I remembered Nora said she always liked it, and so I gave it to her. I wanted Cecelia's memory to stay present. I wasn't ready to let her go either."

Wedding photo. It was a delayed reaction but a reaction nonetheless, like an actor who's missed his cue and has to rush to get on stage. "You were having an affair," I murmured. "With Nora."

He sagged deeper into his chair. "Everything was falling apart," he said. "You were gone, Cecelia was missing, Sharon was a mess. Nora just seemed like she had it all together. We made it about six months before Sharon figured it all out, but by that time, Nora was pregnant. She took a weekend with a doctor in Mexico and then flew back east to be with her family. Sharon and I tried to make it work after that, but we got divorced about a year later."

I wasn't going to hold the affair against him. What happened in his bedroom was none of my business, just so long as I could trace the path of Cecelia's painting. "Surprised Sharon let Janie go live with her," I said.

"Nora can be very persuasive," he said. "And Sharon knew she was in a low place, that Nora could give her more than we could. Or maybe she just wanted to get Janie as far away from me as possible. To punish me. She never told me her reasons."

I hated what I was about to do, but it had to be done. "Did you ever hear about Nora and Janie having problems?"

He narrowed his eyes. "What are you getting at?" he said.

"Just following up on something you said," I replied.

Ron sighed. "I didn't want to say anything," he said. "Didn't want to drive a wedge between Janie and me so quickly – she didn't know about what happened when she was a kid – but when Nora came out to LA to say goodbye to Sharon, she threw herself at me. It was embarrassing. I had to turn her down. I mean, Christ, my ex-wife was dying, I wasn't exactly in the mood to fuck."

"How'd she take that?"

"She was furious," he said. "She left the next day. I suspect the only reason she didn't tell Janie about the affair was because it might make *her* look bad."

"Did Nora and Janie have a good relationship?"

"As far as I could tell," he said. "I mean, she was strict, but I think Janie needed that. Someone to give her the structure we didn't."

"Did she ever say Nora was too strict?"

He looked at me like I had just torn out his soul and was displaying it for him like a new suit. "Her sophomore year at Interlochen," he said slowly. "She called and asked if she could come home. Said it wasn't for her, said she missed us, said that Nora was pushing her too hard. Sharon was really going through a tough time, but I had been clean for two years at that point. I offered to come out for her recital, then take her home for the summer. Even made up a whole bedroom for her with her things from her mom's house. What Sharon didn't sell for coke, anyways."

"So what happened?"

"I flew into Baltimore and Nora met me at the airport," he said. "We all had dinner that night, I went back to the hotel, the next day Nora picked me up for lunch ahead of the recital and that's when I told her I was taking Janie back to LA at the end of the week." He leaned his head forward and pinched between his eyes. "At the restaurant, she insisted on ordering a bottle of champagne to toast to the success of 'our little girl.' I thought I could handle one, just to be polite, but…"

I knew that line all too well. "But it's never just one, is it?"

He shook his head. "I showed up at her recital completely trashed," he admitted. "I don't remember it, of course, but Janie didn't speak to me again until her mother was dying. Nora cried and tried to tell me I was the one who ordered the booze, that she begged me not to, but I know that wasn't the case."

I let myself smirk. "Because you hate champagne," I said. That much I remembered. Other than a couple of sips on New Year's Eve as tradition, he avoided it, going so far as to ban it from our green room. But those couple of sips can easily turn into trouble. I should know.

"Exactly," he replied. "Didn't do me any good, of course. I apologized as much as I could and went home early. Hate to admit it, but I spent the next six months drinking my shame. Got a DUI, plead it down, got back into a program." He snorted and held up his beer as though he was toasting me. "It's not as easy as you make it look."

I wished he hadn't said that. Because every second in that room was agony. My skin ached, my whole body was begging me for a drink or a line of crushed-up Oxy.

"What about drugs?" I asked. "Did Janie ever have problems?"

"I wish I could say for sure," he said. "Nora never mentioned anything, but if she did, I'd probably be the last to hear about it."

I had another photo to show him, but this one was a risk. You never know how a father is going to react to seeing his little girl half-naked. "Did she tell you about her other band?" I asked.

He shook his head. I pulled up the photo that Valerie had found and turned my phone to him. "Machine Gun Snatch," I said. "Guess that's inevitable when your dad plays Black Flag as your lullaby. She called herself Joyride."

He reached out and touched the screen like she might feel his fingertips on her cheek.

"That's my baby girl," he whispered. "Right there. None of this orchestra bullshit. That… that's my Janie."

In an alternate timeline, maybe the two of us would be standing in the back of Topsy's or the Pitt, Cokes in hand, watching Joyride snarl and scream up on the stage. You're not the old guy at the club when you're a proud papa watching your daughter set your shaky legacy right.

"She called me," he said. "The night before she died. Left me a message. I… I can't bring myself to listen to it. Not sober, anyway."

"Now's as good a time as any."

He wiped his eyes. He got up and retrieved his phone. He fumbled to get his voicemail started. He played through a few messages from people I didn't know. One from Nora asking him to call her. And then the final one.

Janie's voice.

"Dad," she said, her voice soft and slightly slurred. "I'm sorry. I made up my mind. I want to come home. Please let me come home, Dad. Please."

Everything I wanted to say caught in my throat. No wonder Ron fell to pieces. "It wasn't your fault," I managed to croak out. "You couldn't have saved her..."

He started sobbing. "My little girl died because I wasn't there," he said. "She finally decided to come home and she thought I rejected her."

What could I tell him? What could I possibly say that wouldn't break his heart further? Was the best-case scenario that it was an accident, not a murder or a suicide? "Janie knew you loved her," I said. "That's why she called you."

He didn't respond. After a minute he wiped his eyes and got up and rummaged around in his coat pocket. He pulled out a baggie with two pills in it and I was on my feet in an instant, grabbing his wrist. "Not while I'm here," I said. "Please."

He shook me off. "Then leave," he said. "I never invited you or your damn photos."

He wasn't wrong. He washed the pills down with a last swig of his beer and flopped onto the bed. In a few minutes he wouldn't even know I was in the room. I wondered if I should get a seltzer from the vending machine and hang around to make sure he didn't OD. But I knew better. Any longer and I might be tempted to join him again, a microcosm of my last days in LA. My sobriety had to come first. I had to make that choice to get up and leave.

"Are you still here?" he snapped.

I thought of something I heard in a meeting once, from a woman who had gotten sober when her boyfriend refused.

How he begged her back time and time again and she kept taking him back, only to find her CDs stolen or his friends shooting up in her living room. How she took care of him until the one day she came home and found him cold on the couch. In that moment learned the lesson we all have to learn when we make the choice to get clean.

Junkies will always break your heart.

35

VALERIE

Melanie was a paralegal at a law office on the Raines side of the city, a stately brick building with a small brass sign that indicated it had been a law firm since it was built in 1884 and would likely be so until the end of the world.

The women of Machine Gun Snatch cleaned up nicely. Melanie met me in the lobby in an unadorned black suit that could have been from H&M or Nordstrom. Normally I was a sucker for a woman in a suit, but she looked too cold, too slick. "Can this wait?" she demanded.

"I'm afraid it can't," I said. "Let's go someplace we can talk."

"Here is fine," she replied.

A lawyer with a briefcase that cost more than my car brushed past us. "No, I don't think it is," I said. "Unless you want everybody here to hear me say your band name out loud."

She gestured me out a side door and into an alley. There was a coffee can that most of the cigarette butts had missed. "What?" she demanded.

I held up Janie's phone in its dark red case. "Dott and Gordon know about this?" I asked.

She seized up tighter than a club girl's bandage dress. "Where did you get that?" she hissed.

"You all put me on the case, remember?" I asked. "But you failed to mention that you and Janie hated each other."

"I didn't hate her," she said. "We had a fight, that's all."

"'Go fuck yourself, you spoiled cunt,'" I read aloud from the text message I'd found. "If that's how you talk to your friends, I'd hate to hear how you talk to your enemies."

She leaned against the brick and exhaled slowly. "She was going to fuck it all up," she said. "I've got a connection with a label in Portland, they wanted to hear our demo, so I sent it. He absolutely lost his shit, loved it, wanted to sign us. But when I told Joyride, she started screaming at me, told me I had no right, that I should have asked her first. If Gordon hadn't shown up right then, she probably would have stormed out of rehearsal. How was I supposed to know she had this whole second life, that we were a big secret to her? I get it, she's got classical shit to fall back on, but this is my band too, and I sure as fuck don't want to work for my dad the rest of my life."

"So where were you the night she died?" I asked.

She didn't answer right away. I got cold between my shoulder blades. "I went over to her apartment around four," she said. "I rang the doorbell, but Nora wouldn't let me in. Said Janie was busy, that she couldn't see anyone."

"Did you see her at all?"

"No," she said. "Not even in the window. The next time I was even in the same room with her was her funeral." She wiped a tear I didn't believe on the cuff of her satin shirt. "Afterwards, I came here. I had some work I had to catch up on. I was going to meet up with Gordon to go see Dott play at the Pitt, but by the time I got out of here, it was midnight and I was just *done*. I went home and crashed."

If she was anyone else, I could threaten to subpoena video footage from the building and key card logins. But I wasn't about to try and bullshit a woman standing outside her dad's law office. I'd have to try a different tactic. Janie's phone had offered nothing else, no nudes or sexts or even a love note, but Melanie had planted a seed that needed to be watered. "You mentioned she might have a secret boyfriend," I said. "Any clue who that might be?"

She shrugged. "Joyride, as you've discovered, excelled at keeping secrets," she said. "But whoever he was, I think he had a girlfriend. I thought I heard her say something like, 'I think she knows.' I don't know who *she* is. They must have broken up, though, because I saw her crying over him a few days before she died. I asked her what was up, and she told me to go fuck myself."

So our good girl had a bad streak. A jealous girlfriend would be as good a killer as any. The question was whose girlfriend she was, and what exactly she knew.

There was music I didn't recognize coming from Martin's office when I got back. I knocked on his half-open office door and he reached over and turned down the volume. "Didn't hear you come in," he said. "Was just listening to some of Janie's performances at Raines. She was quite talented."

"You should have heard her at Topsy's," I said. "Might be a little more your speed."

He snickered. "I was never much for hardcore," he said. "Don't forget, I was a young man in Minnesota in the Eighties. You either loved Hüsker Dü or the Replacements. I was always more into the 'Mats myself."

"You and my Aunt Gina," I said. "You'll have to put *Pleased to Meet Me* on the jukebox next time you come by the bar." I immediately regretted the words that came out of my mouth. If Martin was smart, he'd stay away from any bars for right now. I still had that hard little knot of worry in my stomach that wasn't going to abate until I knew this case was solved and Ron was back on a plane to LA.

He didn't seem offended. "Does she have *All Shook Down*?" he asked.

"Might be out of rotation at the moment, but I could call in a favor."

"Please do," he said with a small smile. "What did you find?"

"I've spoken with all of Janie's bandmates," I said. "They have alibis even if they did turn on each other a bit. But Melanie had the most interesting thing to say – she thinks that Janie had a boyfriend... and that her boyfriend might have had a girlfriend." I didn't want to tell him about Dott, or the locker full of costumes. It almost seemed like a red herring at this point.

"That'll do it," he said. "Any idea who it might be?"

"None," I said. "But I did see that she placed a call to Ron the night she died. Any idea what that was about?"

"She told him she wanted to move back to LA. She didn't exactly sound sober, but we knew that already." He turned his laptop to me.

"I wonder if these two might know," he said. "Proctor Monroe and Laurel Price. The last time Nora saw Janie was at a show in Ithaca, where their chamber ensemble was performing. Maybe they would know a little more about where she went afterwards – and what condition she came home in."

Procter stopped playing his violin when Martin and I came into the auditorium. "Can I help you?" he sneered.

"Heard you at Janie's funeral," Martin said. "You're good."

"I know," he said. "And you are?"

So it was going to be like this. "Friends of the family," he said.

Laurel was so languid and pale when she drifted out from behind the curtain, I was surprised she didn't shrivel and melt when she hit the light. She smirked, slimy and mean. "Her cokehead mom's side or her junkie dad?"

Martin didn't react. "We're following up on Janie's death," he said, flipping open his wallet to show his PI license. "And we'd like to ask you a few questions about the night she died."

"What's there to question?" Proctor asked. "I thought it was an accident."

I handed him one of Martin's cards. "Family wanted us to follow up on a few leads," I said.

Laurel let out a bark that might have passed as a laugh. "I'm sure," she said. "I'm sure her dad is trying to get the insurance claim settled as quickly as he can so he can cash out."

I've learned not to resort to my fists first, but Laurel was testing my patience. How did she know the first thing about Janie? Surely she wasn't friends with this bitch. I turned my focus to Proctor instead. "Did you see Janie the night she died?"

"At the performance, yes," he said.

"How did she seem?" Martin asked. "Was she having trouble playing, was her behavior... off?"

There was a momentary flicker across Proctor's face. "No," he said. "No, she seemed fine. But it's not like we talked. It was better that way."

"What makes you say that?" Martin asked.

"I thought she was a mediocre player who didn't earn her chair," he said. "Everything she had was because Nora pulled strings for her."

So Proctor saw her as his rival. Then why lie about her performance that night? The ME's report showed that she ingested the pills and the alcohol sometime around 8:30pm, probably at intermission. Say she was a junkie, say she got fucked up, exaggerate if you have to, but don't lie. It didn't do anyone in the room a single goddamn favor.

Martin was done. "You're underselling her," he said coldly. "And overselling yourself. I've heard you play. Your technique is perfect, I'll give you that, but you don't have the heart. You don't have the phrasing. If it's not printed on the page, you don't play it. That's what fourth-graders do in band practice."

I was sick of arguing with him. "How did she get home?" I asked.

Proctor and Laurel exchanged a glance. "I have no idea," he said. "She arrived with Nora, I assume she left with her too. Forgive me if you think I'm speaking ill of the dead, but Janie and I were not friends. So unless you have any other questions, I have a recital to prepare for."

"Janie's benefit, correct?" Martin asked.

"Yes," he said. "I'm playing Tchaikovsky's Violin Concerto in D Major. It's the centerpiece of the whole show."

"I saw a video of Janie playing that last spring," Martin said. "You'll have a lot to live up to."

That seemed to cut Proctor more than any other knife we'd thrown at him. He'd underestimated us. Good. I handed Laurel a card. "Call us if you think of anything useful," I said.

"Sorry we couldn't be more help," Procter said.

I couldn't read the tone of his voice. It wasn't quite remorse, hardly a lament, but nowhere near as cold as Laurel's.

"I hate him," Martin said as soon as we were out of the auditorium. "Too bad being a smarmy little creep isn't a crime."

"Laurel's the one who got on my nerves," I muttered. "You believe what they're telling us about the concert?"

Martin didn't say anything. He opened the car door and got inside, and I did the same and we sat in resigned silence for a minute until my phone buzzed. "JoJo's awake," I said. "Maybe he's got something to say."

36

MARTIN

JoJo was ravenously hungry. I'd only done crank a few times – I'd been raised to politely accept what your host offers, and when your host is Evan Dando, that's a couple hits off a pipe – but never enough to keep me up for three straight days with a two-day crash. JoJo kept burning his tongue on the coconut chicken soup we'd brought him from Flower House – Malee's secret cure-all recipe that could fix colds and flu and nourish hangovers especially.

"Guess it'll be a while before I get another rose petal," JoJo lamented, glancing up at Deacon.

"Relapses aren't uncommon," I assured him. "I just had one myself. But it doesn't have to mean a backslide. That's why we're here. To help."

I think he needed to hear that. He wasn't the only one. "You can tell them what you saw," said Deacon. "You can trust them."

JoJo took another swig of Gatorade. "I was with a *friend,*" he began. "I got up when we were finished, and out of the corner of my eye I saw someone in the shallows. I went over to help her; I turned her over but… I knew it was too late. She must have floated there; I know she wasn't there before." Tears filled his eyes. "I called the police. I didn't want to, but you can't just leave a girl in the river. They could tell I wasn't high when they talked to me, so I guess they took my story at face value. But I kept seeing her body when I closed my eyes, so…"

"So you stopped sleeping," I murmured.

When I was in rehab, I sat next to a recovering speed freak named Leon in group therapy. Leon had been a long-haul truck driver who used meth on occasion to help make up driving time. But one night, he witnessed a violent accident where a toddler was thrown through a car windshield. Every time he closed his eyes, he told the group, he saw her little body smash through that windshield, like a movie cowboy being tossed through a sugar-glass saloon window. Like JoJo, he stopped sleeping, staying up for days at a time before using a fistful of sleeping pills to crash, and ended up in rehab with the rest of us after he attacked his landlady with a rake. I found myself wondering whatever happened to Leon. Wherever he was, I hoped he was OK.

Valerie brought us all back to the present. "Did you notice anything about her body?" she asked.

"It was dark, but I saw she had a shaved head," he said, rubbing the top of his own blond hair to demonstrate. "Except for one stripe of hair down the center." He drank a little more Gatorade to give him some time to think. "And she had a black eye. Not, like, a full one, but like someone had punched her sometime that evening."

I didn't remember seeing anything about any facial injuries in the Medical Examiner's report. I'd have to go back and look; head trauma might explain why the alcohol and Xanax hit her as hard as it did. Valerie muttered, "Jesus Christ," under her breath.

He finished the last of the soup with a slurp. He wiped his mouth and turned to Deacon. "I'll be good now," he said. "I promise."

"I'm not mad at you," he said. "I just want you to be safe, that's all. Do you need someplace to stay? Someplace clean?"

For a moment I thought about volunteering to let him stay in my guest room. I could take him to meetings, make sure he was eating and staying sober beyond the regretful day after. It was a passing fancy. I had my hands full enough with a murder investigation and my own recovery; the last stress I needed on my hands was trying to keep JoJo from chasing. And if word got out that I was playing house with a rent boy, my professional reputation would never survive no matter how good my intentions were.

"I've got a friend I can stay with," he said. "She's clean."

"Have her come pick you up," Deacon said. "I want to meet her for myself."

"And leave us your number," Valerie said. "In case we need to get in touch with you."

It would have been easy to miss the head trauma on the ME's report. It was a small note and not attributed to her death. But they didn't know what we knew – a second life, a secret boyfriend, a jealous rival. That blow could have come from one of them as easily as it could have come from anywhere.

I called Hollander and put him on speakerphone. "Got a few more questions about Janie Lovette's death," I said.

Hollander sighed. I heard him shuffle papers. "Go on," he said wearily. "I don't know what you think you've found, but I assure you, we've covered it."

"Pretend it's for an insurance claim," I said. It was the only acceptable lie in this situation; for all I knew, it was true. "ME's report shows a bruise on the left side of her head, right around her eye. What's that all about?"

He paused for a minute like he was trying to catch up. "ME thought that came from a rock that she hit when she was in the water," he said. "He thinks it was less than half an hour before she died. Maybe she fell on the beach."

"Or someone knocked her unconscious," I said.

"There's no fracture," he insisted. "Barely a bump. Martin, I know what you're doing, and I'm telling you…"

I didn't care what he was telling me. I hung up. "We're going to need him to make the arrest if we do find out she was killed," Valerie warned.

She wasn't wrong. "We'll cross that bridge when we come to it," I said. "Hollander isn't so petty as to let a murderer go free just to spite me. And even if he was, District Attorney Jack Lorenz likes me, for whatever reason. He'd be happy to indict. Last I knew, he was getting bored writing pleas for drug dealers. Nothing would make him happier than a murder."

There was a small silence between us. Valerie glanced at her cell phone and got up out of the blue chair. "I've got to get over to Topsy's," she said. "Janie's benefit is tonight and I told Aunt Gina I'd help tend bar."

"Have a good time," I said. And I meant it. I just wished I could go with her. Live music can cure just about any ill; it's difficult to be sad or anxious when you can't hear your own thoughts.

She glanced at me like she didn't trust the words she was about to say. "You… you wouldn't want to come with me?" she asked. "Would you?"

"I would," I said. "But I really shouldn't. It's just…"

She reached over and squeezed my shoulder. "I get it," she said. "I'll send you some pics."

It had been a long time since I had someone around who could read my thoughts. "I'd like that," I said.

She went out to the front room to get her coat. It was now or never. I grabbed the folder from my outbox and followed her. "Before you go," I said, holding it out like an offering. "I did some digging. On Memphis. Hope you don't mind."

She took the folder. I couldn't read her expression. "She's alive," I said. "The details are all in there, but Katy's alive and you're safe. Cops didn't think anyone else was in the house, believed that the wounds were self-inflicted. Don't worry, there aren't any crime scene photos. I just thought…"

"...it would put my mind at ease," she finished. "Thank you."

I watched her leave. I wished more than anything I could have said yes to her offer. There was nothing waiting for me at home except leftovers and an unfinished song and the anxiety of a case that I didn't know yet how to solve. But her world wasn't my world. She knew that as much as I did.

37

VALERIE

The last time I saw Topsy's this packed was when Aunt Gina used some of her old touring connections to get the Dandy Warhols to stop in for a set. The bar was packed to fire code with punks of all stripes, from scenesters in Forever 21 plaid to CBGBs originals in black jackets that no longer hung loose on their teenage shoulders. Rodney came to the bar for a beer. I let him have one free for his trouble. He didn't tip.

I kept hoping Martin might show up, maybe in jeans and a T-shirt that would show off just the smallest hint of the swallow tattoo on his left bicep, the sole permanent piece of his long-lost lifetime. I'd only seen it once, back when I was interviewing him for *High Wire*. Supposedly Cecelia had the same one on her right shoulder; it was how he believed she was still alive, that no body had ever shown up in the LA morgue with that ink. Hell, I would be fine if he brought Ron with him. Just for a chance to say goodbye. To see Janie's legacy played out in front of a hundred screaming fans, to witness firsthand that she was loved, that she was praised, that she found her soul in music the same way they had. But I knew it was better for both of them to stay away from temptation.

"You want to go tell Machine Gun Snatch they're on in ten?" Aunt Gina yelled over the chainsaw rockabilly of Strict Nine.

The green room was behind a door next to the jukebox, painted the same flat black as the walls, blending in so no one accidentally slipped through looking for the bathroom. I would have knocked if I thought they could have heard me over the music.

"This is a fucking coup, Melanie!" Gordon was screaming.

"I can sing just fine!" she snapped. "There's no fucking reason we should dissolve."

"Our frontwoman died!"

"The frontwoman who didn't want us going any further than the same six fucking clubs? This is our *chance*. There's interest in our demos, we'd be assholes not to take this!"

I don't think they noticed I was even there, or if they did, they didn't care. They had bigger problems, clearly. I should have known this would all come to a head at some point. Janie's death had exposed all of their secrets.

"This might be a way to carry on her legacy," Dott said.

"Oh shut up," Gordon sneered. "You're the one who had the fucking photos taken."

"How was I supposed to know she was hiding a whole separate life, Gordon?" Dott demanded. "You could have clued us in!"

"It wasn't any of your fucking business!" he yelled. "What she did outside of this band had nothing to do with us."

I wanted to jump and defend Dott. I could hear applause and screaming back in the bar. This wasn't my fight. "Hey, you guys, uh, think you're going to be ready to go on in ten?"

They all looked at me like a pack of cartoon prairie dogs. "Guess so," Gordon spat. "Our final fucking bow."

You can hide a lot of anger inside music. It becomes part of the show, channeled through chord changes and pounding drums, a monster fed by an unwitting audience. But I could see the fractures between the members of Machine Gun Snatch, the fault lines that radiated out from Janie's empty space on the stage.

At the end of "Canyon," Gordon stepped up to his mic. "We really appreciate you all coming out tonight," he said, choking back tears. "You all meant the world to Joyride, and this means everything to us."

The audience cheered. He continued, "As most of you have guessed, tonight will be our last show," he said. "It's just not right to carry on without her. But we've got merch, and we made some copies of our demo to remember us by. All the proceeds are going to a scholarship at the Perrine High School. Playing music saved our lives as teenagers, and we want to make sure other kids have that chance too."

I wondered if anyone else caught the glare between Gordon and Melanie. Dott swept in and kicked up a hard line on "Bitch Bitch." A handful of kids started slam-dancing. I just wanted it all to be over.

The audience was down to about a dozen college kids when the Reach-Arounds took the stage at midnight. Melanie left immediately after Machine Gun Snatch went off stage; Gordon stuck around long enough to have a beer and man the merch table, told Aunt Gina he'd settle up the door with her tomorrow and left out the back. I didn't see where Dott went, but she wasn't in the audience, wasn't in the green room, didn't seem to be anywhere.

The last drinks were poured around 1am. The last of the late-nights staggered out around an hour later. Some of them were still singing, moshing alone out the door. But there's no silence quite like an empty bar at the end of a long loud night; you can still somehow hear the broom on the floor even though you swear your ears will never stop ringing. I gathered up all the empty plastic cups and tied off the overflowing garbage bags. I just wanted to get out of there. I still had to go to the office in the morning.

"We raised about three thousand from the door and merch,"

Deacon said. "It's a good start. Might have to make this a yearly thing."

"I wouldn't say no," Aunt Gina said. "They only drank beer, but they drank a lot of it. Don't worry, Val, I'll clean the bathrooms."

Good. I'd had enough shit tonight without having to mop up the men's room. It was finally starting to hit me, all those long nights. I don't think I'd gotten a full sleep since this case started. I hadn't even unfolded my sofa bed in two weeks, slept curled up on the cushions because anything else just took too much energy.

I took the garbage to the alley. Dott was waiting with the equipment van. "Have you been out here all night?" I asked.

"No," she said. "Well, I mean, sort of. I've been driving around. I just… didn't want to go home."

She lifted her eyes to meet mine. My breath caught in my throat. It didn't matter that all I had was a couch bed, didn't matter that I was tired and my head hurt and my clothes smelled like cheap beer. Anything she wanted, anything at all, was hers for the taking.

38

MARTIN

I settled in for the evening with my records. No other medium sounds quite like vinyl; it's an almost-living thing in a way that cassettes and CDs and digital can't replicate. It moves and breathes, it gets dirty and sick, it gets injured and broken and limps along without ever fully giving up a ghost.

My phone rang around 8pm. I had to turn down The Housemartins' *London 0 Hull 4* to answer it. I could hear "Fifty Below" playing in the background. "Ron?" I asked. "Everything OK?"

"Why did we ever break up the band?" he asked, his words sagging.

I knew I shouldn't play along, that I should tell him to go to bed and hang up. It wasn't the first drunk dial I'd had from him, might not even be the last. But I was soft tonight. I was patient and I was just as much in need of hearing his voice as he might have been of hearing mine.

"Because we were falling apart," I said. No sense romanticizing any of it. "Not just as a band, but as people. Our fourth album tanked and we hated each other." For a band that began in the cramped basement studio of the campus radio station, two beer-soaked freshmen cracking each other up over novelty records pulled from a half-forgotten vault, the most insulting part of our implosion was how cold it all was, a hungover proclamation that surprised even our manager,

Todd, who'd come to bail me out of the drunk tank after Ron and I nearly bashed in each other's faces outside the Century Lounge. If the cameras hadn't been there, I think Todd would have killed me right there on the steps of the cop house.

"No," he said. "No, it was something else. Something more."

The landscape was changing around us back then; we weren't grunge like Nirvana or Mudhoney or the soundtrack-friendly power pop of Matthew Sweet or the Gin Blossoms, we were just another in an endless series of Replacements clones, too old to be college rock, too fucked-up to send on the road for the handful of fans we still had. We'd had our moment and we'd let it blow by. But he probably didn't want to hear that either. "What else do you think it was?" I asked.

He didn't answer. "We should get back together," he said. "The band. Our fans have money now. They're old, they got kids. I bet they'd buy tickets and T-shirts and all that *shit*."

"*We're* old," I joked. "I'm not sure I'm still up for the touring life."

"Fuck you," he spat. "Keith Richards is still out there, he's a thousand years old. No excuse."

I had to laugh. I *did* miss playing music, more in the last few days than I had in nineteen years. The years had softened most of the bad memories; I occasionally let myself think fondly on the good times we did have, but it had never occurred to me to cash in on the Nineties nostalgia and tour clubs again. "We'd have to call in Vic," I said. "And get a session drummer."

"Fuck Vic," he said. "Never liked him. Just you and me, like the old days. I'll bring some session guys. Young guys. Guys who know where to get the good shit."

I knew then where this was going and it hurt like I'd swallowed a handful of driveway gravel. "I don't think so," I said.

"Why not?"

"It's just not who I am anymore. I've got my agency, I've got Valerie..."

"Your agency." He snorted. "You mean that horseshit divorce factory? Yeah, you'd hate to leave that behind."

"I'm hanging up, Ron."

He was alternately begging and telling me to fuck myself when I turned off the call.

Maybe I should have told him the truth, but what good would that do? Was the possibility that his daughter was murdered supposed to make him feel *better*? Either way, she was dead, the only thing it might have done was remove the blame he cast on me. I was little more than a vessel for his rage and the dreams we both knew had no chance of coming true. The only thing more hollow than the plans of an addict was their promises.

39

VALERIE

I couldn't remember the last time I woke up with someone lying next to me. Dott was still asleep; I didn't want to shower or start the coffee maker or get ready for work, anything that might wake her. I was terrified that when she did wake up, she might be consumed with regret. Maybe I should have resisted, sent her home, convinced myself that she was too vulnerable, that I was a brute for even suggesting she come back here with me. But she was worth unfolding the couch for.

I was getting dressed when she opened her eyes like a sleepy kitten. "Good morning," I said. "I was about to make coffee."

"I could go to Iris's," she said, stretching out one long, slender arm. "Get us bagels and lattes."

"I'd love that," I said. "If I didn't have to go to work."

She sat up. She kissed me. "Raincheck, then," she said. "This time, I'm holding you to it."

I gave Martin only the briefest rundown of the show, how many people showed up, how much money we raised. I mentioned the fight enough to alibi everyone and left out the part about Dott coming to bed with me. Even if your boss is a detective, there are some things he just doesn't need to know. I asked how his night was and he said "Fine," and I didn't quite believe him. Maybe he thought there were some things your assistant didn't need to know either.

The phone rang with a local number. I picked it up. I could hear yelling in the background and more than a few sobs. "It's Nora," came her frantic voice. "Ron is here and I'm scared. Please, Martin, come quickly!"

"Ron!" Martin shouted, pounding so hard I thought he would put his first through the door. "Open this goddamn door, Ron!"

After a long fifteen seconds, Nora opened the door. She had obviously been crying and she fell against him, clutching his lapels like a shield. Behind her, Ron was red-faced with alcohol and exertion, eyes wild, weaving in place back by the bookshelf. "What are you doing here?" he sneered.

"Nora called me," Martin said. "You're out of control."

"I just want the violin back," he said. "It was my daughter's and I want it back."

"I don't have it," Nora shrieked. "I told you that on the phone and you didn't believe me!"

Martin was in no mood for her hysterics. He shook her out of his arms. "Sit," he ordered. "Both of you."

I was surprised when they both obeyed, Nora on the couch, Ron slumped in an armchair. I took up a position by Ron, my hand on his shoulder in case he tried to jump. "You lied to me about Janie at the recital," Martin said. "Why didn't you tell me she was intoxicated?"

"She didn't use drugs–"

"I didn't ask if she used drugs," he said. "I asked if she was intoxicated, and before you tell me no, remember that I have the ME's report and it tells a whole different story."

She sighed. She pulled herself up off the side of the couch like it took all the energy she had. "She had a travel mug backstage," she said. "She drank a little of it before she went on stage, and at intermission, she finished it. We had a champagne toast, as usual, but it hit her very hard. All I can think is that she either took pills or there was alcohol in the mug. She was a wreck, so I left her on the green-room couch. Proctor had to take her solos."

Martin and Ron had that same drained look on their face. "Xanax," Martin said. "Any idea where she got them?"

"I haven't the faintest idea," she said. "I have some in my medicine cabinet, I suppose she could have taken them from there, but she stayed away from drugs. She saw what it did to people."

She shot Ron a glare that should have slit him wide open. But he wasn't paying attention. He had that prospector gleam in his eye. I tightened my grip on his jacket. I couldn't stay silent any longer. "Why didn't you tell us this?" I blurted.

"I didn't want to taint her legacy," she said through tears. "I was trying to protect her. If I had told the police, they would have just seen her as another junkie in a city full of them. That wasn't her."

Taint her legacy. As though Janie was a marble statue, a piece of artwork, a beautiful cloud. Her legacy was more important than her life, the network of loves and hates and passions and experiences that made her fully human, no matter what that looked like on paper. Her legacy was more than a few concerts. Her legacy was her voice and her promise, her rage and her beauty, her friends and those she wronged and those she left behind.

Martin picked up where I couldn't find the words. "So you've got a girl who's passed out, how did she get home?" he asked. "She certainly didn't drive back here."

"I don't know," Nora insisted. "I stayed with a friend."

"Sure you did," he said. "With someone who doesn't exist."

She sighed in a short, hard huff. "His name is Roger," she said through a fringe of fresh tears. "Roger Dillinger. He's married. That's why I didn't tell you. Please don't tell his wife."

"You certainly have a type," Ron sneered.

"Shut up," I said.

The cracks were starting to show. Martin smoothed his tie, one of a handful of nervous tics I had come to recognize. "Mr Dillinger have a phone number?" he asked, trying to recover.

She picked up her phone off a stack of sheet music and scrolled through her contacts. She read off the number and Martin began to dial. "You're going to call him *now*?" she said.

"Why wait?"

Nora went pale. She sank onto the couch. I almost felt sorry for her.

"Hello, Roger, this is Martin Wade, an investigator with the Wade Agency. I'm calling about Nora Archwood. No, she's fine, I just need to confirm she was with you Saturday night." Some murmuring. Martin turned his back. "Well, if you want, I can come by your place tomorrow morning," he continued. "Maybe talk with your wife." There was some shouting I couldn't make out.

"Hang up," Nora said. "Please."

Martin ignored her. She got up and rummaged through her desk and pulled out a folded piece of paper. "My hotel receipt," she told me. "Is this enough?"

I took the paper and crossed the room and handed it to Martin. Roger was still yelling; I could hear a woman's shrieks in the background. Glad Martin was getting another taste of what awaited him on the other side of this case. He hung up and looked over the receipt. He folded it up and put it in his pocket.

"Who gave her the pills, Nora?" he asked again.

"I don't–"

"You have Xanax in your cabinet," he said. "I've seen them. So, either you tell us who gave them to her, or I'll call the cops in here myself. You've lied to me every step of the way. I don't mind it; I've told enough lies in my life. But don't lie to me about this. Not about Janie. She deserves better."

Ron was hanging on the silence like a cliff's edge. She hung her head. "Proctor," she finally said. "Proctor Monroe. I don't know if he gave her the pills, but he was the one who gave her the mug – I recognized it from practice when I saw her drinking from it – he was the one who drove her home. He was the one…" She paused to look up at Ron. "He's the one who has her violin."

I should have known that smarmy little blond was our killer. He had the motive and he had the opportunity; if I checked his cabinets, I'm sure I'd find Xanax in there too. Playing his victim's violin was like something out of a serial killer documentary or an episode of *Law & Order: Obsessed Jerkoff Unit*. "Why didn't you tell us this before?" I asked.

"I didn't think it was possible," she said. "I believed the police when they said it was an accident. But with what you're telling me, that someone might have dumped her, I can't think of anyone it could be *other* than Proctor. God, I feel *sick*."

I think we all did. Ron sagged under my hold and glanced up at Martin. "Get the violin back," he said, gripping Martin's wrist. "I'm begging you. My grandfather made it. It needs to come home with me. With Janie's ashes."

"Come home with you?" Nora said. "Ron, you can't be serious…"

Now wasn't the time to iron out Janie's final resting arrangements. "We'll get the violin," Martin assured him. "But I've got one more question for you, Nora."

"I can't imagine what else you want to know."

"Tell me again where you got that painting," he said.

"I told you, I bought that damn painting."

Ron lifted his head. He looked like someone had reached inside his chest and torn his heart out. But before he could protest, Martin stepped up. "And I don't believe you," he said. "You don't think I wouldn't recognize a piece of Cecelia's artwork? The one that hung in my best friend's living room for half a decade? Ron already told me everything – the pregnancy, the weekend in Mexico – so there's no point in lying about any more of it. Just tell me it's hers, Nora. Just tell me the truth about that."

"Is that what he told you?" she hissed. "That I terminated my pregnancy?" She reached into her pocket for a tissue and dabbed her eyes to better sell the scene that neither of us was touched by. "I *miscarried,* Martin. I lost that baby at fifteen weeks and he used that as an excuse to go back to Sharon. We were going to *be* together."

"Nora..." Ron breathed. "Nora, why didn't you tell me?"

"It wouldn't have changed anything," she said.

"It would have changed everything."

How fucking romantic. But Martin pressed on. "Is that why you took Janie?" he asked. "The child the two of you never had? That you thought might bring you back together?"

"I took Janie because she needed a mother," she said. "I could provide a life for her that her own parents couldn't. I loved her."

Martin looked wrung out. "Just tell me it's her painting, Nora," he croaked. "Just tell me that one truth."

"Of course it's her goddamn painting," she snapped.

I wished I could read the storm of Martin's thoughts. Not only did we have a murderer running loose with only the word of a liar to sell us, we were opening wounds that had been scarred over for two decades, cuts too deep for the sutures we had on hand.

"C'mon," Martin said, gesturing to Ron. "I'll drive you back to the hotel."

Ron let out a long, tired sigh. I let him stand. He was unsteady on his feet, and Martin handled him with something between disgust and concern and maybe the last lingering aches of tenderness. I would have been fine with letting him fall on his face.

"That's it?" Nora bleated, rising to her feet. "You come in here, you practically accuse me of murdering Janie, and then you *walk out of here*? Like it's all nothing?"

"That's it, Nora," he said coldly. "Thanks for your time."

40

MARTIN

Ron was quiet when I drove him back to the hotel. "You really think someone murdered Janie?" he finally asked.

"I think so," I replied.

"Why didn't you tell me?"

Why didn't I tell him, right from the start? Too afraid to make him a promise of justice I couldn't keep, perhaps. Unsure of what he might do with the information, if it would destroy him further to know that she was a victim of just one more person's cruelty after a lifetime of the same.

"I want to go with you," he said. "When you confront him. I want to look this Proctor kid right in the eyes. I want to see the man who killed my baby girl."

"Not a chance," Valerie piped up from the back seat. "If we can make this case, you can see him at arraignment."

He acted as though he hadn't heard her, as though she wasn't even there. "This man took the last thing I had to live for," he said. "You have to at least let me see him."

My throat felt like it was turning to stone. I couldn't get the words out either way, to back up Valerie or to make an exception.

"There's still some work to do before we confront him," I said. "Might not be for another couple days." Maybe that would give him a lifesaver to cling to. "In the meantime, you should see a doctor, try to get into treatment…"

He waved me off. "Not a good time," he said. "Besides, if they toss me in a clinic, I'll be stuck behind those walls thirty days minimum. You better not plan on waiting that long to see this asshole get arrested."

"You won't be there to confront him if you're dead, Ron."

He was silent as I pulled into the parking lot of the hotel. Ron got out of the car. He was weaving, but he could walk. "I'll get clean when I get back to LA," he said, leaning in through the passenger window. "I promise. I've got a good doctor there; he'll take care of me."

LA was full of good doctors. Like the doctor who got me hooked on Percocet, or the plastic surgeon who shot my former drug dealer, Charlie, after he blamed him for his club kid daughter's overdose. I had no doubt Ron could find a good doctor there. But what he needed was the *right* doctor. Those were a lot harder to find.

"I'm sorry," I finally managed to say. "For all of this."

"Yeah," he said. "I'm sorry too."

I watched him walk away. He didn't look back. He stumbled a little on the curb but carried himself inside just fine. A drunk man always acts like he's sober. A broken man always pretends that he's whole.

41

VALERIE

Martin shut himself in his office. I had a missed call from Deacon. No message. This was serious. "JoJo got picked up," he said when I called him back. "Loretta said she went out to get groceries and when she came back, he was gone. Cops found him in the park with rock in his pocket."

"How much is bail?"

"Five thousand," he said. "They added a solicitation charge because they're dicks. This might even be his third strike. He's in real trouble."

Five thousand dollars was more than either of us had access to. But Martin's friend Malee might be able to spring him. I hung up and followed the sounds of Elvis Costello wailing "Let Them Talk" into his office to make my pitch. I was surprised when I found the doorknob loose.

Martin was smoking out the window like a teenager. "Thought I had locked that," he grumbled.

In researching the French Letters, I came across a profile of the band in *Alternative Press* titled "Gutter Ball." The band was photographed at a candlepin lane in Brunswick, Maine; Vic throwing a ball down the lane, Kurt tying on bowling shoes, Ron with his feet on a table, drinking a beer and Martin watching the game with his elbow on the jukebox, cigarette half-forgotten in hand. He was younger then than I was now, gorgeous and lost and lonely. He didn't look much different these days; nicer clothes, sure, but that same sad defiance wasn't something he could just shake off.

"Just got off the phone with my brother," I said. "JoJo got picked up in the park. Third strike on rock with a solicitation topper. Bail is five grand."

"Wonderful," he said as he took a drag. "Just what we need."

"He was never going to be our star witness," I said. "We don't even really need him, now that we have Nora."

"Nora." He snorted. "When this is done, I hope I never see her again."

I couldn't argue that. "What's our next move?" I asked. "To get Proctor?"

He finished up his cigarette. He ground it out on the windowsill and tossed it in the trash can with a flick of his skinny wrist. "I want some evidence," he said. "Nora lied to me the first time I asked her about Janie; I can't trust that she won't move to protect Proctor when the cops close in. I need something to back us up, something we can take to Hollander."

"Like a pill bottle," I said. "Prove he gave her the Xanax."

"A pill bottle, a prescription, something like that," he said. "The travel mug itself would be good; there probably wouldn't be any residue, but Nora might be able to put it in his hands the night Janie died. The question, of course, is how to gather it up legally."

I had an idea of where to look. The legality was debatable, but those gray areas were my specialty. I'd handle this part.

Proctor lived in a small rental house at the end of a cul-de-sac about two miles from Nora and Janie's apartment, with ivy crawling up the walls like a goddamn storybook. I parked my car in the Denny's parking lot two blocks down and walked over under cover of darkness. It didn't look like anyone was home. I crept around back and turned on my phone's flashlight and hoped to hell he recycled. I just needed to find those Xanax bottles, a receipt for car detailing, something I could take to the DA. Anything that could prove that Proctor was involved.

There were junk mail envelopes and catalogues and Pennysaver newspapers. There were a few takeout menus. Nothing incriminating. Nothing of use. Not unless I was willing to really dumpster dive. How much time did I have?

A car came up the street. I flattened myself against the house, hoping whoever was driving past didn't see me and call the cops. I turned my head to look for an alternative exit, a fence to climb, a loose board to dive under like a frightened rabbit.

Headlights filled my vision, blinding me as they came up the driveway. I froze, but they didn't. They just kept coming closer.

And then, there was darkness.

42

MARTIN

I almost didn't take the call. Didn't recognize the number, didn't want to break my stride on mile four of my treadmill run. I had been ignoring my workout for too long, but I needed to do something to make up for my transgression this afternoon. That cigarette tasted far too good for my comfort.

Something was nagging at me to pick up. I slowed the treadmill and swiped my thumb across the phone screen and tried not to sound too out of breath when I answered.

"Mr Wade, this is Andi Curtis, I'm an LPN at Perrine General Hospital," she began. "I'm calling on behalf of Valerie Jacks..."

I didn't even hear the rest of what she had to say. I was starting my car before she even finished the call. It wasn't until I was halfway across town that I realized I had put my hoodie on inside out.

Valerie was stretched out on an emergency-room bed with a bandage wrapped around her head. She got this look like a stone had been lifted off her chest when she saw me. "What happened?" I asked.

Before she could answer, a nurse in Minions scrubs spoke for her. "Police brought her in around 10:30," she said. "Found her wandering downtown. She had a concussion and some bruising on her ribs and back but she came up negative for drugs and alcohol."

"I wasn't drinking," she insisted.

I wouldn't have cared if she was. It didn't matter. I was just relieved she was safe. We could figure out the rest later, the how and the why and what happened. All that mattered was that she was still with me.

"You don't want to keep her overnight for observation?" I asked.

"We need the beds," she said. "She's fine to be discharged and she told us to call you."

Not Gina. Not Deacon. She said to call me. I would have been flattered if I hadn't been so goddamn worried. "Sure," I said. "Sure, Valerie. I'll get you home."

The nurse left to get the discharge papers. I pulled up a chair next to her bed. "Mind filling me in on why you're wandering around Perrine in the middle of the night?"

"I... I don't remember," she said. Her words had that faint sedative slur. "My brother called me. He told me... he told me *something*. Wait... JoJo. The cops picked up JoJo."

Whoever had hit her had done so hard enough to knock a couple hours loose. I got this horrible sinking feeling that she had been out looking for evidence; I had let her go after our likely killer alone and he had attacked her. Maybe I wouldn't let Hollander know I was going after him for murder. Maybe I'd just strangle him with my bare hands.

Her purse was missing, so she didn't have her keys. I took her back to my place; the Ativan made her just woozy enough that she hung onto me the whole way up the stairs onto my porch. For a flicker of a second, I wondered if I should just sweep her up in my arms and carry her like a storybook princess, a new bride.

Once inside, I left her in the living room while I searched around for a few necessities: a dentist's-office toothbrush in a fresh wrapper, a pair of pink-striped pajamas my niece left behind, laundered and forgotten, a clean towel. Might as well make her feel at home. I wasn't the best host the last time she was here.

I made up her bed while she went to the bathroom to change. I tucked in her sheets and fluffed up her pillows, spread out her blanket and got a glass of water. "They used to tell you to not let someone with a head injury fall asleep," I said, when she came back in. "Now they say you need to sleep to help heal. So we'll split the difference and I'll stay awake."

"You don't need to stay," she said.

"Of course I do," I said. "You'd do the same for me. You *did* the same for me."

She gave me a crooked little smile. "You gonna read me a bedtime story?"

"I could," I offered.

She got under the blankets and I resisted the urge to tuck her in. I always secretly liked taking care of Cecelia when she had the flu. I would put on cop show reruns and order Chinese food and sit next to her in bed; she would always ask me to read to her, *Cosmo* quizzes or articles from the *LA Times*. I liked feeling useful. I liked feeling needed. Putting Valerie to bed helped fight back that horrible feeling that I could have lost her. I should have never let her go. This was not her fight, she never signed up for any of this, and yet she had taken a blow likely meant for the back of my skull.

I turned off the lamp. I plugged in my phone and pulled up the jazz station and put it on softly. It was too late for anything raucous, anything with lyrics that might turn over in her brain. I sat with her until I was sure she was asleep.

And then I sat a little longer.

43

VALERIE

My head throbbed from the outside in. I tried to put together the pieces of last night, but they felt like scenes in a movie I had fallen asleep watching, unable to determine what was on the screen and what was in a dream. My throat was raw. My back and my ribs hurt. Where had the headache come in and did it have anything to do with the hospital? I remembered lying on concrete. I remembered neon and garbled voices. Somewhere I remembered the back of a car, leather on my cheek, then Martin's hand on my arm, and then jazz, softly.

There was still music, but it wasn't in here. Maybe I was still dreaming. I threw back the covers and stood and I could still hear it. I was wearing pajamas I didn't recognize. I got changed into the clothes I found folded on the nightstand. I followed the sound up the stairs, gripping the railing so I didn't fall to my death.

There were three doors at the top of the landing. Through the first I could see the corner of a bed that didn't look slept in. Through the second I could see an office. And through the third was the music; Martin's back and a grand piano swooning out the sweetest notes imaginable, plucked out like daisy petals on a summer afternoon. Every chord was unexpected, each note resonating in such a way that I felt quivering inside my blood cells, a sort of crystalline magic.

How could one man create music that was so pure, so sonically radiant? It was better than sex, better than a fine meal or the first flush of wine. It could heal me. I never wanted it to end.

"You don't have to wait out in the hallway," he said without missing a note. "Come on in."

I obliged his invitation. "Hope I didn't wake you," he said as I sat on the edge of his piano bench. "It's usually just me in this house; I don't exactly know how far sound can travel through these walls."

"It's fine," I said. "A perfect wake-up call."

"Glad you got at least one," he said. "You woke up screaming earlier."

Did I? He had no reason to lie to me. Then I remembered the moment in question. I dreamed about Katy. I thought I was back in Memphis. And it wasn't until I smelled sandalwood and heard his voice piercing my darkness that I was able to put together the fragments of at least *where* I was long enough for the adrenaline to die down and the rest of the Ativan to knock me back out. "Hope I didn't hit you," I said.

"You calmed down eventually," he said. "How's your head?"

"Pretty awful," I said. "And it's not just my head. I feel like a heavy bag at the end of practice."

He stopped playing. He turned to face me. "Valerie," he said slowly. "Did you go to Proctor's house?"

I hadn't been hit hard enough to lose the hours before whoever worked me over. "Yes," I confessed. "I thought I could find the evidence we needed."

"Even if you could," he said, "it would be illegally obtained and therefore inadmissible."

I sighed. The last thing I was in the mood for was a lecture. "Doesn't matter," I said. "I didn't find anything."

"Do you remember how you got hurt?"

I had a faint memory of headlights and pavement. "I think they hit me with their car," I said. "Don't remember anything after that."

"The cops found you wandering downtown," he said. "They must have dumped you somewhere."

"I'm sorry," I said. "I didn't mean to compromise our case."

He stopped playing. He didn't look at me. "I don't know what I would do if something happened to you," he murmured.

I got hot with embarrassment. My heart ached inside my busted chest. "It didn't," I said. "I'm OK."

"This time," he said. "But… just… be careful. In this kind of work. Believe me, I've been hit in an alley a few times myself. I shouldn't have let you go out alone like that."

I put my head on his shoulder. "You couldn't have stopped me if you tried."

He snorted and smiled a little. "The good news is that the cops found your purse," he said. "Or rather, some good Samaritan did and turned it in. We can go pick it up if you feel up to it. Only reason I brought you back here was because you didn't have your keys. Did you sleep OK?"

"I guess," I answered. "Except for the nightmares."

He nodded. "I used to have really bad ones," he said, closing the piano. "For the first year after I got sober, I would dream that I was using again. Sometimes Cecelia would be there, and she would overdose right in front of me, and I wouldn't be able to get to her. I'd wake up screaming, cold sweat, the works. A couple times at my sister's I woke up the baby. After the second or third time, Sandy made me get up and rock her back to sleep. I didn't mind. It helped, I think. They started to dissipate after that."

"Know where I can find a baby?" I joked.

He let me have a laugh. "Are you hungry?" he asked. "I already ate, but I could make you breakfast."

I wasn't sure I could handle breakfast just yet. I dodged the question; he seemed to have a lot of them this morning. "What were you playing?"

"A new piece," he said. "Working title is 'Joyride.' First I've written in a while, but who can say when the muse strikes."

"It's gorgeous," I said.

He closed the piano and I was a little mad at him for doing so. "You might be the only person to ever hear it," he said. "C'mon, let's go get your purse and I'll take you home. You need to rest up. If you want to take Monday off, that's perfectly fine."

Like hell it was. I was going to get over this and be ready to get back onto Janie's case. I was looking for something. But what? I had to remember. Janie was still counting on us, even if she couldn't count on anyone else.

We got my purse and my phone. My car had been located, parked in a Denny's parking lot, no clue how it got there. Martin made a call to his lawyer, Vinny, but not to Malee. "Much as I hate to say it, jail might be the safest place for him right now," he said. "Vinny will get him into drug court, but if we bail him out, he'll just take off again."

I didn't like it, but he wasn't wrong. The last thing we needed was for him to OD on some couch somewhere and find out through the grapevine that he was laying cold and unclaimed in the morgue. His testimony was likely useless, but that didn't mean he was disposable. I just hoped he understood that when Vinny explained it to him across the steel slab in the visiting room. No one likes to be abandoned.

Back at my apartment, Martin insisted I call my brother to have him come keep an eye on me. But when the doorbell rang, it wasn't Deacon, or even Gina.

It was Dott.

44

MARTIN

Dott was short and curvy and pretty, carrying a bag from Iris's Coffee Shop and a set of three coffee cups in a cardboard holder. "Deacon couldn't get away from the shop," she said, "so he asked me to come by and keep you company. Besides, I still owed you coffee."

Valerie couldn't have turned redder if she got a sunburn. Before she could say anything, Dott put down the coffee and held out her hand. "You must be Martin," she chirped. "I want to thank you for taking Joy– Janie's case. Is there anything new?"

"Working on a couple leads," I said. I needed to find a time to go over and interrogate Proctor, but it felt wrong to do so without Valerie.

"You don't think whoever hurt her hurt you too?" she asked, sitting on the couch next to Valerie.

Valerie shrugged. "Whoever it was, they knocked their identity out of me," she said, rubbing the back of her head.

Dott touched her bandages tenderly. I got the sense that there was something about her that Valerie had neglected to tell me. I should have warned her never to get involved with someone whose case you're on, but I guess it didn't matter now. She seemed like a nice girl. No sense creating trouble where there wasn't any.

But that meant that it was probably also my cue to leave.

"Call if you need anything," I said, a little clumsily. "I can bring you some dinner later, or..."

Valerie looked at me like I was the only person in the room. "You've done more than enough," she said. "I'll see you at the office tomorrow."

"I told you not to come in..."

"You know better than to tell me what to do," she said.

She had me there. "I guess you're right," I conceded. "But I want you to be careful about driving. You've had a head injury. I'll come and get you if you insist on coming in, but please consider taking a day off. You've put in a lot of hours."

"It's an important case."

I sighed. There would be no arguing with her. We said a few limp goodbyes and Dott gave me a coffee for the road. I drove home feeling terribly alone. In the back bedroom I stripped off the sheets and picked up the pajamas from where Valerie had folded them clumsily on the chair. I threw it all in the wash before the faint scent of her made me cry.

A man doesn't realize how lonely he is until he almost loses the one person he really cares about. For the last two weeks the two of us had been attached at the hip. She'd seen me at my worst. I'd nursed her back to health when some monster threatened to take her from me. Now being without her, even for just a few hours, felt like someone had torn out a piece of my soul.

I distracted myself by playing through "Joyride" a couple more times and made some minor adjustments at the bridge. I'd have to write some lyrics at some point. When it was all finished, when Ron was clean again, I'd play it for him like a reward for good behavior. Sure his plan of getting back on the road again was the chatter of bourbon and pills, but ever since he'd said it, the idea had hummed in the back of my head like gnats at a picnic. A couple club gigs wouldn't kill us, they might even be fun. Hell, we had plenty of songs from our aborted fourth album; put together a *Sidewinder* reissue with those demos and some rarities and maybe a couple of live tracks. Valerie could finally publish her profile – I wouldn't trust it to anyone else – and I could let the album sales pad out my bank account with a few extra bucks. And maybe Cecelia might see our name again wherever she was hiding out, know that I was still alive. If I could write a song for Janie, I could write a song for her, like a lighthouse, a beacon in the night.

45

VALERIE

The Ativan was beginning to wear off, allowing me to feel human emotions again. Too bad all I felt was anxiety and shame for the mess I was. I was unshowered, in yesterday's outfit and with a bandage still wrapped around my head. But Dott didn't even seem to notice. "Iris makes *amazing* soup, plus there's some bagels in there for later," she said. "Or now. Whenever you want a bagel, there they are."

"You didn't have to come over," I said.

"Sure I did," she said. She went over to the kitchenette and began to unpack the bag. "I told you I would get us breakfast and I am a woman of my word. How are you feeling?"

I was starving. I felt like I had been asleep for days. I had the worst craving for junk food, tacos and potato chips and Cadbury bars. I wanted to eat everything I could get my hands on. But, for now, the soup she was heating on the stovetop smelled pretty damn good. "Better now that you're here," I admitted.

She laughed. "That was corny as hell," she replied. "I'm kinda into it."

She brought the food over and sat next to me on the couch. I put my head on her shoulder. "I'm glad you're here," I said.

"I'm glad I am too," she replied.

I sat back up. "So what now?" I asked.

She took her coffee cup and shrugged with a distant little look in her eyes. "Not sure," she said. "Gordon and I talked the next morning, said our apologies, but the band isn't getting back together. We left the door open, but I don't think he's going to be ready to play without Joyride for a long time. They were soulmates, you know?"

I read once that Courtney Love got her band name from something her mother told her – *you cannot live your life with a hole running through you*. But that hole in your soul is so real, it's something you're born with and you spend your whole life trying to fill it back up, with love, with sex, with drugs or video games, stray cats or reality television or imaginary relationships with Instagram influencers. If you're lucky, you never get a second hole torn open, the way I did when my parents died, and if you're really lucky, you meet someone who has the tools to fix that hole. And then you realize you've got the tools to fix that same empty ache they've been lugging around their whole lives. *Soulmates* was too cheap a term, language for wedding vows that would end in divorce five years down the line. But just because every Facebook housewife had watered it down didn't mean it wasn't a foundational truth of human existence.

"Where does that leave you?" I said.

"The Chirmps are going on tour in a couple weeks," she said. "They're not as good as Machine Gun Snatch, but we have fun together. As long as I get to play music, that's all that matters. I have no illusions that it's going to be a career. I think that's where Melanie and I could never quite see eye to eye. I'm open to it, but I'm not going to push it. There will always be a band that needs a drummer, and I'm happy to fill in."

I hated the idea of her going on tour, leaving me before anything could really get started. She might never come back, she might think better of what we had, she might realize she didn't need me after all, once the case was solved and we had nothing else in common. But we had this moment, and we might as well make the best of it.

She brought me the soup. She unwrapped a bagel for herself. She turned on the TV and sat down next to me. We didn't kiss but we were close enough that our bodies were touching. We ate and watched TV like this was a weekend morning and not the Wednesday comedown from a brutal attack. I liked having her there, a friend, maybe a girlfriend one day. We were still in the nebulous aftermath of that first night spent together, but I had to love a girl who brought me soup when I was sick.

When the bagels were crumbs and the coffee was just a few stray droplets, I excused myself to go shower and change while she insisted on tidying up. I winced as I rinsed my hair. I had been so woozy on love and sedatives that I almost forgot I had a head injury until my fingers brushed across my scalp.

Once the shower was done, I got the photo album and Janie's cell phone off my dresser. I'd send myself the screenshots of Melanie's texts for Janie's file. The DA would want everything when they indicted Proctor; they'd probably seize the phone as evidence and comb over it to find what I already had, but the photo album, at the very least, should go back to Dott.

"I'm not even going to ask how you got Joyride's phone," she said.

"I couldn't tell you if I wanted to," I joked. "Top secret, you know. Very hush-hush."

Five messages down from Melanie's chain was one marked only PM. It was the same message every time: *Practice? Practice? Practice?* There had to be a dozen of them, varying in frequency. Some were two weeks apart, others were only a day or so. PM was surely Proctor Monroe, but he had never mentioned anything about the two of them practicing together. The lyrics to "Razorfuck" pounded themselves out in my head. *Love like a bloody knife, desire so wrong that tastes so right.*

"Dott," I said slowly. "Can you do me a favor?"

"Sure," she said.

"Can you drive me over to Lido Avenue?"

46

MARTIN

I shouldn't have been surprised to see Valerie at my front door. "I thought I told you to stay home," I said as I opened it.

"Too important," she replied, pushing herself inside. "You didn't go talk to Proctor without me, did you?"

"I wouldn't dream of it."

She took a phone that I knew wasn't hers out of her bag. I wasn't in the mood to chastise her, it was too late now anyway. "Look at this," she said, passing me the phone. "All Janie's texts from Proctor were about practice. There are a dozen of them, dating back about three months."

"It makes sense," I said. "Trust me, you can put aside a lot of animosity for music. The Eagles, the Replacements, the Beatles, Fleetwood Mac, we all hated each other by the end of it, but we still got in the studio."

She smirked. "How much practice do you think they're doing at 10:30 at night?"

Proctor was, as usual, holed up in one of the Raines College rehearsal spaces, playing through a Beethoven piece I couldn't quite place. I didn't bother knocking. He nearly dropped his violin when he heard me.

"I have a performance in three hours," he spat. "Can this wait?"

"Sure it can," I said. "I'll just have the cops come back while you're on stage, take you out in handcuffs in front of the entire audience, if you'd prefer. It'd be a hell of a show."

"What are you talking about?"

"Janie's death," Valerie said. "Nora told us everything. Well, almost everything. The text messages took a little decoding, but we figured it all out in the end."

"It's a story that has everything," I said. "Sex, drugs, murder, jealousy, with a preppy veneer over the top of it. A little too pulp for my tastes, but the papers will devour it."

"Nora?" he stammered. "Nora told you I drugged her?"

I nodded. He sank into a chair like a punch-drunk boxer. I could feel my blood beginning to pound in my face as my *case solved* self-satisfaction melted into rage. I was sitting in the same room as Janie's killer, face-to-face with the boy who set her adrift in dirty water. Valerie straddled a chair like a youth minister, but I remained standing. I wanted to loom over him; a specter, a childhood nightmare.

"You were jealous of her," I began. "You thought she had everything – Nora's favor, an antique violin, the solos and the praise. And to make matters worse, she put a stop to all your little 'practice' sessions a week before she was killed. So not only was she playing circles around you, she wasn't fucking you. So you plot, and you scheme, and you decide to humiliate her. You drug her tea. She can't perform, so you get to shine. You even get to look like the gentleman when you offer to drive her home. She vomits, she starts to choke. Maybe you thought she was already dead when you dumped her. But she wasn't. She drowned, Proctor, cold and lonely under the waves of the Leslie, floating half a mile before a meth-addled hustler found her in the shallows. He, at least, had the courage to call the police, even if it wound up with him in lockup after they caught him with a pocketful of crank. Then you came back here as though nothing happened. You even had the *nerve* to play her funeral. Like one final 'fuck you.'"

"Stop saying I killed her!" he shouted. "I loved her!"

Neither of us expected *that*. "It didn't start that way," he admitted. "Yes, I was jealous of her. Hated her, even. She hated me too, but one night, that just boiled over into…"

"Murder?" I said.

"Desire," he said. "It was just the two of us in the green room, the leftover champagne and… sparks."

"I think the kids call that a hate-fuck," Valerie said sarcastically.

"If you insist on being vulgar about it."

I was going to have to insist. "Nothing more vulgar than murder," I said.

"Please quit saying that," he said through tears. "Christ, you have no idea what these past few weeks have been like for me. I feel like I'm completely rattling apart."

Martin took pity on him. He handed him a handkerchief. "Tell us what happened."

"Yeah, she broke up with me," he said. "Said she'd made the decision to move back to LA, try to get her other band going. Said she was giving up the violin. I told her not to, that she was too talented. And… and she told me she thought I'd be happy to have my rival gone." He laughed grimly. "But that wasn't it at all. I was devastated."

"So why did you drug her?" I asked. "Revenge for blowing you off?"

"I wasn't the one who gave her the tea."

"Who was it, then?"

He worked the words around his mouth like marbles. "Laurel," he finally said. "Laurel drugged her."

"Why?" Valerie asked.

"Because she found out about us," he said through tears. "She was furious. I thought she was going to confront Janie at the concert, but she was very sweet to her. Too sweet. I saw her give her the mug, tell her it was tea. When Janie passed out, I asked her what was in it and she told me – two of her Xanax dissolved in vodka, spiked into the tea."

That would explain the two drinks in her system. Enough honey in a cup of over-brewed tea and she wouldn't even taste the bitterness of the pills, wash it all down with a champagne toast. She drank her poison willingly, even thanked her killer for it. And it might even explain why he was such an ass when we interrogated him the first time. He was covering, for himself and his girlfriend, the way all cowards do.

"I was furious with her," he continued. "But she told me if I told anyone, she would report us both to Nora, tell her that all those practice sessions were anything but. I knew Nora would punish Janie more than she would me. After the concert, I offered to take her home. And I took her *home*, tucked her into bed and everything. I even left her a bottle of water."

"Where did Laurel go afterwards?"

"She came home with me," he said. "And stayed all night."

"So why did you hit my partner with your car?" Call it an educated guess, a shot in the dark.

"That was also Laurel," he said. "She was coming home from her practice and she saw someone in the driveway. She recognized you, Valerie, and she hit you. Then she came crying to me, and I… I dropped you off in the park. I thought someone would find you and help you."

"Such a gentleman," Valerie sneered.

"I'm sorry," he said. "For all of it. I'd take it all back if I could."

His tears were plenty, but I wasn't ready to buy his whole story just yet. "Why would Nora tell us you were responsible for her death?"

"I don't know," he said. "I'm sure to her, it was the only thing that made sense."

Except it didn't. If she thought Proctor had killed Janie, why ask him to play at the funeral? Why let him have the Carlock violin, a family heirloom? I wasn't ready to ease him out of the chair just yet.

"Call Laurel down here," I said. "We've got some questions for her too."

The wait for Laurel felt like hours. Before she could even open her mouth to protest, Proctor silenced her. "They know, Laurel," he said. "All of it."

Gone was the antique-doll fragility, replaced instead with a face like cold cement. "I guess I should call a lawyer," she said.

"Plenty of time for that when the cops come in," I said. "Right now, I want you to walk me through the whole night."

She sighed. She sat down in a chair with her ankles crossed. The statement she gave was a lot like Proctor's, but less emotional. She gave Janie the tea. Janie vomited in the car; Proctor stopped briefly to clean her up without realizing that she had inhaled some of it. She helped carry Janie upstairs and put her to bed just before midnight. "I only wanted to humiliate her," she said at the end. "She shouldn't have fucked my boyfriend."

"So why not humiliate him?" Valerie asked. "He's the one who cheated on you, not her."

She didn't have an answer for that. She looked at Proctor, but he wouldn't look at her. "I should have never let you talk me into any of this," he said. "I should have told Nora what you did from the start."

"I could say the same," she replied.

They could fight it out later. "What about Valerie?" I asked. "Any reason you decided to try and run her down?"

She shrugged. "Call it self-defense," she said. "I saw someone rummaging through my garbage cans. How was I supposed to know they weren't breaking in?

Theoretically, she wasn't wrong. Hell, the cops might not even charge her – but they might charge Valerie for trespassing. I felt sick inside. I've been in this business long enough to know that justice doesn't always come with the bang of a gavel. Sometimes it didn't come at all.

"Go home," I told them. "Both of you."

"But the concert…"

"To hell with the concert," I spat. "The cops can either question you at home or they can pull you out of the show in front of everyone. Your choice, but you will have to face them. I'll make sure of that."

The truth is that I didn't know when the cops would get around to interviewing them. I didn't have my killer like I thought I would; I had a cruel prank and a stack of lies that came tumbling down like a Jenga tower, but it's hard to prosecute a half-finished puzzle. Maybe she did just walk into the river, drugged up and woozy. Maybe the cops could get more out of them than I could or maybe a lawyer might shut them both up. I had gone as far as I could today and it wasn't far enough.

Laurel didn't say anything. Proctor got up and put the violin in a case lined with green velvet. The *click* of the locks was louder than anything in the room. He handed it to me. "Janie's violin," he said. "For what it's worth… I'm sorry. I really am."

I had only ever heard tales of the Carlock violin, built by Janie's great-grandfather when he arrived in New York City, the very same one he played in restaurants to help feed his family. Her grandfather played in the Omaha Symphony and Ron was supposed to play it next, but instead chose the guitar, a destiny left unfulfilled. Now I was holding a legacy in my hands. I've never felt more unworthy of anything in my entire life.

We were halfway across the parking lot when my phone rang with Ron's number. I picked it up, but before I could say a word about the violin, I heard heavy breathing. "Ron?" I asked. "Ron, are you all right?"

"She took her," he said. "My little girl. Took her from me." His voice was gummy, his words soft and slow. "Bitch took her," he kept repeating. "Took my baby girl."

"You left Sharon, remember?" I said.

"Not Sharon. Not Sharon. Sharon's my wife. I love her."

Valerie kept a good pace beside me. "Ron, I'm coming over there," I said. I threw her the keys and got in the passenger-side door of my car. "We'll talk. Ron. Ron? Stay on the phone with me. Ron? Ron!"

47

VALERIE

Martin's keycard still worked for Ron's room. Good thing too, because we found Ron slumped against the bed with his eyes sagging shut. Martin was on his knees next to him in a heartbeat. "Ron, wake up," he said, shaking him. "C'mon, Ron, don't do this. Not right now, damn it. Wake up!"

I took a quick survey of the room. The whole place smelled like piss and vomit and dirty sheets. There were a few fingers left in the bourbon bottle on the nightstand, but only dust in the pill bottle next to it.

Ron's eyes fluttered open and Martin let out a Category Five sigh of relief. "Thought you were a goner," he said. "C'mon, let's get you to a hospital. You're a mess. We gotta get you back into detox before you kill yourself."

Ron gave him a sloppy smile. "She killed my baby girl," he said again. "Said I couldn't have her. Walked right in, took her away, left her in the river to drown."

We couldn't have been more stunned if Ron had spontaneously confessed to the murder of Hae Min Lee. "Who killed her?" he demanded. "Who killed Janie?"

Ron didn't answer. He dropped hard from Martin's arms, falling against the bed like a jacket at the end of a long night. Vomit dribbled from his mouth down the front of his shirt. It wasn't the first stain.

"He's overdosing," Martin said. "Call 911, go downstairs, see if they have a Narcan kit. Meet the ambulance and bring them back up here."

He laid him out on the floor, wiped his mouth and pinched his nose and started rescue breathing. "Ron, please," he pleaded between breaths. "Please, hold on. We're getting the band back together, remember? We're going back on tour – hell, we'll record a new album, I just need you to come through this. Please, Ron, c'mon, don't do this to me, Jesus Christ, Ron, please!"

I got on the phone and left the room. I could still hear Martin begging for his friend's life, each plea getting more desperate as I got further down the hall. No one at the front desk had what I needed. The paramedics arrived and I gave them the room number, but I waited in the lobby, pawing over his last words. *She killed her.* There was only one woman he would let into his room, but it was hard to tell if his words were a final outcry or the incoherent ramblings of a man in a dark state.

Half a clock later, Martin came downstairs, weaving like a drunk from the shock of it all. One look at him told me everything, but he shook his head just to drive the message home. I took his elbow and eased him into a low chair. "Martin, I'm so sorry," I said, crouching in front of him so I could hold his hands in mine. Felt like I said that a lot these days.

"Pills and alcohol," he said, looking right through me. "Too much of both. He didn't stand a chance."

I only left him for a moment, got him a glass of lemon-cucumber water from the lobby to wash the taste of Ron's mouth of out his. He'd barely taken a sip when Roland and Rue came into the lounge. That brought him back to life, a surge of adrenaline in his veins. He stood up and faced them down. "Don't come in here looking so smug," he snarled. "A man is dead up there."

"Do all your clients end up on the slab?" asked Rue. "This is, what, the second in three weeks? You know, they never caught the Zodiac Killer. Starting to think I might have."

"You're getting a bad reputation," said Roland. "Might be time to find a new line of work."

"We don't have to talk to you," I said. "And we sure as hell don't have to stand here and take your bullshit."

Roland pointed at me. "See he brought his little girlfriend along to protect him," he sneered. "You always let women do your dirty work?"

Martin started to walk past them, but Rue shoved him back. "What *were* you doing here?" he asked.

"A man's got a right to visit his friend," he said.

"He *was* your friend," said Roland. "But he's *our* corpse."

Terry, the medical examiner, came over with his black bag and a bored look. "Evidence at the scene looks like an accidental overdose," he said. "There's drug paraphernalia at the scene, evidence of alcohol use. I'll will run a tox screen, but there's no note, no sign of any external trauma."

Roland looked at Martin with a sneer. "Just another junkie," he said. "Just another goddamn bum."

Martin lunged at him, but I grabbed his jacket and held him back with everything I had. "It's not worth it!" I said, yanking him around to face me. I put my hand to his face; his cheek was burning hot. "It's not worth it."

Martin pulled out of my grip and straightened his tie. He ignored Roland and Rue laughing. "Come on, Valerie," he spat. "Let's go back to the office."

We went out to the car without another word. But he didn't start the engine right away. He took a deep breath and leaned his head against the steering wheel. I rubbed between his shoulder blades. "I'm sorry," I repeated. "You did everything you could."

He took a long slow breath and sat back. He was shaking. He reached into his pocket and pulled out an orange bottle.

This was not the Martin I knew, the Martin who, just a few hours ago, had lectured me about the same thing. "You can't remove evidence from the scene of a crime..." I chided him.

"And it's not like they're not going to know he overdosed. The ME already called it. You're setting yourself up for Roland and Rue to kick down your door."

He dropped the pill bottle in my lap. "Xanax," he said. "Four milligrams. Look who the prescription is made out to."

I turned over the bottle.

Nora Archwood, the label read.

48

MARTIN

The Raines auditorium was packed. The girl at the card table out front told me the show was sold out and I wasn't in the mood to hear *no* right now. Valerie pulled me down a hallway before I could make a scene. "Keep it together," she hissed. "We're so close; you can't fall apart on me now."

I knew she was right. I sucked in a breath through my teeth. We followed the music down the hallway to the green rooms. I heard Nora's voice: "Has anyone seen Proctor and Laurel? The show starts in ten minutes." I reached for the door handle. It gave under a flick of my wrist.

Nora came out of the theater's wings and looked at us like rotten meat. "What are *you* doing here?" she spat.

"Ron's dead," I said without fanfare. "Drug overdose in his hotel room. Looks like he kicked back a bottle of Xanax with most of a bottle of bourbon."

It took a moment to sink in, but then she pitched forward into my arms, wailing. If I was less of a gentleman, I might have shoved her back; it was all I could do not to just let the whole scene crumple to the floor. But instead I held her, letting her weep against my chest. A few of the performers leaned out of doors, trying to see what was wrong. I didn't want anyone rushing to her aid, didn't want her to have a single note of sympathy. I all but dragged her into the empty rehearsal room and set her down in a chair like a shabby doll. "I was there when he died," I said. "I gave him CPR until the paramedics showed up. At least he wasn't alone."

"That's of little comfort," she moaned, gripping my arms. "First Janie and now Ron. Do they think it was a suicide?"

"The cops are ruling it an accident for now," I said. "But they don't know what we know."

Her eyes darted to Valerie, stone-faced, and then back to me. She tried to move away, but I held her tightly. "What do you mean?" she asked.

Valerie displayed the bottle like a prize on a game show. "We found this at the scene," she said. "My guess is that if we went into your medicine cabinet, I'd find one of those three bottles missing. My guess is the Zyrtec is still in there. And you're going to need it. I can hear that ulcer growing."

"He must have stolen them," she stammered. "When he was there the other day."

I let her go and she stood, backing up towards the soundproofing panels on the wall. I took one step forward. Valerie moved to block the doorway. "No, Nora, he didn't," I said. "You offered to come over to make up after your fight. You brought the pills, maybe you had a few drinks together, and you left. You knew he wouldn't be able to resist cracking those open, you knew it was just a matter of time. You just waited here for the news to get back to you that he was gone. You had those tears all saved up, didn't you?"

"It wasn't like that!" she shrieked. "I loved him, I would never hurt him."

"Sure you loved him," I said. "And you loved Janie too. But you still killed both of them."

She moved to slap me and I grabbed her wrist. "He told us, Nora," I continued. "Told us how you told him, one last torment as he overdosed in my arms."

She pulled back from me. I let her. Gone was the wailing widow act, replaced with something cold and quiet. "It was only a matter of time," she said. "If not today, tomorrow, perhaps, or the day after. You and I both know how that story ends."

I was shaking. My throat was so tight I could barely get the words out. "He had four years sober," I hissed. "Four years until you murdered his daughter. That would send anyone over the edge."

"You were the one who went back to the hotel bar with him, weren't you?"

Ron used to say that Nora was a sniper. She knew how to find your weakness and her aim was true. She had me dead to rights and she wasn't about to let me go. "Janie never forgot finding you," she said. "Four years old and she found a grown man blacked out in her bedroom in a puddle of his own vomit. She used to have nightmares about it, even up into her teens, even when she'd all but forgotten your name. You were a ghost that never left her, Martin, so spare me this white knight charade."

She'd smashed my knees out from under me, but Valerie was immune, a blank slate. "Doesn't change the fact that you killed her," she said. "So what pushed you over the edge? Did you find out about her punk band? Her secret affair with Proctor?"

If she couldn't be cruel, she could be defiant. "She told me she was going back to LA with her father," she said. "After *everything* I'd done for her, she was going to throw it all away for *him*, the same way Sharon did."

I remembered what Janie told me, sitting in my office what seemed like months ago: the fear of making the wrong decision, the need for the space to clear her head against the factions of her family. She had made her choice, the loose gear that popped off and sent the whole whirling merry-go-round flailing in all directions. "You lied to her," I said. "You told her he was using again, that he wanted money. And she believed you."

"I was doing it to protect her," she insisted. "If she went back there, who knows what would have happened? We both knew it was only a matter of time before he started using again, and he would have dragged her down with him. She might have ended up just another junkie."

I had recovered from my reel and was back on the attack. "Or she might have been a star," I said. "But you couldn't let that happen, could you? Not without your name attached. You worked too hard, you sacrificed too much to let her capitalize on her father's scene. He had the connections, the producers, the works. Everything you couldn't give her for the life she hid from you. That was the biggest insult of all."

I had scored a blow she couldn't deflect. "I didn't send her to Interlochen, to Julliard, for her to wind up in some dirty nightclub," she said. "I watched that life destroy her parents, two people I *loved*. I wasn't going to let that happen to her, not when she had the talent she did. Not for that *noise*."

It was Christmas break when I announced to my parents that I was dropping out of school to take the French Letters on the road. They tried to be as supportive as they could, but I could sense their apprehension. At their annual Christmas party, my Aunt Gracie came up to me and loudly decried my choice, using that exact same word: *noise*. She went on and on about how I was wasting my *beautiful piano talents* and I just stood there frozen until Sandy came to rescue me. Sandy, at least, thought it was cool that her brother was an up-and-coming rock star. The next year we had a record deal; two years after that, a hit single. Maybe Joyride would have never risen above a local band. But maybe Janie wouldn't have gotten any further than a local chamber ensemble. Talent was no guarantee of success. I was living proof of that.

"That wasn't your call to make," Valerie said.

I couldn't tell if the tears that began to roll down her cheeks were genuine or just another performance. She sank into a chair like a boxer on the ropes. "Tell me about the night she died," I said quietly.

She sighed. "I'll tell you everything," she said. "I just have one request."

Valerie snorted. "You're not in a position to negotiate," she said.

I waved her off. I was willing to listen. "What do you want?"

"Let me start the concert," she said. "Just the opening remarks. For Janie. She didn't deserve any of this, but tonight is for her. They're all waiting, please, just let me do this one last thing and I'll tell you the whole story."

"You've got to be shitting me," Valerie snapped.

Any minute one of the performers was going to knock on the door, wondering where she was and when the show would begin. Maybe it was empathy for my fellow musicians; the wait to go on stage was a heady rush of anxiety and excitement and prolonging that would be torture. Maybe I bought her *do it for Janie* sympathies, atonement for my own sins in this mess. Or maybe I just needed a minute to catch my breath and get the cops in place.

"I'll be watching from the wings," I said. "If you make one move to the exit, I will chase you across the stage while Valerie tells the whole audience why."

She got up. She wiped her eyes and took a deep breath and stilled herself remarkably. Once she hit those stage lights you wouldn't know that she'd done anything but meditate in a field of lavender for the last ten minutes.

I followed her into the hallway, through the gathered performers and into the wings. The applause she garnered curdled in my stomach. They'd all be shocked tomorrow when they read the papers, all the gasping and murmuring and *we had no idea*. Let them exchange the adulations tonight. The hangover of disbelief would be waiting on their doorsteps at dawn.

"Thank you all so much for coming," she said in a clear, calm voice. "I'm Nora Archwood, Janie's mentor. The performers tonight have all volunteered their time and talents to celebrate her legacy as a musician, and all proceeds will go to a scholarship in her name, here at Raines College."

More applause. I held my breath, waiting for her to bolt, waiting for her to spontaneously confess in front of everyone. Instead she took a small bow and returned to us. A little color had returned to her face. A spiderweb soprano and her pale accompanist took the stage and began to sing in Latin.

"Thank you," she said. "Shall we continue?"

49

VALERIE

We went to Nora's office. Away from the crowd, away from the music, away from anyone who might disturb us. She sat at her desk; Martin let me take the jade velveteen accent chair while he stood, blocking the door. I doubted she was going to run. I think we'd all gone as far as we could go.

"What I told you about the night of the concert was partially true," she said. "I saw Laurel give her a tumbler and sometime after she drank from it, she became intoxicated. It wasn't like her to drink herself to that condition. I'll admit, all I could think was, *well, she's finally become her parents' daughter*. I was so furious with her, I decided she must have done it to punish me. Proctor, of all people, defended her, insisted it was a bad reaction to something and took her home."

"Laurel gave her the pills," Martin said. "Two Xanax dissolved in vodka. It was a mean-girl prank."

I didn't know if I was comfortable with how unemotional she was. I saw a lot of tears in this job; women who found out their husbands were cheating on them with the babysitter, dads who couldn't help their kids get clean no matter how many times they called us in to track down missing stereo equipment. It's always awkward for everyone when a stranger is sobbing and you can't do anything to comfort them, but somehow, her weary demeanor was worse. She had the blood of two people on her hands – people she claimed to love – and she was confessing as though recounting a movie that she had seen, but hadn't particularly enjoyed. "From there, I went to the Hotel Ithaca to meet with Roger," she said.

"But you didn't stay at the hotel all night, did you?" I said.

She shook her head. "Roger had to get back to his wife," she admitted. "I got home around one. Janie was already home. She was awake. Intoxicated, but awake. She… she was bald, except for this… strip of hair down the middle of her head. It was like she was someone else, someone I didn't recognize. She told me she was going back to LA with or without her dad, that her band was going to make it big, that she didn't need me. My little girl… she… she didn't need me, and worse, she was choosing a life I saw destroy the lives of people that I loved. Not just Ron and Sharon, but you and Cecelia and too many of my other friends. I *rescued* her from that life, and she was going to throw it back in my face. Why? Because she had a few nice dinners with her father? After everything he'd put her through. I couldn't believe it. She tried to go back in her room, and… and I… I lost it."

Lost it isn't a murder confession. *Lost it* is what you say when you cannot find your keys, or your phone, or the sweater you borrowed from a friend and then spilled beer on. No one ever marked *lost it* as the cause of death. This was going to be the hard part.

"What did you do?" Martin asked quietly.

I don't think either of us really wanted to know what happened. No matter what she said, it would be an image we could never get out of our heads. But it had to be told. Might as well take a deep breath and get it over with, hold it at arm's length and hope it doesn't destroy you when it wakes you up in the middle of the night.

"I shoved her," she said. "She fell into the corner of a table and hit her head, and she… she just went limp. There was no blood. Nothing at all. I thought she was dead; I began to panic. I couldn't call an ambulance, couldn't risk the police getting involved. So I picked her up and carried her down the back stairs. I kept hoping she'd wake up, that she'd be OK, but she didn't. The river was just outside our building. I just… set her adrift. It was the only option."

I could feel tears, molten-hot, boiling up in my eyes. *Only option* my ass. It wasn't the only option. She could have called an ambulance. But she didn't, because she knew the police would arrest her for assault. Better to polish away the fingerprints, chalk it all up to a drunken fall and let the river take the rap. Even that wasn't enough. She framed one of her students for the crime and topped it all off by killing her ex-lover. Roger might have dodged a bullet slipping out of the hotel when he did. Who knows what might have come of him.

Martin flexed his hands in and out of a fist next to me. "Except she wasn't dead, Nora," he hissed." There was water in her lungs, and that bump on the head wasn't hard enough to kill her. Hell, she could have woken up the next day if you'd just thrown a blanket over her and let her sleep. But you couldn't have that. Couldn't risk it. So, you drowned her. She might have even been awake when you did."

Nora stared hard at him. She folded her hands in her lap. "She was," she admitted, her voice like a snowbank. "She was groggy, mumbling for her dad. But what I did was better than what awaited her in LA. At least it was quick."

Martin's cold calm was more terrifying than if he had boiled over in rage.

"What about Ron?" he asked.

"The man I loved was dead," she said. "The man who came to my house demanding the violin back was someone I didn't recognize. I knew it was only a matter of time before the body caught up with the soul that was already long-lost. I told him I was bringing the violin. I thought, at first, I might stay with him so that he wouldn't be alone. But when I arrived, he was already high; I felt sick just looking at him. I went inside the room, he asked to see the violin, I told him it was in the car and that I'd get it for him later. We had a drink, he took a few of the pills, then a few more. And when I thought he was far enough gone that he wouldn't be able to hit me, I told him about Janie. I thought he had a right to know. I… I didn't expect that he'd have enough sense left in him to call you."

"But he did," Martin said. "His dying words."

"He's with Janie now," she said, almost dreamily. "And Sharon. They're the family they always wanted to be."

Martin sighed. He turned and left the room. Through the door I could hear him on the phone with Hollander. Nora reached over and tapped on her laptop. Music filled the small space. "She was beautiful, wasn't she?" she asked. "Such precision. Such talent."

I wasn't in the mood to be romantic. "She was," I said. "Until you killed her."

The cops arrived. Martin let them in. They read Nora her rights and led her away. I was surprised by the emptiness I felt. I was expecting some measure of triumph, a ray of light to pronounce that the case was solved and the good guys won. But Janie and Ron were dead and no grand trial or newspaper headline was going to bring them back. There was nothing so profound, nothing so exalting. Just a quiet sense of passing, like the opening night of a performance that nobody bought tickets to.

"Thanks for taking this case," I said after a year-long minute.

"I couldn't have done this without you," he replied.

"Same here," I said.

"We're a good team."

"We are."

And then, there really wasn't much more that either of us could say.

50

MARTIN

Ron didn't have any family left, so I claimed his body from the morgue. It didn't seem right to bury him here, a place where he had no connection. Who would come to his funeral? Valerie, maybe a couple of Janie's friends out of respect. No, that wouldn't do. But I didn't have the time or desire to fly back to LA to settle his estate there. I spent an afternoon with Ravi, the funeral director at the Singh Brothers funeral home. He owed me a favor; a couple years back I caught his makeup artist pocketing jewelry between the services and the burial. I would have Ron cremated, same as Janie. Someday I'd return to LA and scatter their ashes over the Pacific. Someday.

Hollander gave me everything from Ron's hotel room. His luggage, his wallet, the New Year's Eve photo they found propped up against the lamp on his bedside table. I wouldn't let myself believe that I was the only one left, forced myself to hope against all odds that Cecelia was still out there somewhere. I ran a perfunctory search for her social security number and came up, as always, with nothing. It was just one more way to distract myself from the sad tasks that awaited me.

An obituary was included with the cost of the service. I'd have to let Vic know; *Rolling Stone* might run a short blurb that the *Huffington Post* would rewrite as clickbait for Nineties nostalgia. But when I forced myself into my chair to try and write it, I realized there was so much about him I didn't know. Nineteen years is a small lifetime.

> *Ron Carlock, 53, the former guitar player and founding member of the French Letters, died Wednesday, Sept. 23.*
>
> *He was born to Cheryl and Paul Carlock in Omaha, Nebraska. A guitar prodigy from an early age, Ron played in several bands in high school. He attended the University of Minnesota, where he formed the French Letters in 1982. Their debut album, Sidewinder, garnered three Grammy nominations in 1986, including Best Rock Single. The band produced three more albums, Fait Accompli, God Machine and Bullets for Breakfast before disbanding in 1996.*
>
> *He married Sharon Lovette on May 9, 1990 and their daughter, Janie, was born January 11, 1992. Both predecease him.*
>
> *In his later years, Ron worked as a producer and session musician, composing music for the TV shows Murder by Law and Here's Two Eggs, as well as the film Driver's Ed.*
>
> *He is survived by his former bandmates, Martin Wade and Victor Van Owen.*
>
> *Services will be private.*
>
> *Arrangements are entrusted to the Singh Brothers Funeral Home.*

A hundred and fifty-one words. Hardly enough to sum up a man's whole life. But I didn't know what else to say, didn't know what else to do. I didn't even know if he had a lawyer or what would become of whatever estate he had. That was for another day. Today was just for goodbyes.

There was no one else in the funeral home. The very definition of a private service. I hadn't even told Valerie. Ron was in a closed casket, presumably in the dark blue suit I brought for him, the same suit he had worn at his daughter's funeral.

"Take as much time as you need," Ravi said, closing the parlor doors behind him.

For the first ten minutes, I just sat there. I didn't know what to say. It wasn't like he could hear me, but silence didn't seem right either. When I was really sick, when the band was falling apart, I used to lie in bed wishing I'd never met him. If I'd never called into our college radio station, if we'd never formed the band, maybe I wouldn't have been shivering and jonesing, a hundred and thirty-five pounds of bone and misery in a fetal position on dirty sheets. I might have lived a quiet normal life, never knowing what it felt like to love someone as deeply as I loved Ron. He was a piece of me that I didn't know had been missing until it was 2am in a booth at the college radio station, drunk on cheap beer and a broken heart and laughing in spite of it because Ron kept playing "Pico and Sepulveda," over and over, each time with a different dedication. *This next one goes out to Sheila St Bernard; I know she's missing her boyfriend, Ted Peachy. This one goes out to our remedial dodgeball team, you're gonna kill at the state tournament next Thursday. This one is for Christina LaRoux from Martin Wade, congratulations, he hates you*. Right off the top, he could read me and I could read him, like we were brothers, like we were pieces of each other that had been cut apart and finally pieced back together. I had been in love with Cecelia – crazy about her, craved her, wanted to spend the rest of my life with her – but to say I felt anything other than love for Ron would be a lie. And by extension, I had loved Sharon and Janie especially, because they were a part of him. Even when I left LA, cut off all connection, part of it was out of that same stupid love that wouldn't let me stand by and watch him destroy himself. But now he was gone, nineteen years later, and he died the same way I always feared he would. At least I was here to say goodbye, not reading about it the way Vic would have to. I just couldn't bring myself to call Vic yet, wasn't ready to say out loud what we had always feared would happen.

"We didn't have enough time together," I finally said. "And I'm sorry about that. But I wouldn't take it back, Ron. Not one second of it. Because it all came to an end too quickly. We should have retired together, become those old men in diners. Like we promised."

When we moved to LA, we used to go to a diner called the Spot. We wrote a song about a waitress there, Jessica, who had a thick blonde braid and white hi-tops and a sunny disposition at 2am, waiting on a couple of punks with ringing ears and big dreams and a couple of bucks from the door between them. It never made an album, but I caught myself humming it on and off through the years. *When we're old,* Ron used to say, *we'll find some Tom Waits kinda greasy spoon and get breakfast every morning. We'll have our own table and our own waitress; we'll flirt with her and leave a big tip every time.* Maybe when this was all over, I'd go to the Red Top, order steak and runny eggs and burnt hash browns in his honor, drink my coffee black and smoke half a Lucky Strike in the parking lot, passing it back and forth with his ghost. I still had the pack from that night at the Vanguard in my office. For emergencies. For special occasions. For goodbyes.

I didn't realize I was crying until I felt a hand on my shoulder. I looked up and there were Valerie and Joan, both in black dresses. Joan held out a box of tissues and I took a handful. "How did you find me?" I asked, wiping my eyes.

"Valerie's a good detective," she said.

"I saw the obituary," she admitted. "I called Ravi and he gave you up. We didn't want you to be alone."

I laughed. A real laugh, from somewhere deep in my gut. "I'm glad you're here," I said.

"I'm sorry about Ron," Joan said as she sat down next to me. "Valerie told me you had been friends for a long time."

She took my hand. I let her. Valerie put her head on my shoulder. I let her do that too. And we sat, quietly, for another half hour, until all the goodbyes I needed to say were silently said. I stood up and Joan embraced me. "Thank you for coming," I murmured into her shoulder. She smelled like gardenias and coffee. I never wanted to let her go.

"Please call if you need anything," she said. She reached into her purse and pulled out a slip of paper with her number written on it. "Day or night, you understand?"

I tucked the paper into my breast pocket, close to my heart without even thinking about it. "I know where to find you," I said with a smile.

She squeezed my hands and leaned in and gave me a kiss on the cheek. And then she was gone, leaving just me and Valerie, and Ravi in the back office. "You didn't have to do that," I said.

"Of course I did," she replied. "I know he meant a lot to you."

"He did."

"Aunt Gina and Deacon send their condolences," she added. "Aunt Gina especially. She said she always thought he was cute."

I let myself laugh. "She wasn't the only one," I said. "The guitar player always gets the girls."

"You want to get a bite to eat?" she offered.

"I've got a little more to do here," I said. "And I think I'd just like to be by myself for a bit."

"You gonna be OK?"

"Yeah," I said on a sigh. "Yeah, I'll be OK. Sad, probably for a long time. But I'll be OK." I knew what she was getting at and she didn't have to worry. I had her to stay clean for, her and Joan and Ron and Janie. I could think of no better way to honor their memories than by not surrendering to what stole him from me.

After she left, I went out to my car, but I didn't drive home. I reached into the back seat and retrieved Janie's violin and the New Year's Eve photo. I took them inside and handed them to Ravi. "Please put these in his casket," I said. "And let me know when I can pick up his ashes."

51

VALERIE

Katy's letter was still waiting, unopened, when I got back from Ron's funeral, relocated to the file of Memphis-related articles Martin had prepared for me. I was suddenly ashamed I hadn't opened it. I didn't want to end up like him, burying my former best friend without a real chance to make up what had been lost. I didn't know what to expect inside. There was only one way to find out.

Hey Val,
I'm sorry. There's just nothing else to say except that I'm sorry for everything. I don't know where you are, but I figured Aunt Gina would know how to get this to you. Just knowing you're reading this, that you even opened the envelope instead of chucking it in the garbage, is more than I deserve.

I fucked up. You tried to save me and I just fucked it all up. But I'm getting help now; on some real meds, not just a bunch of shit from some dude named Yaz. I've got a therapist, her name is Sally, like the rag doll in The Nightmare Before Christmas. She's really cool. I told her about you and she was the one who suggested I write to you. But she told me to tear up the letter and never send it. Fuck that shit. You need to hear it from me.

I don't expect you to write back. I don't expect to ever see you again and I don't even deserve to. But I want you to know that I love you, that I never meant to hurt you and

that I'm sorry. I hope wherever you are that you're safe and that you have people around you who can take care of you. I'll always remember the awesome times we had together.
Love always,
Katy

PS. Sorry if I fucked up your tattoos. Guess that means I owe Deacon an apology too.

Katy had never been good at apologies. Her mom hadn't been either; an alcoholic who was in and out of jail, always because it was someone else's fault – a shitty boyfriend, a coworker who thought she was better than her, even Katy. Katy learned how to say *sorry* enough to get her out of trouble, but she never learned how to make real amends to the people she'd hurt. "I've said I'm sorry enough times in my life," she once told me. "The world owes me an apology for once." I used to forgive her because being mad was more effort; I could get another dress, another book, another lipstick, another CD. I had a family, I knew I was going to eat when I went home, I knew no black-toothed jerk-off named Craig was going to ask to see my teenage tits. But somewhere – rehab, maybe, or drug court or detoxing on the floor of a jail cell – she finally understood what it meant to ask for absolution. And I wasn't going to be so cruel as not to grant it to her.

I tore a piece of paper out of the end of one of my work pads. I wished I had something prettier, lilac-scented stationary with my name at the top. But I didn't want to waste time getting a card, didn't want to think too much about what I was going to do.

Katy,
I forgive you.
Love always,
Val

* * *

I folded up the letter, I repurposed a junk-mail envelope from the recycling bin, taped the return address of Katy's letter over the top of it and added a stamp. I walked it down to the box on the corner of my street before I could change my mind.

I put the letter she'd sent me into Martin's folder and put the folder in a file box underneath my desk.

Then I sat down on my couch and had a good long cry.

Dott had cried when I told her on the phone about Nora. I wished I could have told her in person, held her while she sobbed, but I didn't want to wait, didn't want her to see it on Facebook and have to wonder if it was just another hideous rumor. I offered to call Gordon and Melanie, but she said she wanted to tell them.

I didn't hear from her again until Saturday morning. I was reading an article on the oral history of *Yacht Rock* in my pajamas when she knocked on my door. "I brought coffee," she said, holding out a pair of cups like a sacrificial offering. "Can I come in?"

Of course she could. I gestured her to the pile of blankets and pillows on my unmade bed and hoped she didn't take it as a come-on. "I'm sorry I haven't called," she said. "It's been… a lot to process."

I couldn't be mad at her. Even if she had called, I might not have had time to see her; between Ron's funeral and meetings with Hollander and District Attorney Jack Lorenz, I'd kept too busy to do much of anything else. I hadn't even seen Aunt Gina and Deacon except for a couple of quick calls congratulating me on breaking the case.

"Look," she began. Nothing good could follow that word; I braced myself for the worst. "I like you. I *really* like you. But I don't want to jump into something when I'm dealing with all these complicated feelings. I don't want *this* to be always tied to something so awful."

It made sense. It hurt, but it made sense. "I like you too," I said. "And I get it."

"That doesn't mean I regret anything that happened," she said. "I hope you know that."

That was a relief. I wouldn't have been able to live with myself if I thought I had taken advantage of her, if she had fallen into bed with me out of desperation.

"The Chirmps head out next week," she continued. "I figure six weeks will be the time I need to get my head back together. It's kind of a dick move to tell you that I don't want to start a thing and then ask you to wait for me… but I guess that's what I'm asking. I'll understand if you say no, though. And I won't be mad if you do."

It had been so long since I'd felt like this for anyone that I was starting to doubt it was even real. It would be easy to tell her no, to get bitter and tell her that she was a one-night stand and that was all. But love was never easy. A couple million songs all had that same tune. Maybe she'd spend the whole tour pining for me. Maybe this was her way of asking for permission to fuck around with a different groupie in every city. Hell, maybe she'd never even come back. I couldn't speed up time, couldn't see into the future. All I knew was that I was going to be here when she got back, however she would have me, if she would have me at all. I'd waited all this time to even meet her. Six weeks was a blink, a speck of dust in the eternal etching of time.

I hugged her. She held me for a little longer than she might have if this was a regular goodbye. I wished her luck on her tour. She kissed me and I kissed her back and there were tears on both of our cheeks. I watched as her car pulled away from the curb. I swallowed a lump like a geode in my throat. This had been a long fucking week.

When I could finally breathe again, I did the only thing I could do when my heart was broken.

I called my brother.

52

MARTIN

There was a group of theater kids crammed into two of the back booths, ordering in bad Shakespeare from a waitress who was making a valiant effort not to roll her eyes. Joan was ringing out an elderly couple holding hands while the man paid from a leather wallet that looked like it had held bills for his whole life. If I'd been quicker, I would have paid their ticket. I was feeling strangely generous.

She smiled when she saw me. "Have you come back for that promised milkshake?" she asked.

"Not tonight," I said. "And don't worry, I'm not here to recite a soliloquy, unless you'd like me to. I probably still remember a little bit of high school *Hamlet*."

"Think table nine has that covered," she said. "What can I get you?"

I was never good at asking a woman on a date. Hell, I only got together with Cecelia because she left me her number after a show. But not one of the familiar anxieties were there, no sweaty palms, no heart palpitations, just the delicious anticipation of a *yes* in the waiting. "I'm thinking dinner," I said. "Tomorrow night at the Café In. That is, if you'll join me."

She beamed. "I would love that," she said. "I was starting to think you'd never ask."

I could feel my cheeks getting hot, but I didn't mind. "Sorry I kept you waiting," I said. "What time can I pick you up?"

She scribbled her address on the back of a receipt and handed it to me. "Seven," she said. "I like to eat late."

"I'll make a reservation," I said, tucking it into my shirt pocket. I swore it was warm across my heart. "I'd stay for dinner tonight, but I've got some work to do."

"I guess I'll just have to wait until tomorrow." She leaned across the counter and gave me a peck on the cheek. "I'll see you at seven."

I drove home listening to New Order. For the first time in a long time, I felt good, good enough, at least, to sooth my heartache about Ron. At home I played "Joyride" once through on the piano before I went into my office. I had a lot to think about.

I had started the Wade Agency with the intent of being a solo act. But when Valerie arrived with her voice recorder and her notepad, when she saw through all of my dodges and got me to tell her everything I'd been running from for the last two decades, I knew I'd met someone I didn't even know I was looking for. And when she declined to run the piece – I have the only copy in existence, printed off and stashed in my filing cabinet – I knew I could trust her. And the more I trusted her, the more I liked her. She was funny and she was smart and she was caring in a way that didn't put up with the backstage remnants of my petulant bullshit. For the first time in a long time, I felt like there was a future to look forward to. And it would start, I realized, with some paperwork and paint.

53

VALERIE

Nora was indicted for Janie's murder. Ron's death was ruled an accidental overdose. Guess they bought her story that he stole her pills. Martin didn't press the issue. Vinny got JoJo a spot in drug court; he was moved to an in-patient rehab in the Adirondacks. Laurel was charged with distribution of a controlled substance and assault, and who knows what happened to Proctor. My bruise, in time, healed.

I was getting ready for work when Martin called and asked if he could come by. He said he had something for me. What a coincidence. I had something for him, too.

I unlocked the door and about a minute later he was in my apartment, carrying a large frame with both hands. He turned it around to reveal a bright canvas of bold lines and soft shapes. I didn't know shit about art, but I was instantly lost inside of it. I could have stared at it for hours and seen something different each time: a rose garden, a jungle, a cityscape at night. "It's beautiful," I gushed. "I love it."

"It's…" He hesitated and cleared his throat, and I hoped he was about to say what I thought he might say. "It's one of Cecelia's. My favorite, actually. She painted it around the time I wrote 'The Storm Before the Calm.' It hung in our bedroom, but it's been in storage for years. I… I thought it needed a good home."

Tears welled up in my eyes. I couldn't believe he was trusting me with something so personal, so intimate, so meaningful to him. I took a shaking breath and smiled and hoisted it up against the back wall. "Let's hang it here," I said. "So it'll be the first thing I see when I wake up."

"Perfect," he said. "It lights up the whole room."

"Were you able to get the other one back from Nora's apartment?" I asked.

"I did," he said. "The super let me in."

"Gonna hang that at your place?"

"No," he said. He shuffled his feet, put his hands in his pockets. "I, ah, burned it. Scattered the ashes. Didn't seem right to keep it. There's a lot of heartache and grief in that painting. I'd never be able to look at it the way it was intended."

"Oh, Martin…"

"It's all right," he said. "I found another one of hers that I liked, hung it in the bedroom. Deviates from my clean lines and dark colors aesthetic, but I think she'll appreciate that."

"She absolutely will," I said. "Let me see if I can find a hammer, we'll get this one up…"

"I've got a hammer and some wire out in the car," he said.

"You always come prepared," I said.

We hoisted the painting onto my wall. My sweater sleeve slipped, revealing plastic on my forearm. "New ink?" he asked.

He'd beaten me to it. I rolled back my sleeve further. "Fixing some damage," I said, holding it out to him.

It took him a minute to translate the artwork, my scar hidden by a scroll of vines worked into eight bars of music, with a small gold leaf on each end. "Valerie," he said slowly. "That's…"

"'Joyride,'" I said. "I snapped a picture of your sheet music. The two leaves are for Janie… and Ron."

He was so silent for a minute that I worried I might have offended him. "I don't even know what to say," he stammered. "I'm honored, Valerie. I know how much your tattoos mean to you."

"I know how much Ron and Janie meant to you," I replied.

That was the simple answer. The real answer was more complicated. Working with him on this case, as brutal and as frustrating and as heartbreaking as it ended up being, made whole what was torn apart inside me. Fixing my scar was the last bridge to cross in forgiving Katy. It was only right that the remaining space be dedicated to the man who, in his own way, helped me repair that.

He wiped his eyes. He laughed a little to cover. "C'mon," he said. "I'll give you a ride into the office. There's a couple more things I want to run by you."

A man in a painter's uniform came by a little after ten. He wasn't on the books, but Martin ushered him into his office and closed the door. I finished up the case notes in Janie's file and felt a small sadness when I put it in the cabinet with all the other closed cases. It was all over, with two dead bodies and half a dozen lives ruined. Didn't seem right to just sum it all up on a few pieces of paper, but that was all that was left to do. There would be other cases for the Wade Agency, robberies and divorces, a small scandal if we got lucky. But our names would never appear in the paper, we would always remain a whisper, an incognito search in the dark. We'll look into your books, sir, see where that money has gone missing. You may want to consult a lawyer, ma'am, have him call our offices and we'll send over the file.

The painter came out of the office. Martin gestured for me to come inside. "Let me guess," I said. "He thinks his supplier is giving him lower-quality paints than he ordered."

He gave me a half-laugh. "I've been thinking about some things," he said. "And I've decided that I no longer need an assistant. What I need is a partner."

I had a brief vision of getting coffee for some other dolt in a hundred-dollar suit, teaching myself to decipher his scrawl while silently resenting him each time he went out the door on *my* stakeout. But before I could ask any other questions, he continued.

"The truth is, you're a better detective than me," he said. "You saw a case that I didn't and you solved it when I couldn't. And beyond that..." He paused to take a sip of his coffee. "I came into the office on Friday and it just felt... wrong. Too quiet. And I realized that it was because I didn't have you to talk to. Because you *are* my partner, and have been for a while now. That means it's my duty to make it official. I've pulled a few strings at the state office, guys I've done favors for, you know the drill. All you have to do is fill out the paperwork in this folder and they'll process your license. That is, if you agree to it."

So he did mean me. I didn't know what to say. *Thank you* didn't seem like enough. Except for that brief moment of spite it had never occurred to me to get my license, to do what Martin did in any capacity beyond what I was already doing.

"Please say yes," he said. "Please say *something*."

Partners. Not just associates, but *partners*. Wade and Jacks, Private Investigators. It had a nice ring to it. "Of course!" I said. "Holy shit, you had me so scared there."

He let out a sigh of relief that spoke for both of us. "Not my intent," he said. "And it's a good thing you said yes, because that painter is out there peeling off my name in order to put both of ours on the door. It would be terribly awkward if you said no."

My name on the door and everything. This was too good to be true. "Is that all I need to do?" I asked. "Just the paperwork?"

"That's all you need to do," he said. "I've written your letter of recommendation, and they'll need a photo, but in six to eight weeks, you will be Valerie Jacks, licensed private investigator."

Most of the cases we worked didn't have happy endings. Best-case scenario, someone got their stuff back, but always with the knowledge that the sanctity of their home had been violated in a way that we couldn't put back together. The worst-case scenario was still sitting half-completed in a folder on my desk, waiting to be typed and filed away with the rest of them. But I liked the way he said those words. I'd like them even more when I said them out loud for the first time.

The phone rang. Martin glanced at me between digital bells and gave me that left-sided smile. I picked up the receiver. "Wade and Jacks," I said. The words tasted like honey on my tongue. "How may I direct your call?"

ACKNOWLEDGEMENTS

To my beloved husband, Ian, for his love, care and cat-wrangling while I'm trying to write, and to my family for their lifelong support on this journey.

Thank you to my agent, Jim McCarthy, my editor, Daniel Culver and everyone at Datura and Kaye Publicity for all their hard work in making this book a reality.

Thank you to Janet Hutchings, Ellery Queen's Mystery Magazine, Jackie Sherbow at Alfred Hitchcock's Mystery Magazine and Rusty Barns at Tough for introducing the world to Martin and Valerie on the pages of their magazines.

And, of course, my eternal gratitude to all the friends who have read, fed and encouraged me.